Rafel Nadal Farreras is an award-winning Catalan journalist and author. This is his first novel to be translated into English.

www.transworldbooks.co.uk
www.transworldireland.ie

THE LAST SON'S SECRET

Rafel Nadal Farreras

English translation by
Mara Faye Lethem

BLACK SWAN

TRANSWORLD PUBLISHERS
61–63 Uxbridge Road, London W5 5SA
www.transworldbooks.co.uk

Transworld is part of the Penguin Random House group of companies
whose addresses can be found at global.penguinrandomhouse.com

Penguin
Random House
UK

First published in 2015 by Columna Ediciones as *La Meledicció dels Palmisano.*
First published in Great Britain in 2017 by Black Swan
an imprint of Transworld Publishers.
Published by agreement with Pontas Literary and Film Agency

A CIP catalogue record for this book
is available from the British Library.

ISBN
9781784162269

Typeset in 12/15pt Adobe Caslon by Jouve (UK), Milton Keynes
Printed and bound in Great Britain by Clays Ltd, Bungay, Suffolk

Penguin Random House is committed to a sustainable
future for our business, our readers and our planet. This book
is made from Forest Stewardship Council® certified paper.

1 3 5 7 9 10 8 6 4 2

To Anna. To Sílvia. To Raquel.

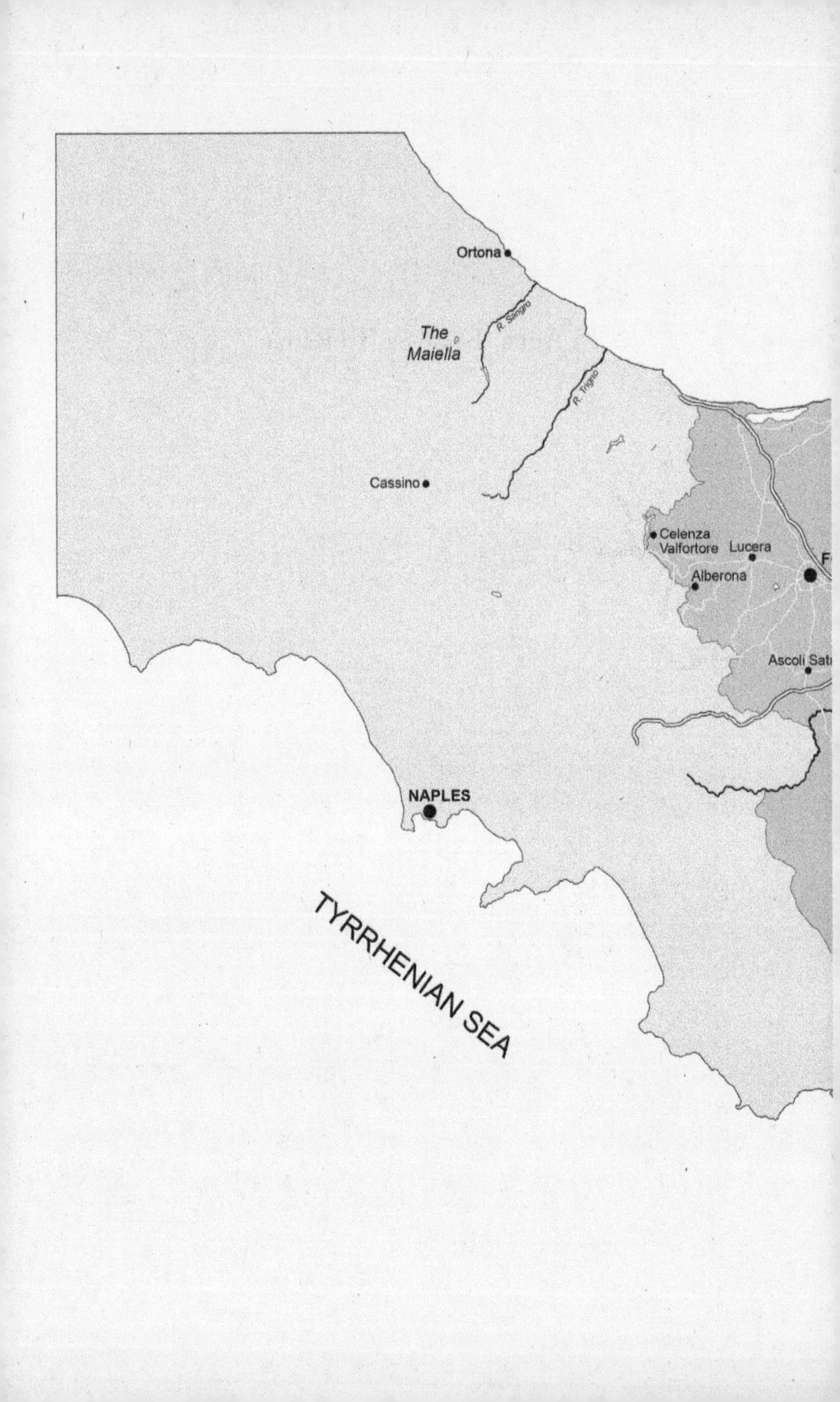

Ortona
R. Sangro
The Maiella
R. Trigno
Cassino
Celenza Valfortore
Lucera
Alberona
NAPLES
TYRRHENIAN SEA

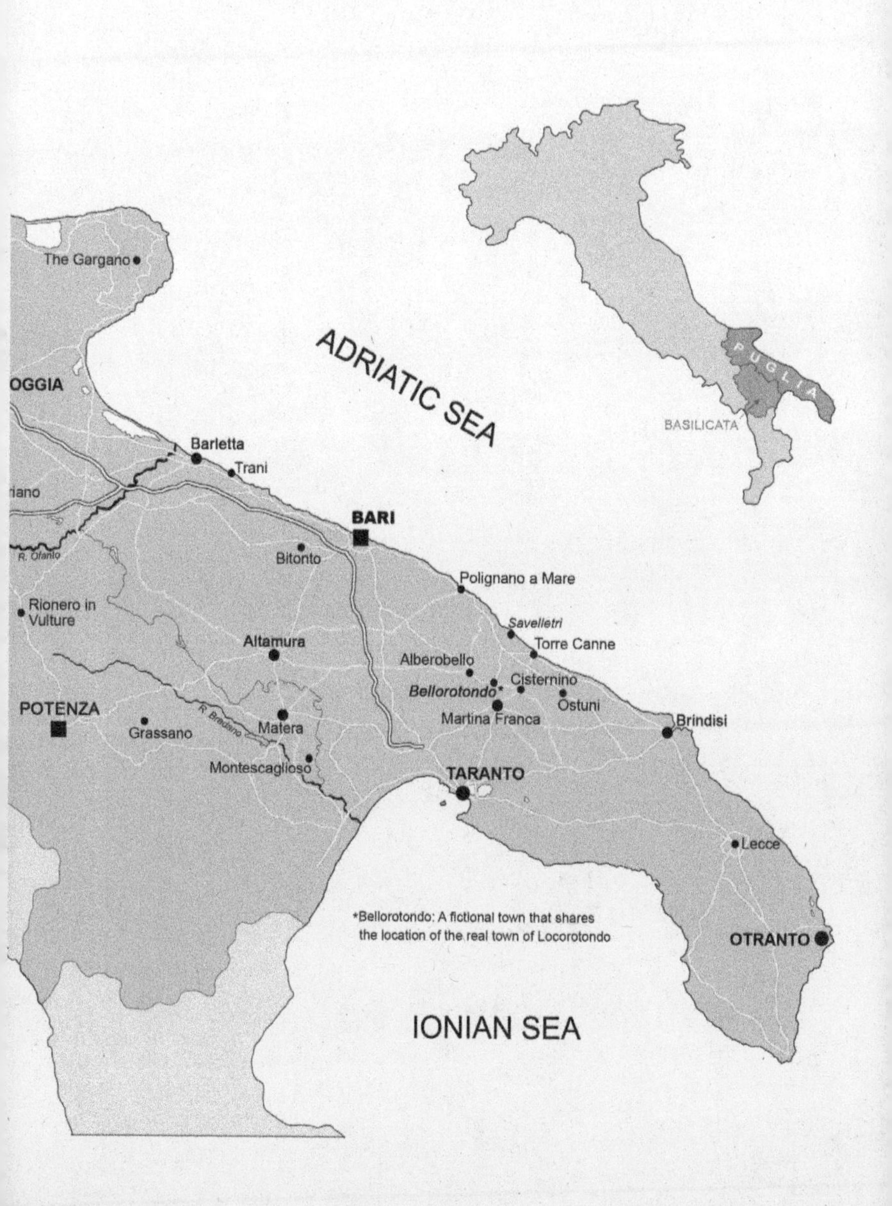

The Gargano
OGGIA
ADRIATIC SEA
PUGLIA
BASILICATA
Barletta
Trani
riano
BARI
R. Ofanto
Bitonto
Polignano a Mare
Rionero in
Vulture
Savelletri
Torre Canne
Altamura
Alberobello
Cisternino
Bellorotondo*
Ostuni
POTENZA
Martina Franca
Brindisi
Grassano
Matera
R. Bradano
Montescaglioso
TARANTO
Lecce
*Bellorotondo: A fictional town that shares
the location of the real town of Locorotondo
OTRANTO
IONIAN SEA

Prologue

24 August 2012. Midday.

At first, the town seemed abandoned. The only sign of life was a couple of dogs sleeping on a dusty old mat, in the shade of some bins. But around the corner, the town square appeared, filled with large balcony-clad houses that opened on to the valley of vineyards and olive groves, granting a panoramic view over the Puglia countryside, stretching almost to the Adriatic. Three carob trees and two holm oaks presided over this small oasis, and in the shade of the large, leafy branches two monuments rose, each covered with floral offerings and adorned with bows and ribbons striped in the colours of the Italian flag.

On a wooden bench with peeling paint sat an old man who had dozed off: his eyes were closed, his head tilted to one side and his mouth half open. He seemed to be having trouble breathing, or maybe he was already sleeping the sleep of the just and no one had realized; either way, it looked like he might never muster the strength to get up again. At his feet lay a dog, stretched out in that way only Mediterranean dogs can, in the paltry shade of the summer during the sunstroke hours. All around rang out the repetitive song of the cicadas scratching their bellies on some high branch of the carob trees in the windless air.

One of the monuments in the middle of the square was a monolith dedicated to the fallen of the First World War. A stone pillar engraved with a list of the local victims showed forty-two names, but a careful reading revealed something more: half of those dead had the last name *Palmisano.* Twenty-one men from the same family.

'Guseppe Oronzo Palmisano (one); Donato Fu Francesco Paolo Palmisano (two); Silvestro Palmisano (three); Gianbattista Di Martino Palmisano (four); Nicola Di Martino Palmisano (five); Giuseppe Fu Vito Palmisano (six) . . .'

The other memorial was dedicated to those fallen on the fronts of the Second World War. There wasn't a single Palmisano on this list; perhaps the family and the last bearer of its name hadn't survived the losses of the first war. This time, half of the dead were Convertinis.

'*Ventuno . . . sono ventuno!*' The old man on the bench sat up, awake, and said it again to the empty square, '*Ventuno . . . sono ventuno!*'

His face was grooved with wrinkles as he gazed at the monument. The dog had woken up as well, but he remained on the ground, his legs stretched out.

'Twenty-one!' he repeated quietly to himself. 'All victims of the First War. *La maledizione dei Palmisano!*'

PART ONE

The Curse of the Palmisanos

The Great War

THE FIRST TO die was Giuseppe Oronzo Palmisano, the most belligerent of all the Palmisano men. He had long been preparing for the moment his homeland would call him to arms. He fell on 23 May 1915, the same day Italy declared war on Austria-Hungary and joined the Allied coalition in the First World War. Poor Giuseppe Oronzo always maintained that fighting on the front offered men a great opportunity: it taught discipline, strengthened character and allowed youngsters to channel appropriately their natural-born aggresion. He believed that the battlefield was the only place where brute force could be brought to bear in a natural, organized manner. Like a noble art, he used to say.

Giuseppe Oronzo was loyal and reliable. His problem, though, was that he had always preferred to resolve differences with his fists. But despite this violent streak, he wasn't an entirely bad sort: he was the first Palmisano to enlist, and was assigned to a volunteer corps, quite an honour for someone from a small town like Bellorotondo. Shortly after, he was the first to head to the Carso front, in north-east Italy, and the first to enter into combat. He was also the first of his detachment to go over the top to attack the Austrian positions. And he was the first to get a bullet to the chest, right in the sternum. When he felt the impact, accompanied by a sound like two pieces of metal colliding and a very unpleasant burning sensation, he assumed the bullet had just grazed the buttons of his uniform tunic and he tried to carry on. His legs refused to move, they folded under him and he collapsed. When the Austrians stormed the trench, a corporal with a curled moustache stepped over his body and rammed his bayonet into his heart, but poor Giuseppe Oronzo didn't feel it: life had left his body some time before. The first Palmisano died with the banal honour of being one of the first Italians to lose his life, that very first day of war on the Austrian front. That summer he would have turned twenty-two.

Donato Fu Francesco Paolo Palmisano (2) was the second to die. The most cowardly of the family, he would have done anything to avoid being called up, but alas, he wasn't even afforded the chance to experience the full horrors of the trenches. He also died on the Carso front, towards the end of the first summer of the war, victim of a Howitzer shell from the Austrian artillery that was defending the border city of Gorizia. And, a few days later, Silvestro (3) died, pumped full of bullets from the new Austrian machine guns, which, in October 1915, ravaged those troops assaulting the Santa Lucia hill on the north-eastern Italian frontier. Installed in lookout posts far from the line of fire, the

Italian officers drank tea from porcelain cups served by gloved auxiliaries, and from their towers they ordered successive waves of troops to attack the mountain. Until, finally, the commander of the Italian armies, General Luigi Cadorna, realized it was a useless massacre and put paid to the offensive. That was the end of the third battle of the Isonzo, a river squeezed in between magnificent mountains, right by the border with the Austro-Hungarian Empire, a river that had never been heard of in Bellorotondo until that day.

The twins had the most horrific death of them all. As boys, Gianbattista Di Martino (4) and Nicola Di Martino (5) couldn't stand being made to dress identically. They hated when the women in town would stop them on the street to pinch their cheeks and coo over them! 'So cute, like two peas in a pod.'

Growing tired of such maternal effusiveness, one fine day they decided to never wear the same outfits again. They stopped walking to school together. They refused to leave the house at the same time. They wouldn't go anywhere near each other in the school playground. If, during some local festival, the family went for a stroll along the Via Cavour, in the centre of Bellorotondo, they found a way to walk separately, one on either side of the road. And when they were teenagers they did everything possible to differentiate themselves physically: Gianbattista grew a moustache and Nicola opted for a small beard; one parted his hair on the right side and the other on the left. When they began to court girls, Gianbattista went after the exuberant, extrovert ones who laughed a lot. Nicola, on the other hand, eyed the more discreet homebodies.

When they had finally managed to forget that they were twins and the old women in town finally stopped cooing over them, they were called up. They both received the conscription letter on the same day, 1 February 1915, and from the same postman. They were also sent to the same barracks, and once the army had shaved both of their heads and put them in the same uniform, they were once again so alike that it was impossible to tell them apart. From that day on they trained together and slept in bunk beds, one on top of the other. Six months later, they travelled north together, in the same company, and they were also side by side when they received word that they were headed to the front and were to prepare for immediate combat.

The twins had just turned nineteen and once again were like two peas in a pod, but it no longer bothered them. Instead, they grew inseparable: they slept next to each other, they hunkered down together in the muddy trench and they advanced together when they attacked the Austrian positions. No one in the company could tell the brothers apart. Captain Di Luca gave them orders as if they were a single person: 'Palmisano, get behind those trees and shut that damn machine gun up, for once and for all!'

Gianbattista and Nicola didn't ask for whom the

order was meant. They both crawled out of the trench and crept along, stuck together as if they were just one man, to the rocks. Then they ran to the pine forest and half an hour later the enemy machine gun exploded and their fellow soldiers shouted, 'Long live Palmisano!', figuring they would both feel included in the cheer.

In November, the Austrians dropped chlorine gas, right on the front where the twins had just earned a medal for bravery. When the lethal fog lifted, a horrifying carpet of cadavers was discovered in both sets of trenches: the wind had changed midway through the attack and, after annihilating the Italians, the gas had wreaked havoc on the Austrians themselves. Both armies had their work cut out in recovering the corpses of the victims of that piece of military insanity. Captain Di Luca's men found the twins hugging, their bodies so entwined that they couldn't manage to separate them. Their faces were blue from the poison, and contorted from the horror they had seen coming. Thick foam filled their mouths. Their jackets still smelled of gas.

The captain was resolute. 'Stop what you're doing and bury the Palmisano body. I can't bear another minute of this horror!'

The soldiers stared at each other, disconcerted.

'Which Palmisano, Captain? We can't get them apart.'

'For the love of God, can't you see there's no need? Bury them just as we found them. They are one man.'

And they buried Gianbattista Di Martino Palmisano and Nicola Di Martino Palmisano, clinging to each other in their final embrace, in a clearing in the pine forest, together for all eternity.

When the townspeople of Bellorotondo found out that the twins had died in each other's arms, they were deeply moved and commemorated them in a huge, well-attended mass in the church of the Immaculate Conception. They all remembered the twins as little boys, when they still dressed identically, and they left the mass pleased that, before dying, the two brothers had decided to be twins again.

After that tragedy, the Palmisano women wore mourning clothes for the rest of the war. Days later, on Christmas Eve of 1915, they received the news of the death of Giuseppe Fu Vito (6) in Libya, an almost exotic location, far from the various fronts of the war and which, on the face of it, had seemed less dangerous. The boy was slight and he'd endured every sort of illness going as a child. In Tripoli, an infection saw his temperature rocket to forty-two degrees Celsius and after fifteen delirious days he could no longer stand the fever and died.

Fate was laughing cruelly at those peasant farmers punished by the war: the news of Giuseppe Fu Vito's feverish end reached them just as the temperature in town dropped to three degrees below freezing. When the Palmisano women went out on the street to cry, breaking the crisp silence of Christmas Eve, they were met by the coldest temperatures yet that century.

Martino Palmisano (7) died the following March from a bullet wound to the head, in the fifth battle of the Isonzo, a river which by then everyone in the town had learned to place on a map. Most of them had assumed it was a very lovely, but very small river in a corner of Italy so far from Bellorotondo that they doubted it was actually part of the same country.

In the autumn of 1916, Stefano (8), Giuseppe Fu Piet (9), and Donato Fu Francesco (10) fell within a matter of a few days. The first was killed by shrapnel from a grenade; the second, by complications from gangrene in one leg; and the third as a result of a heart attack in the midst of battle. All three of them had girlfriends and all three were thinking of getting married as soon as the conflict – quickly becoming a collective insanity that threatened the survival of families across half of Europe – ended. From the day they received the news of this triple tragedy, the three young women in question walked through the streets of Bellorotondo crying over their misfortune. And from that moment on, the town no longer had any doubt that the Palmisanos were cursed by a terrible *maledizione*. No one could say exactly whether the death of the three cousins in the foothills of the Colline dell'Hermada, the last obstacle to an Italian advance before Trieste, had happened during the seventh, eighth or ninth battle of the Isonzo; they followed one another at a dizzying pace and the line of the front changed position every week. But, after the coincidence of three deaths in a matter of days, the fate of that poor farming family achieved legendary status in Bellorotondo.

Were any more evidence needed that the Palmisanos were plagued by a monstrous curse, it came two months later, at Christmas of 1916. For the second year in a row, tragedy knocked at the family's door on the most important festival night of the year: as they headed out for midnight mass, the news of Giuseppe Di Giovanni's death (11) reached the town. In late September, the eldest of the Palmisanos had miraculously saved himself from an explosion in a tunnel dug by the Austrians beneath the Italian positions on Monte Cimone, but three months later he had fallen in a skirmish near Stelvio. Giuseppe had been sent to the Alps, to the high mountain troops, because he was a specialist in digging mine shafts, an essential skill for the strange war that was going on at the Alpine front: instead of attacking on the surface, the Italians and Austrians dug tunnels and placed explosives beneath the enemy positions. Underground, in the bowels of the mountains, Giuseppe was the most skilled of them all, but patrolling outside the tunnels was different – he never felt comfortable marching along snowy paths that were sometimes at more than two thousand metres of altitude, and where he was finally greeted by a stray bullet in a skirmish.

During what remained of that winter and all of the spring of 1917, no more telegrams arrived and the lack of news seemed to contradict the worst portents. But really, the lull was due to the freezing weather that gripped the entire European continent. When the weather improved, the curse reared its head once again. At Pentecost, they learned of the death of Cataldo (12) in Albania, just as it had become an Italian protectorate and hostilities there had officially ceased.

And in the autumn came the disaster at Caporetto: the Isonzo front collapsed, the Italian army retreated across the entire line of the front from the Adriatic to Valsugana, almost at Trento, and more than three hundred men were killed, wounded or taken prisoner by the Austrians. In just one day, 25 October 1917, and just a few kilometres away from each other, Vito (13), Giulio (14) and Angelo Giorgio (15) were killed – all from rifle shots at point-blank range when they were out of ammunition and their officers had fled en masse hours earlier without even giving the order to retreat. All three of them had just been called up, having only turned eighteen the previous spring. When the news of the latest triple tragedy reached Bellorotondo, the town was convinced that not a single Palmisano man would survive the merciless war, or the family curse.

The town had always considered Domenico (16) a solid sort, a happy chap who took things in his stride. The crueller among them treated him like a buffoon and made fun of him, but he never complained because he saw no ill intent in their remarks. Those who didn't know him were always surprised by his irrepressible smile, which made him seem a fool, but was really just a sign of his guileless contentment. As a boy, at home, he was regularly beaten because he was so easily distracted. The teachers at school also often caned him, due to his inability to concentrate. Eventually, all gave up on him and stopped trying to reform him with either whacks or slaps.

As he grew older, they discovered that he wasn't as simple as he appeared and that he was a tireless, highly capable worker, particularly in the fields, or among the olive trees: he was strong as an ox; patient as the day was long; and the more he worked, the happier he seemed. In the war he also proved himself. He volunteered for the most dangerous operations, never questioned orders and was never afraid. In fact, the idea of dying never crossed his mind. So when the time came for combat, everyone wanted him by their side. In the evenings, in the barracks, he would think about his grandfather, who had always taken him with him to the olive groves and treated him as he would have treated anyone else. He missed him.

'Looks like we'll be heading out to dance again today!' was all Cambrone, his bunkmate, said in greeting when he strode into the barracks after his guard duty. 'They called the captain to the command post. It looks like the *Alpenjäger* are preparing another attack before the bad weather hits,' Cambrone concluded, as he stretched out for a rest.

Domenico had already lost count of the times they'd won or lost on those lousy positions high in the Alps, between Venice and Trento. When he saw Cambrone looking at him from his bunk with a frightened expression, he had no idea of the carnage awaiting them. His bunkmate, however, had noticed some unusual movement on his watch and already sensed that on that morning, 4 December 1917, the assault from the Austrian alpine battalions wouldn't be just another run-of-the-mill attack.

'Let me have a look at your girlfriend for a little while,' his bunkmate said, his voice trembling in anticipation of the battle.

'You're going to wear her out,' answered Domenico with a nervous laugh. He had bought a postcard of a naked lady in Bari, right before boarding the train that would bring him to the front. After two years at war he knew that woman by heart, and he had shared her with half the company. She was posed completely nude, sitting elegantly on a flowery stool, beside an inviting bed with velvety drapery. She had the body of an angel and she had extended her left arm back elegantly, to make her breasts stand gracefully to attention.

'Always picture perfect!' said the boys as they assiduously reviewed the girl's bosom.

Her hair was wavy black silk. It was just long enough for the ringlets to cover the nape of her neck and a big curl also coiled over one ear. Her face rested gently on her right hand, which lay on her shoulder. She had a sweet gaze, focused on some point beyond the camera's lens. No one in the whole company had ever seen a girl as lovely as her. They all called her *Palmisano's girlfriend*.

When the great grey wave of Austrian Alpine troops arrived, the orders and counter-commands came rapidly, and were increasingly contradictory. Soon it was clear to the Italians that the defence of their position would end in disaster, and they began a full-fledged exodus that only bolstered the already overwhelming victory of the attackers and the extraordinarily high death rate among those fleeing. Domenico, however, defended his position for hours, along with Cambrone and another bunkmate, Campana. The three of them had become inseparable and always fought together on the front line. They retreated only when they saw that they were about to be surrounded, and to their shock they discovered that their commanding officers had long since abandoned their positions.

Fleeing down to the valley, there they found the dregs of the battalion that had fled en masse hours earlier. Campana and Cambrone joined what remained of their company, but Domenico kept walking. After two years of fierce combat on the front line, he'd had enough. He'd decided to go home.

It was complete chaos on the roads, and no one bothered to ask him for his papers. Nor did they check that he had tickets or identification on any of the journeys he made by train. But eight days later, when he reached Bellorotondo, the military police were waiting there to arrest him as a deserter.

The next day, when they were taking him to their

headquarters in Bari, a few hours from Bellorotondo, he saw his grandfather for the first time in years, standing on the other side of the avenue.

'*Nonno, Nonno!*' he shouted, unable to comprehend why the guards wouldn't let him go to his grandfather. The young man seemed crazed, he kept screaming. The older Palmisano couldn't bear it and turned to go, desperate at not being able to hug his grandson or make him understand what was going on. When Domenico saw his grandfather leaving he let out a scream that echoed in the clear air of that frozen winter morning.

'*Nonno!*'

The soldier guarding Domenico rammed his rifle butt into his stomach, knocking him out with a second blow to the head. Only then was silence re-established and were they able to get into the car.

The next day he saw his grandfather again at the military court in Bari where he was being tried. He couldn't understand why his grandfather didn't speak, but he reasored that if he was there it meant he still loved him, and he again gave his famously irrepressible smile, which didn't flag even when the military judge sentenced him to death.

'Don't cry, *Nonno*. The war will be over soon!' he shouted to him when they pushed him on to the train that was to take him back north, to return him to the custody of the officers of his company. His grandfather watched him from the other side of the platform. It seemed to Domenico that he had shrunk.

The trip back to the mountain plateau was much faster than the route he had taken down to Bellorotondo. Two days after leaving Bari he reached Vicenza, and by the next day they had already taken him to Asiago and from there to the Col del Rosso, where they had sent what was left of the troops decimated in the disaster of 4 December. A new captain quickly assembled the firing squad from the few survivors in Domenico's unit, including Campana and Cambrone.

When the captain gave the order to fire', the members of the firing squad found themselves faced with Palmisano's innocent smile – he still didn't understand what was going on – and they shot into the air.

'Fire!' shouted the irate captain for a second time.

Again they intentionally missed their target.

The officer threatened the firing squad with a revolver, but the soldiers stood up to him.

'For the love of God, Captain . . . !' protested Campana. 'Domenico has saved our lives a thousand times. Less than a month ago, he took out two machine guns that had us cornered in Valbella, all on his own . . .'

'Shoot, damnit! Shoot! I am following orders. If you don't fire immediately, I'll have the lot of you court-martialled!'

They started to cry and shoot at the same time, and when Domenico collapsed, they could still hear him saying goodbye: 'I'm tired, *Nonno*. Take me home.'

Curled up on the ground, he shook violently, the sight sending a shiver down the spine of every soldier watching. Then, finally, he stretched out his legs and stopped twitching. His comrades surrounded him and lowered their heads to bid him farewell respectfully.

Cambrone was the first to break the silence: 'Son of a bitch!' he shouted, staring straight at the captain. He started shooting, in a rage, at Domenico's inert body. And as he fired he thought about the many contemptible officers who had led them from defeat to defeat through the Alps and who had now forced them to execute their best friend, who had died without understanding what was happening to him.

When the circumstances surrounding the death of Domenico Palmisano – that good egg – reached the town, his grandfather hanged himself from an olive tree.

Giuseppe Fu Francesco (17) had convinced himself that nothing more could happen to him, and he spent the night arguing his theory to his fellow soldier on watch as they shared the eagle's nest from which they had to control that particular Alpine pass. The January full moon lit up a crystal-clear night and the snow of the last few weeks refracted the light, sending it up to all the mountain peaks. It would have been a magnificent sight if not for the fact that Giuseppe was terrified at the piercingly low temperatures that the north wind further sharpened. He had never imagined that the cold could be so painful.

'If there is divine justice, then I'm untouchable,' he declared with conviction. 'At the start of the war we were twenty-one Palmisanos and now there are only nine left! We are protected by the other twelve's misfortune.'

They had hidden Domenico's execution from Giuseppe Fu Francesco, and they also hadn't said anything to him about his other three cousins felled at Caporetto, so he still didn't know that he was now one of only five survivors; for him the last family death had been Cataldo's (12). The other young man on watch didn't answer. When earlier they had been walking to their post, Giuseppe Fu Francesco had realized that his companion for the watch wasn't much of a talker, so he turned the conversation into a monologue that went on through the entire night. He couldn't come up with a better way to combat the cold and sleepiness.

When the day began to dawn he said, 'We can rest easy. They won't be back today.'

He went over to his companion, who still wasn't responding. When he grabbed him by the shoulder and shook him to wake him up, his body slipped from his hands and fell to the floor of the trench; only then did he notice the dried blood around the wound left by the bullet that had pierced his neck. It must have been from the attack they had fought off the evening before: he'd been talking to a dead man all night long.

He didn't even know his name. He closed his eyes, crossed himself and looked at him meditatively, the way the officers did during funeral ceremonies. Then he picked up his rifle, slung his rucksack over his shoulder and started to walk down the mountain, because they should have been relieved hours ago. When he reached the camp there was no one there. They must have fled in such haste that they hadn't even alerted them. He continued walking all alone, searching for points of reference between peaks that where completely foreign to him. In Bellorotondo, every hill, gully and bit of terraced land had a familiar name, but here he was lost. Ever since he had been sent to the Alpine front, he'd moved from one mountain to another, but he'd never known their names. Suddenly, he heard someone shout, 'Halt!'

He had just been taken prisoner by an Austrian patrol.

A week later Giuseppe Fu Francesco reached a prison camp to the east of the small Austrian town of Mauthausen, and he discovered to his horror that the Italian captives there were dying by the thousands in horrible pain and suffering. The guards rationed the food and gave the prisoners only what was sent from their own countries via the Red Cross. The Italian top brass considered those who allowed themselves to be captured cowards and traitors and refused to send them any supplies.

In the camp, he found his cousin Michele (18), who was dying from Spanish influenza. He was one of the more than a hundred thousand Italians who had been taken prisoner in the disaster at Caporetto. Giuseppe Fu Francesco had time only to hug him and close his eyes. A week later, he himself succumbed to starvation, without understanding why his people had abandoned him.

Angelantonio (19), who only had sisters, missed home the most of all of them. And he was the one sent the furthest away, to the Champagne region of France. On the front at the Marne he was so homesick that he started to lose his mind. The Italian soldiers in General Albricci's 2nd Army Corps had trouble understanding what the hell they were doing there, on a French front. No one had explained to them that after the Caporetto fiasco the Italian Supreme Command had asked the Allies for help: five French and English divisions had come to Italy's aid and, in return, to symbolize the reciprocity of the alliance, close to forty thousand Italians were sent to Champagne and the Chemin des Dames.

That was how Angelantonio found himself in a hellish trench in the Vrigny forest, near Reims, surrounded by magnificent vineyards, charged with defending Point 240 to the death, as it was bombed non-stop by the German artillery's howitzers. From his trench, turned to mud by the horribly bad weather, Angelantonio saw columns of civilians evacuating the capital of Champagne, fleeing from the collapse of the cellars where they had taken shelter from the German bombardment since the start of the war. He also saw his trench mates fall one by one, flattened by shells or poisoned by gas, from which the masks the Italian army provided – barely some gauze soaked in a sodium carbonate solution – were no protection.

Soon he began to display strange behaviour, and around the feast of Corpus Christi in 1918, he lost his mind. One night when he was on watch and everyone was trying to take advantage of the artillery truce between the two armies to get some rest, he confused the rats running between the sets of barbed wire with an attacking enemy detachment. He ran, shouting, to wake the company. Disconcerted, the Italians and the French, who were sharing a trench, started to shoot at the enemy lines and soon after the German positions returned fire, without really knowing what was going on. After an hour of exchanging gunfire, in a manner more hysterical than effective, Captain Monfalcone called for them to cease firing.

'Go back to sleep. I don't see any movement, and it doesn't look like they're preparing an attack.'

The next night, Angelantonio mistook an owl for the covert signs of another surprise attack and he woke the company up again. Half an hour after a fierce shootout, in which no one was killed but the nerves of the soldiers on both sides were shredded, the Italian captain decided again to call for a ceasefire. Calm settled over the Vrigny forest, but few of them were able to get back to sleep.

On the third night, before curling up under his blanket, Captain Monfalcone, a philosophy student from Lucca who was also unsure as to how he'd ended up in Champagne, called Angelantonio over.

'Look, Palmisano, if you think they're attacking us, let me know. But unless you want me to have you executed right here, don't wake the whole company up again.'

The captain hadn't even closed his eyes before he heard a shout:

'For Italy!'

He leapt up and saw Angelantonio running, all by himself, towards the enemy positions. Since Angelantonio had been told not to wake the others, even if he thought they were being attacked, he'd decided to launch his own counteroffensive. The German sentries sounded the alarm and when the soldiers saw a single man approaching with his gun drawn, they aimed their weapons, concentrating all their rage on to that madman who wasn't letting them sleep. They riddled him with bullets. Angelantonio shuddered in a macabre dance, and when the Germans stopped shooting he fell to the ground. An expectant silence hovered over both trenches. Both sides were wondering what would be the next twist in that outlandish succession of events.

'Thank you!' shouted Captain Monfalcone to the German trench, in a burst of sincerity. He immediately sensed that he shouldn't have said it, but it was already too late. He ordered his men back to bed.

'Tomorrow we'll try to recover the poor chap's body. Now let's try to get some sleep.'

On the night of 29 June 1918, the company of Ignazio (20) – the youngest of the Palmisanos, not yet eighteen – was asleep in a clearing in the woods at the foot of the Col del Rosso, just above the patch of land where six months earlier they had executed poor Domenico. Unaware of his proximity to his brother's remains, at dawn, he played a decisive role in the reconquering of the highest and most symbolic of the Tre Monti. Ignazio died a hero, victim of a stray bullet just as he was reaching the peak and the Austrians were about to surrender their position.

The Last Palmisano

VITO ORONZO PALMISANO, the last Palmisano, had survived the eleven battles of the Isonzo river one after the other, and he'd fought heroically without suffering the slightest injury over the three and half years since the war began. He seemed destined to be the family's only survivor. He was a vocal opponent of Italian participation in a conflict that had nothing to do with the peasants of Puglia, but even so he hadn't tried to avoid conscription. He had a strong sense of duty, always fighting bravely, but also never lapsing into recklessness or excessive zeal. In fact, he was the most prudent of his family and the one in whom war inspired a cautious respect.

On the front, he lived in the moment and carefully focused on his actions with an extraordinary survival instinct. He always acted on the idea that you shouldn't take any more risks than absolutely necessary on the battlefield, but that it was even more dangerous to hesitate or let yourself be overcome by fear. It wasn't that the pain and misery of war didn't affect him; in fact, he felt keenly the remoteness, hunger and panic of the trenches. And especially he missed Donata, who seemed only half his wife having been, in a promise of lifelong fidelity, wed in a rush on the morning that he set off for war; the marriage had yet to be consummated. For more than three years now, the soldiers of the 164th Company had been his only family.

In the last few months he had shared a trench with a wealthy chap from his home town, Antonio Convertini, and they had become inseparable. Fate had brought them together – first in the same battalion, and finally, right before the changes brought about by the defeat at Caporetto, in the same company. Their wives, Donata and Francesca, were first cousins, both from Matera, a two-day trip from Bellorotondo, and had been best friends since early childhood. The men received notification on the same day that they had been granted leave, their first leave since the start of the war, thanks to an initiative by the new Chief of Staff, General Armando Diaz, who was looking to improve morale among his dispirited troops.

As Vito and Antonio were preparing to go on leave, the soldiers from the battalions camped in the Piave heard rumours of an imminent offensive and were regaining their optimism.

'You blokes are really going to miss out,' joked their fellow soldiers as they enviously bade them farewell. 'By the time you come back we'll have won the war. The Austrians will have surrendered or legged it, and you'll have to come looking for us all the way over in Ljubljana.'

Indeed, everything seemed to indicate that the war

was coming to an end, and when on 17 October 1918 Vito Oronzo Palmisano arrived in Bellorotondo with Antonio Convertini, it also appeared that he had cheated death for good and saved himself from the family curse. Three of his brothers and seventeen of his cousins had died in that futile war; Vito Oronzo was the last man left in his family.

Nonetheless, he felt unsettled when he arrived in Bellorotondo. It wasn't anything like he'd been remembering it at the front. Families were in mourning. The abandoned olive groves and vineyards were a pitiful sight. Nor did the older men seem to admire the young men's sacrifices on the battlefields; they were just waiting for the war finally to end. Vito was also upset to discover that the sons of the richest men in town had avoided being called up and that, consequently, their vineyards were thriving. It all gave credence to the rumour that had run through the trenches: the powerful paid to escape the front, the leading example of this being Antonio Salandra; the prime minister who had vehemently supported Italy entering the war had also ignominiously manoeuvred to ensure that none of his three sons went anywhere near the battlefield.

Vito Oronzo didn't want to dwell on it, or breed bad blood. Putting any such distressing thoughts from his mind, he threw himself, body and soul, into enjoying the week's leave that he'd been dreaming of for three years: the magnificent autumn light in Puglia and Donata's company. He wanted to savour them both.

Each day early in the morning, they walked along

the vineyard path up to the olive grove. Donata was proud of her Verdeca grapes, among the few that had been harvested during the war in all the valley: she and the women in her family had worked from sunrise to sundown to compensate for the lack of men and, contrary to the whole town's expectations, they'd been rewarded with a magnificent crop. Every morning, once they'd reached the largest olive grove, Donata and Vito would meet up with the women and old people from the neighbourhood, who gathered in groups to help them. Vito Oronzo and Donata were always at the head of the first group, with Antonio Convertini and Francesca, who had also come to lend a hand. Concetta, the widow of Vito's brother Stefano (8), led the other group. In just a week of leave, they harvested the remaining *nuzarol* olives on almost all the *rossa* trees.

When it grew dark that first evening of leave, they returned to the large farmhouse from the back, through the *oliastra* olives, which were also ripe. Seeing them out of the corner of his eye, Vito warned Donata, 'Next week you'll have to harvest these *ñastre*; they're ready.'

That evening, they made up for the time they had lost during the three years the war had kept them apart: they locked themselves in and kissed each other all over.

The week passed in the blink of an eye. On 24 October, Vito Oronzo and Antonio had to take a train to Bari, to go back up north to rejoin their company, which had moved with the entire battalion to the outskirts of Vittorio Veneto, just north of Venice. The Italian offensive had begun.

At the break of dawn, Vito Oronzo and Donata said goodbye in the kitchen; she was helping him into his uniform jacket, but every button he fastened she immediately unfastened.

'Do you mean to say that they really need *you* to win this stupid war? You can't stay a few more days?'

'Before you know it the war will be over and I'll be back here to nibble on you.'

Vito Oronzo started to kiss her neck. Then he bit open her lips and sought out her tongue. He untied her ponytail and her long hair fell over her breasts, and he kissed them too, as he undid her blouse. Lifting up her skirt, Donata stretched out on the kitchen table and he frantically covered her entire body with little bites.

Afterwards, they got up from the table, Vito kissed her on the lips one last time, and they both rushed out of the house, still buttoning up their shirts. Panting, they reached the train station just as Antonio and Francesca did, running from town. They too had got carried away in the kitchen of their house on the Piazza Santa Anna, in the centre of Bellorotondo. The night before they had dined in the Convertini palazzo and hadn't been able to slip away from their family until late. When they finally got home they couldn't sleep.

'You certainly made the most of it!' both men said simultaneously as they settled into the train carriage, just in time, and they realized each was out of breath. And they laughed as they stuck their heads through the compartment window to kiss their wives one last time.

'We'll be back before Christmas!' shouted Vito Oronzo to his wife as the train that would take them to the regional capital started of.

Donata and Francesca watched their husbands as they laughed like madmen and leaned wildly out of the window to say goodbye. The women stood on the platform, hand in hand, trying to hold on to the laughter of the men, who grew smaller and smaller down the track. The train took a bend, they saw them wave one last time and then they were out of sight.

On 3 November, the Austrians signed the armistice. The news reached Bellorotondo in the late evening of a sunny Sunday, unusually warm for the time of year. People rushed out on to the streets to celebrate the news, so long hoped for, with hugs and shouts of euphoria. The next day the town council decreed three days of public holiday, and the festivities exceeded all official expectations. Many families wavered between their grief over the fallen and their happiness at the end of the fighting, but soon they opted to forget their pain: the dead were left behind, buried far away in the foggy northern lands; the time had come to celebrate peace. Each evening, the balconies filled with the farmers returning from the valley, anxious to dance to the rhythm of the small orchestra and rejoice at the return of the survivors.

Donata and Francesca, who had also come out to mark the war's end, didn't dance: they paced back and forth, trying to find out when the men were due to return from the front.

'Rome doesn't have the money to feed the soldiers; they'll be home in a few weeks!' they were assured by the local priest, who prided himself on always being well informed.

That Sunday, Donata fell asleep very late, with her head resting on her arms folded on the kitchen table. She dreamt that Vito Oronzo was kissing her neck and unbuttoning her blouse, until she was woken up by a stranger knocking on the door. When she opened it, the town official didn't dare meet her eye; he put the letter into her hands and fled, mumbling something under his breath.

Donata read:

The mayor of the town of Bellorotondo, in the district of Bari, is hereby asked to communicate to the family members of Private Vito Oronzo Palmisano, son of Giorgio and Brunetta, with ID number 18309, of 164th Company, 94th Infantry Regiment, of the 1892 levy, that he departed the world of the living on 4 November 1918 . . .

Donata didn't understand what they were trying to tell her. She searched for the letter's heading, which she had skipped in her rush to see if they were notifying her of the date of her husband's return. On the upper part of the official form there were large printed letters: *'94° Reggimento Fanteria. Consiglio di Admministrazione. AVVISO DI MORTE.'*

Her heart stopped beating. She felt her legs folding under and she fainted on the front steps. At that moment, the same town official was heading quickly towards the Via Cavour with an identical letter for Francesca: the news of Antonio Convertini's death. Unbelievably, the two friends had fallen at midday on 4 November, just as the batallion was waiting for the ceasefire, signed the night before, to come into effect that very day at 2 p.m.

The official notification of these final two senseless deaths reached Bellorotondo three days late, when they were already dismantling the stage used by the little orchestra that had joyfully accompanied the armistice celebration. Having already decided to turn the page on the tragedy of war, the town's nine thousand inhabitants forgot to mourn the two poor men's bad luck. Donata was left to come to terms all on her own with the death of the last Palmisano, the death that marked the fulfilment of the family curse, and she took refuge in the house of Francesca, the only person with whom she could share her grief.

From that day on, Donata and Francesca spent their time together, keeping each other company, but still unable to accept that their husbands were never coming back. If the war was already over, how could they have died?

In December, Giuseppe 'Skinny' Vicino returned from the front. He had worked for the Convertini family before the war and in the final months of the conflict he had been transferred to Vito Oronzo and Antonio's company. The captain had charged Skinny with delivering the dead men's personal belongings to their widows. He told them about the two men's final hours and how they had become the last two victims of the war.

'On the twenty-sixth of October, when Vito Oronzo and Antonio came back from leave, we had just begun our last offensive, under pressure from the Americans and the English: "The last few weeks you've held up well against the Austro-Hungarians; maybe now you can do something more," they said. The Italian generals were offended and ordered the attack. Surprisingly, the enemy seemed to be made of butter and we easily made it through their lines of defence at the gates of Vittorio Veneto. After just a few days we had liberated Trento and the Austrians were barely shooting back. They were too busy running away . . .'

Donata and Francesca listened with eyes filled with tears. They gripped their husbands' wallets in their hands, as if they were treasures; in them they had found their own photos and the last letters they had each written to the men. They hung on skinny's words, feeding the irrational hope that they might lead to a happy ending: as if the telling of the tale had the power to refute reality and bring their husbands back.

'. . . On the fourth of November we decided to continue our advance so that by the time the armistice was signed we would have the most territory possible under Italian control. We were marching, but no one had fired a gun in some time; both sides of the front were watching the clock, because at two in the afternoon the ceasefire would officially come into effect. But at around two, a stray shot hit Antonio in the leg. Before he fell, a second bullet hit him below the shoulder. We all took cover, but he was left exposed to the shots of a sniper hidden in some house. Vito Oronzo didn't think twice: the two had been inseparable since they'd returned from leave, and he ran out to drag Antonio to cover. The sniper shot at him, too, and it was a miracle he didn't take him down. It would have been suicide to run out into the open again, so they both had to stay hidden behind some ruins for more than two hours. During that time we tried to clear the houses of snipers, but a group of Austrians prevented us. Antonio was bleeding to death and Vito decided to move him.

'"I have to get him out of here. He needs a doctor . . ." he shouted from their hiding place.

'It's too risky, don't try it,' I warned him.

'He won't make it, we have to try,' was his reply.'

Skinny paused. Before continuing he shifted his gaze and looked down at the table, as if he wanted to apologize.

'With Antonio in his arms, Vito Oronzo started running, looking for a wall to hide behind. We heard a second shot and he collapsed. But before we could react, the sniper hit Antonio again. Later, we saw that they had both been shot in the head. They would have both died instantly.'

Donata had turned towards the window. She had

closed her eyes some time earlier and was trying to imagine the final moments in the life of her Vito Oronzo: the last Palmisano had died when the war was officially over, but he had died without knowing it. Without suffering. It was cold comfort: she hid her face in her hands and wished she were dead.

PART TWO

The Garden Full of White Flowers

The Widows' House

AFTER THE WAR, Bellorotondo was a town filled with widows, but the term was reserved for Donata and Francesca. When they decided to move in together to share their grief, the town pointedly began calling Francesca's house in the Piazza Santa Anna *the Widows' House*. In towns like Bellorotondo, young, beautiful widows were highly valued and these two were the most desirable among them. Donata had a serene beauty, with bright chestnut-brown eyes, and she was very kind and quick to laugh. The widow of the last Palmisano never tried to hide her humble roots: she had the discreet charm of a Matera shepherdess. The Convertini widow, on the other hand, in just three years of marriage, had already merged her physical beauty with the seductive elegance of one of the wealthiest families in Puglia. Francesca was gorgeous: she had very long black hair, dark skin, incredible green eyes and shiny, moist lips like ripe fruit. And she had a beautiful body: firm, round breasts like hard peaches; strong shoulders; fleshy thighs and a reed-like waist that swung to the rhythm of her long, long legs.

During the first few weeks after their husbands'

deaths, the widows cried constantly. Eventually, they learned to stifle their tears, but they still spent their days wandering about the house like lost souls. Until one day, a few weaks later, Francesca entered the kitchen smiling widely, something Donata hadn't seen since their husbands had been in town on leave.

'I'm expecting!'

Donata leapt up and hugged her. Her smile was as broad as her cousin's, but when she sat down at the kitchen bench she began biting her lip. Noticing her nervous gesture, which didn't match the joy of the moment, Francesca knew something was wrong.

'What is it? Aren't you happy?' she asked.

'Of course I'm happy . . .' Donata hesitated for a moment. Finally, she said, 'It's just that . . . I'm pregnant too!'

'Really? Why were you keeping it to yourself?' Francesca let out a loud laugh. She took her cousin by the hands and pulled her up. 'Let's dance! If we have a boy and a girl, we can marry them.'

'Don't joke, I haven't slept for days. Francesca, I'm really scared.'

'I don't understand.'

'What if it's a boy?'

'What do you mean? Don't you like little boys?'

'I can't have a boy, he would be cursed like all the Palmisano men. I can't bring him up thinking about how he'll be killed when he grows up. I don't know what that family did to deserve such a fate, but I won't have a child just to sacrifice him!'

'That's in the past, the war is over.'

'Wars are never over. They always come back! A war that was officially over robbed half of our lives from us.'

Francesca wasn't usually superstitious, but she knew that Donata was right: for some unknown reason, God had decided to take vengeance on the Palmisanos and had condemned all the men in the family to death. Hugging her cousin, she wondered how it was possible that a new life could already be so burdened with bad omens.

They stood in silence, leaning on one another, for a long time. Then Donata emerged from Francesca's embrace, looked into her enormous green eyes and said, 'You have to promise me that, if it is a boy, you'll pretend he's yours and bring him up as a Convertini. We'll name him Vitantonio. Only you and I will know that it's in honour of my Vito Oronzo, his father, and your Antonio, who will give him his surname and his chance to survive the curse.'

The months passed, and while Francesca showed off her growing belly in the streets of Bellorotondo, Donata hid her pregnancy two days' journey from Bellorotondo in the Sassi caves, the ancient neighbourhood of Matera, where all her family came from, and where people might well assume she had gone simply to grieve. When the moment of birth drew near, she discreetly returned to Bellorotondo, to the Widows' House. Both women had their baby on St Anne's feast day, on the morning of 26 July 1919. Dr Ricciardi, the only one who shared their secret, attended to them. Luckily, all the townspeople were distracted by the town's patron saint's feast, even though it would be very modestly celebrated that summer, as many families were still in mourning.

Donata was the first to give birth, shortly after midnight. When the baby was born, the doctor took him in his arms, putting off the verdict as long as he could. Finally, with great sorrow, he told her, 'It's a boy.'

She closed her eyes and stifled a scream. It was as if she had just been split in two by a razor-sharp sword. Then she opened her eyes, full of tears, and asked, 'Let me hold him, Gabriele.'

Dr Gabriele Ricciardi was the family doctor for both the Palmisanos and the Convertinis, and had attended to all twenty-one of the dead Palmisano men's births. He was the only doctor in the region who saw both rich patients and the poor peasants who couldn't afford even a measure of quinine. Placing the boy on her chest, he went out into the hallway. Donata hugged the baby so tightly that he started to cry. Listening from behind the door, the doctor wondered whether Donata would have the strength to go through with the cruel pact he was about to condone. Taking a deep breath, he went back into the room.

'Are you sure you want to do this?'

'I might die of grief, but he will survive the curse.'

The doctor said nothing, but he turned his head to wipe away a tear. The little boy continued crying.

'What a pair of lungs! And to think that all this life is condemned by a cruel curse!' Donata said bitterly.

'It's best if I take him to Francesca so he can get used to her,' he said gently. 'She's still got a few hours to go.'

When he went to take the boy into his arms, Donata wouldn't let him go.

'Just one moment more,' she begged. And she started to kiss the baby and promise to love him for ever. 'Maybe one day you'll understand,' she said to him. 'No mother has ever loved a child as much as I love you right now . . .'

Ricciardi had taken a seat in a corner of the room, in the shadows, and was silently weeping, unable to control his rage at the cruelty of the situation. Then he got up decisively, kissed Donata on the forehead, took the boy in his arms and carried him to Francesca.

From her bed, Donata could hear how the baby began to settle in his new mother's arms. The doctor stopped pacing and went into the kitchen. He occasionally heard the baby's cries. He also thought he could hear Donata's sobs in the distance. Finally, the house having fallen silent, he took a nap in a chair. When he woke up, he washed his face and prepared Francesca for her imminent birth. Donata had stopped crying and, when Ricciardi went into her room to make sure everything was all right before tending to Francesca, he discovered that she had slipped out of the house while he was sleeping.

Francesca gave birth at around six in the morning to a girl. The next day the town got the surprising news that the widow Convertini had had twins. A week later, Father Felice, the family priest, officiated at a very solemn ceremony at the baptismal font of the church of the Immacolata and christened the two little ones: Vitantonio and Giovanna Convertini.

Zia

AFTER THE BIRTHS, Donata spent all her time at Francesca's house, so much so that when the 'twins' began to talk, they soon started to call her *zia*, auntie. In actual fact, they grew up with two mothers, who secretly shared all the work of raising them. When they breastfed the babies, Donata tended to pick up Vitantonio, her own son; Francesca, on the other hand, usually chose Giovanna. Every once in a while, though, they switched, and that way the children grew accustomed to their two mothers: *Mamma* and *Zia*.

At Francesca's house in Bellorotondo they were able to enjoy both the convenience of living in the centre of town and a more rural life. The main façade looked out on to the Via Cavour, but behind the house there was a small courtyard backing on to the square and the church of Santa Anna. So the neighbours, when they didn't call it the Widows' House, referred to it as the house on the Piazza Santa Anna. From the upstairs back window, they had an exceptional view over the olive groves and the *trulli* huts of the Itria valley, all the way from the hills of Alberobello to the slopes of Cisternino. Seen from a distance, Francesca's house stood proudly smack in the middle of the majestic skyline of Bellorotondo, the circular town on top of a hill, like a watchtower always ready to defend the most fertile valley in all of southern Italy for its modest farmers. If the house on the Piazza Santa Anna had been a bit taller, Donata and Francesca might have seen, to the south, the homes and palazzos of the town of Martina Franca, which clung to its own hill, the first one beyond the Itria valley.

The Widows' House was ideally situated, but the two cousins longed for more. They missed the sheep herding they'd done outside Matera when they were girls. In a bid to combat their nostalgia they decided to fill the courtyard with animals: hens, rabbits and pigeons soon became Giovanna and Vitantonio's favourite playthings.

The twins also grew up under the influence of their grandmother, Angela Convertini, née Orsini, a Venetian who had moved to Puglia as a child when her father, who was a lawyer, was sent there for work. Her subsequent marriage made her the matriarch of the Convertini family and she never forgot that the twins were her eldest son's children and, as such, her own blood. Antonio's tragic death in the war didn't make the children any less true Convertinis. The family had prospered thanks to timber, becoming one of the wealthiest in the region. The old sawmill had done well since the day Antonio Convertini senior had decided to import Austrian fir and started dealing in large stocks of chestnut from the forests of Tuscany and the Gargano. His early death was an unexpected blow; but just when the decline seemed inevitable, his widow surprised everyone by taking over the business and relaunching it with even better results – especially when she decided they should also buy fir from the Volga region of Russia, more desirable than Austrian wood.

As Angela quickly showed exceptional resilience, and an instinct for business far superior to that of the men she was competing with, the townspeople started to call her *Lady Angela* and soon just *the Lady*. And, indeed, no one doubted that Angela Convertini was *the Lady of Bellorotondo*.

On 26 July 1923, the twins turned four. Again, it was also the town's patron saint's feast day and the whole of Bellorotondo was celebrating. But just as the various birthday parties were in full swing, Francesca fell ill, and from that day on the doctor's visits became more and more frequent, until the X-rays confirmed the worst: tuberculosis. Donata left the Palmisano house on the outskirts of town – where she only very occasionally lived with her sister-in-law Concetta – and moved definitively into Francesca's house in Bellorotondo to take care of the twins and her sick cousin. Lady Angela made a desperate attempt to send Francesca to a sanatorium, but her daughter-in-law refused point-blank: she said that there was nowhere she would be more comfortable than in her own home and that no one would take better care of her than her own cousin. She would have said anything: there was nothing in the world that could come between her and her little ones.

From the autumn of 1923 to the following spring, Francesca spent long periods bedridden with only occasional, sporadic improvement. Donata remained by her side. Together they fondly recalled times in Matera and made plans for when Francesca was well again, although they both knew that she wasn't going to get better and that death was only a matter of time. Even so, Donata refused to give up: each week she killed a rabbit or a chicken and made sure Francesca ate the kind of food that might restore the energy of which the illness robbed her. In the evenings, she prepared pigeon broth and didn't leave Francesca's bedside until she had drunk it all. As summertime approached, Francesca had one of her good spells, which arrived unexpectedly, and on Santa Anna's feast day they were able to take her rocking chair out into the courtyard to celebrate the twins' fifth birthday and watch the annual fireworks.

It was a false dawn. In September, Francesca had a relapse and was confined to bed indefinitely. As she rapidly deteriorated, Dr Ricciardi prepared them for the end. Francesca had grown so thin that she was barely recognizable. When she coughed, she stained her handkerchiefs with blood, and her rattling wheeze echoed through every corner of the house.

But despite the doctor's prognosis, Francesca improved slightly and survived all of October and November. Until one December evening, on the eve of the Feast of the Immaculate Conception, she realized that the moment had come: she called for Fini the notary and dictated her last will and testament. The next day, at the crack of dawn, she sent for Father Felice, who happened to be Angela Convertini's brother; he gave her the last rites. That afternoon she called for her mother-in-law, Lady Angela herself, and they locked themselves in her bedroom. Two hours later they let Father Felice in and shortly after the mayor and the notary arrived at the house and joined the meeting.

The group left the house at seven in the evening. When they had all gone, Donata went into the bedroom and found that Francesca was barely breathing. She seemed to be asleep, but wore an enigmatic smile. Hearing Donata come in, she opened her eyes. She took her cousin by the hands and her inexplicable smile grew wides.

'Don't worry, Donata, everything will be fine. And now bring the children to me, I want to say goodbye.'

She had never made any distinction between the twins and she hugged them now as if they were both hers. She held them close for a little while: before she died she wanted to breathe in their scent to remember it for ever. Then, Donata took them and put them to bed. When she returned to her cousin's side, Francesca still wore an enigmatic smile, but her eyes were closed.

'Are they sleeping?' she asked in a thin wisp of a voice.

'They prayed to their guardian angel and fell asleep right away. For several days now they've been fighting sleep and staying up until they can't keep their eyes open. They don't know what's going on, but they can tell that something's wrong.'

Donata knelt by her cousin and gently kissed her eyes and cheeks. Their tears mingled together. Francesca wanted to pull back so she could look Donata in the eyes, but she didn't have the strength. She had one last breath and she used it as she brought her lips to Donata's ear.

'I fulfilled my promise with Vitantonio. Now you have to swear to me that you will always treat Giovanna as if she were your own daughter.'

And just as Donata said, 'I swear it,' Francesca fought, unsuccessfully, for another breath. In its stead, an faint sigh escaped her as she died.

The Funeral

AT FRANCESCA'S FUNERAL, Donata Palmisano presided next to Lady Angela and no one batted an eye, because by now they all considered Donata part of the Convertini family. When she entered the church of the Immacolata, she held little Giovanna and Vitantonio by the hand and she didn't let them go throughout the entire funeral. Two hours later, at the Bellorotondo cemetery, they still hadn't been separated: standing before the Convertini family vault, at the highest and most central part of the graveyard, they held hands tightly, heads bowed and fearful. Donata and Giovanna were dressed all in black, Vitantonio in a white shirt that contrasted with his mourning tie and armband.

Everyone came over and gave their condolences to Donata as if she were the deceased's closest relative. Then they gently touched the children's faces or ruffled their hair and started to cry. The tiny, helpless twins awakened a compassion in those rough, calloused Puglian farmers that they wouldn't have allowed themselves in any other circumstances.

After the funeral, Donata went over to the Convertini

brothers and kissed them one by one. First, Angelo, who had taken Antonio's place at the sawmill and had become heir to the family fortune after his death. Then she kissed Matteo, Marco, Luca and Giovanni, known as 'the four evangelists': all four had studied in Bari, married there and stayed. Matteo worked with his father-in-law as a shoemaker; Marco was a lawyer; Luca worked at the Banca Popolare; Giovanni was an engineer, but he had just set up a chemical company with his brother-in-law from Otranto and was about to move there. She also kissed young Margherita, who had married the son of a Venetian notary and gone to live up north, mirroring in reverse the journey her mother had made years before. Lastly, she went over to Lady Angela. The two women looked into each other's eyes for what seemed an eternity to Donata. Finally, Angela Convertini put her hands on Donata's shoulders, pulled her towards her and kissed her twice on each cheek.

Still holding both children's hands, Donata turned to leave the cemetery. The three of them moved forward with small, hesitant steps through the groups of neighbours who were discussing the tragedy in sombre tones. The crowd opened to let them pass and when Donata and the children reached the gate and began walking up the long avenue lined with cypress trees that led to the centre of town, everyone found it perfectly normal that Vito Oronzo Palmisano's widow, a poor peasant girl from Matera, had left with the two children of Francesca, the widow of the eldest son in the wealthy Convertini line. Nor were they surprised when neither the twins' uncles, nor their aunt, nor their grandmother Angela, the true head of the family, moved to stop her.

To the Notary's

THE DAY AFTER the burial, Donata was on her hands and knees washing the back porch of the Widows' House on the Piazza Santa Anna when Giovanna and Vitantonio ran out, shouting for her.

'*Zia*, there's a man asking for you! He's very well dressed.'

On her knees, their aunt watched Fini the notary come in and, without really knowing why, she was immediately on her guard.

'Is something wrong?' she asked without getting to her feet.

'Good morning, Signora Palmisano. I need you to come to the office tomorrow, to settle poor Francesca's last wishes, which affect you and also the two little ones. Can you come by tomorrow morning?'

'Of course . . . But what is it about the children? As you can see, they're perfectly fine.'

All that afternoon, Donata couldn't eat and forgot to give the twins their tea. When they saw her crying, they leapt on her to wipe away her tears with kisses and caresses. Later that afternoon, she took them both to the church of the Immacolata, where they had been just the day before to bury Francesca.

'Are we going to see *Mamma* again?' asked Vitantonio, a bit frightened when they entered. They had never liked the stone lions that guarded the church door; from a distance they seemed welcoming, but up close they had sharp teeth and a fierce gaze, their menacing eyes warning of all sorts of threats.

Donata headed to a side aisle, on the left of the church, and stopped in front of the chapel of Our Lady of Sorrows. When she lifted her head to look at the wooden image, she fixed her gaze directly on the silver sword that pierced the virgin's heart. Donata felt the same pain that had tormented her every time she went to the chapel to pray for her son, ever since the night she had given birth. She had the twins sit on the first pew as she dropped to her knees. All she could do was beg for the Virgin Mary's compassion.

'From one mother to another!' she whispered.

After praying in front of Our Lady of Sorrows she moved on to the chapel of the Blessed Sacrament. Donata sat down on a pew and lay the children down with their heads on her lap, both facing the huge stone nativity scene that adorned the left side of the chapel. She hugged them tightly and was relieved to find that the nativity figures calmed them: lambs that grazed beside the shepherds, the ox and the mule, and baby Jesus.

She watched as they both dozed off and when she

too fell asleep she had a nightmare: the lions at the door were chasing the lambs from the manger. The lions had sharp claws and fierce, bulging eyes and, as the dream progressed, they took on the face of her brother-in-law Angelo Convertini; the lambs were Vitantonio and Giovanna, who ran from him in terros and clung to their *zia*'s neck for protection. On that freezing December night, Donata woke drenched in sweat and swore that she would never again fall asleep, for fear of waking to find the children had been taken from her.

She arrived at the notary's office the next morning, still holding the children by the hand, ready to argue that they would be better off with her than with anyone else. But when she entered the room she felt her nerve fail her: Angela Convertini and her son Angelo were seated in two armchairs, one on either side of the desk. The Lady of Bellorotondo was dressed all in black, looking very austere, but she wore a chain around her neck with a solid gold Christ pendant, like the one usually adorning the bishop's neck. Angelo had on a dark woollen suit, and from the waistcoat pocket peeked out a gold watch chain that had belonged to his father. Since Antonio's death in the war, Angelo had claimed his right as heir and didn't miss a single opportunity to assert himself as the eldest Convertini son. Nonetheless, in the end, he always had to bend to his mother's overpowering will, which she liked to impose, without too much pomp and circumstance, as the indisputable head of the family.

The four evangelists were also in the room: Marco sat alone, in a chair; Matteo, Luca and Giovanni had settled beside each other on a sofa. Father Felice, Lady Angela's brother, was pacing around the office, with a breviary in his hand, as if the situation was making him uncomfortable. They had also called in Signor Maurizio, the mayor, who was sitting somewhat casually in another armchair at the back of the room. It was his official presence that particularly unsettled Donata.

'Sit in this chair, next to Marco. My mother will take the children to the kitchen and give them something to keep them busy,' said the notary.

Donata resisted letting go of their hands; something about this scene gave her a very bad feeling. When the notary's mother took Vitantonio and Giovanna, her legs buckled slightly and she had to lean on the arm of a chair.

'Let's get to work,' said the notary, calling them to order once he was installed behind his desk.

The four evangelists sat up and Donata saw that all of them were twirling the tips of their moustaches with both hands, in an identical gesture, ready to listen respectfully to Fini's explanations. They looked ridiculous, but she didn't have it in her to laugh. She didn't even react when Father Felice, who had only just sat down, began to snore on the other side of the room. She was having trouble breathing again and she said a Hail Mary in an attempt to forestall the bad omens. She had never before felt so devout as in those last few hours.

'This is all rather unconventional,' the notary began, 'but all those present agree that, if these were indeed Francesca's wishes, we must respect them. Before she wrote them out, I clearly explained to her that her provisions were somewhat irregular and could be taken very badly, but she was insistent. So here are her wishes, in brief. The properties that Francesca inherited from her late husband, Antonio, will be divided into two parts: the two large olive groves by the Martina Franca road, of sixty and a hundred and forty hectares respectively, and their large farmsteads will revert to the Convertini estate and be shared among the six surviving siblings, according to an attached document. The small olive grove, the one on the outskirts of town, consisting of five hectares and a *trulli* hut, and the house on the Via Cavour, which you all know as the house in the Piazza Santa Anna, will be for Vitantonio and Giovanna, who will inherit them when they turn twenty-three. Until then, Donata Palmisano will be the trustee.'

The notary looked up from the will and stared straight at Donata. For the first time he addressed her informally.

'You cannot sell or divest yourself of any property, but you will have use of it until the children are of age, and the children will remain in your custody thanks to this private agreement. Next week the family court judge will call you in to swear your acceptance.

'Father Felice, Signor Maurizio and Lady Angela were there when I first read Francesca the legal provisions and they signed as witnesses, at her express wish.

We all agree that this is fair. As do Angelo, Matteo, Marco, Luca and Giovanni, who will sign the attached document accepting everything set out in the will; Lady Angela will sign by proxy for her daughter, Margherita. The Martina Franca olive groves will revert to the Convertinis, who had given them to poor Antonio before he died on the Piave front . . .'

Donata hadn't been paying attention to the notary for some time. She wouldn't lose her son Vitantonio and she had just gained a daughter, Giovanna. She didn't care about anything else. She was no longer listening to his speech, which had been going on for more than an hour. Nor did she notice the shuffling of chairs when all the Convertinis stood up, nor did she hear how they said goodbye to Fini, nor did she see that they were nodding at her in farewell. Only the voice of Fini the notary eventually brought her back to reality.

'Let's go and see what those two are doing in the kitchen, but first wipe away your tears.'

'I still can't believe it!' she said, taking the notary's hands and kissing them.

Amused, the notary let her do it, adding, 'Nor can I, Signora Donata. I can't believe it either. But Francesca insisted and made the whole family accept it. Of course, the prospect of regaining the Martina Franca olive groves and houses must have helped . . .'

'Who cares about the groves, Signor Fini. The only thing that matters are the children. I thought they would want to take them from me.'

'Well, the only one who thought about fighting to

keep them was Lady Angela. She did everything she could to get Francesca to change her mind; she insisted that the grandchildren should live with their family and not with a friend – even a cousin – who had no blood ties to them. The day before she died, Francesca called for Lady Angela and they spoke for more than two hours; then they called for Father Felice, who also considered it an aberration to separate the children from their family. When they finally called for me, poor Francesca had used up the little energy she had left. Even so, she begged me to draw up her last wishes for the twins right then and there and attach them to the will she had dictated the previous evening. Then she had the mayor come and she wanted everyone to sign the documents before leaving the room.'

Fini the notary stopped. Something was bothering him, and had been since that night. He took a deep breath and continued with his story.

'I don't know what Francesca said to her, but in the end it was Lady Angela who convinced the mayor and the priest to sign as witnesses. She said it was essential so that no one in the family or the town could question the legitimacy of the will, especially with regard to the custody of Giovanna and Vitantonio. That was the evening poor Francesca died . . . I don't know if we'll ever know what was said in that room before the mayor and I arrived!'

Donata could imagine it fairly easily. Thinking about her friend, she gave a wide smile. Out of the corner of his eye, the notary saw her smile and couldn't help but say out loud, as if talking to himself, 'Maybe someday I'll understand how it all played out.'

Donata shrugged.

'By the way,' he suddenly recalled, now addressing Donata directly, 'before she relented, Lady Angela added two clauses to the will that you will have to comply with to the letter: every Sunday you must bring the twins for lunch at the Convertini palazzo, and when comes the time to make decisions about their education, she will decide, as their grandmother. And you will have to accept her choice.'

Donata didn't argue. What could she say, when she could barely read and write as a child and was only really learning now as an adult? When she lived in Matera and was being courted by a Palmisano from Bellorotondo, she never even dreamt that one day her children would go to school; where she came from you had children to work in the fields.

In the kitchen, Vitantonio and Giovanna were eating biscuits and giggling. Donata considered Lady Angela's clauses a very small price to pay for keeping the treasure that Francesca had just entrusted to her.

Food for the Dead

AS THE FIRST anniversary of Francesca's death approached, Donata missed her more and more. On the eve of All Saints' Day in 1925 she lit candles in every window of the house and after supper she left food on the table in case any of their dead ancestors decided to make an appearance, as was traditional.

'Don't mention it to your *nonna*,' she warned the children, who were helping her. 'She doesn't understand these things.'

And after that year, every All Saints' Day they would always lock themselves in the kitchen and prepare a big bowl of *grano dei morti*, cooked wheat that they mixed with *vincotto*, pomegranate, nuts, sugar and cinnamon, for the Feast of the Dead the next day. When they'd finished, they would light candles in the windows, which in turn illuminated the back of the house's and gave the Piazza Santa Anna a suitably dramatic atmosphere. To avoid *Nonna*'s disapproval, though, they kept quiet about setting the table with dishes for the dead. Lady Angela may have been a devout follower of religious feast days but in general she distrusted the local traditions, which she considered pagan and superstitious.

Donata didn't believe in them either. In fact, over the years, she didn't perform the rituals out of any sort of religious conviction, but rather out of her need to feel a link with her ancestors.

From the first floor of the house, above the square and the church of Santa Anna, the small family were afforded a privileged view of the cypress-lined avenue that led to the Bellorotondo cemetery. In the first months after Francesca's death, whenever she leaned out of the kitchen window, Donata thought about Francesca, but she still didn't have the heart to go to visit her cousin's grave. She preferred to remember her alive, thinking of her irreverently sticking her tongue into her cheek and bursting out laughing.

In the autumn, Donata finally made up her mind to go to the cemetery. On the Day of the Dead, almost a year on from the burial, they returned to the Convertini vault for the first time. They went early in the morning, when it was just getting light, and as they walked to the cemetery the children entertained themselves by counting the cypress trees along the avenue. In one row, on the right-hand side of the path, they counted 136; on the left-hand side, there were only 132: a year earlier four had died, they had been chopped down at ground height and no one had bothered to replace them.

Once they'd reached the cemetery, they headed to the Convertini vault, to pray at Francesca and Antonio's tombs. Then they repeated their prayers on the other side of the grounds, in front of the modest gravestone for Vito Oronzo Palmisano. And that was the first of their annual visits to the Bellorotondo cemetery, which became a solemn fixture on the calendar of family traditions.

From then on, they always visited Francesca's grave first, so that the twins could jointly place a bouquet of white chrysanthemums there. Then they turned to the right side of the vault and repeated their prayers facing the memorial to Antonio, the father they had never known. Here, Donata made sure that it was Giovanna alone who delicately placed the bouquet of red chrysanthemums on her father's grave. Later, at the other end of the cemetery, when they recited the same prayers in front of Vito Oronzo Palmisano's grave, their *zia* took Vitantonio in her arms and asked him to place the flowers in the iron container that stuck out from her husband's gravestone.

'I can't reach, you have to help me. Climbing is for big boys,' she would tell him.

Then the little boy would stretch with precocious pride and place the bouquet of red chrysanthemums in honour of the man whom Donata often spoke about and for whom they felt sorry, because he had died in the war on the same day as their own father.

The Palazzo

After leaving the cemetery, the twins would have lunch with *Nonna* Angela at the Convertini palazzo, an imposing house that dominated the entire southern side of the square, next to the large terrace that hung over the Itria valley. Their grandmother considered All Saints' Day to be one of the most important dates in the calendar and, while she didn't put out food for the dead, she did lay the table beautifully so that the living would properly remember those who were no longer with them. During those special luncheons all the Convertinis would gather, including the families of their uncles Matteo, Marco, Luca and Giovanni, who came up from Bari and otranto. Aunt Margherita came down from Venice only for Christmas and in the summer, when they all stayed on the coast.

Giovanna always felt at home in the palazzo, among the carpets, wing chairs and velvet curtains. She'd always clung to her *nonna*'s skirt, from a very young age, and her grandmother surprised everyone by letting her sit with the grown-ups. She watched her out of the corner of one eye to correct her and teach her proper manners, just as one would expect of the eldest Convertini granddaughter. But little Giovanna didn't always pay attention: she often demonstrated, just as naturally as she blended in to the family landscape, the early signs of a headstrong character.

Vitantonio, on the other hand, seemed stifled by the family gatherings. He was well-behaved and reliable, and as easy to read as he was rough around the edges. But the boy found everything at his grandmother's palazzo too rigid, and the discipline excessive. Inside the house they weren't allowed to run, they couldn't play and they couldn't shout or even speak in a loud voice. His *nonna*'s office, the dining room, the living room and the conservatory off it were reserved for the adults; children could enter only when they were called in. They were also banned from upstairs, the terrace, the attic and the roof. Before entering the dining room they had to hold out their clean hands and at the table they had to sit quietly and, above all, sit up straight. When they were eating, they had to raise their fork to their mouth, because it was very bad manners to bend over your plate. In the dining room and the living room, they could speak only when spoken to by an adult, and even then they couldn't contradict them or answer too emphatically. Their grandmother kept a very firm grip on the basic forms of polite speech – *please*, *thank you* and *you're welcome* – and there was no excuse for not employing them. When they were summoned by her they always had to answer, 'What can I do for you, *Nonna*?' If they forgot she pretended not to hear them again and would call them again until they used the correct formula.

Vitantonio was only happy when Lady Angela opened up her office and let him rummage through the promotional calendars of the Austrian companies that supplied wood to the Convertinis. He loved the photos of snowy landscapes: forests of fir trees that looked like cotton; frozen rivers; little wooden houses with flour-dusted roofs and meadows piled high with snow that he longed to roll around in. He also could spend hours watching the electric train set that, according to family lore, *Nonna* had brought back from Switzerland to celebrate the twins' birth; it was always laid out in the playroom, ready to travel round the Alpine mountains, fir forests, bridges and snowy stations. The children were allowed to watch it from a distance but only the grown-ups could turn it on.

When the weather grew warmer Vitantonio spent the days in the garden with his cousin Franco, Angelo's eldest son, who was a similar age and also always came to Sunday lunch at the palazzo. The garden was filled with corners to hide in. They entered it through the kitchen door, which looked out on to two very elegant lime trees, with leaves of the softest green. From there, a path lined with a box hedge led to the service entrance, which opened directly on to the square. The side door, intended for the maid and the shopkeepers to bring their deliveries into the house, was used by the boys when they wanted to escape to play on the terrace, far from the adults' severe gaze.

Along the north side of the house, the wall was obscured by glazed ceramic planters filled with huge elephant's ear plants, as well as acanthus, ferns and hydrangeas, the only splashes of colour in the coolest part of the garden. At one end of the planters, towards the far west of the garden, just beneath the kitchen window, there was a glazed ceramic well with an iron pump handle. Beside it was a pond that held red fish and pink water lilies.

In a region where water was very scare – almost non-existent at times – the well and the fish pond were *Nonna*'s Venetian eccentricities. She had had them built on top of one of the palazzo's two small ornamental tanks, which stored rainwater collected from the public square, according to the usage rights of the former owners of the palazzo; Angela Convertini had claimed these just for her garden. As soon as she saw a cloud formation approaching, the Lady would send her maids out to sweep the square clean to make sure that nothing would impede the rainwater as it ran through the channels to her tanks.

At the back of the palazzo, which overlooked the valley, there was a terrace accessible only from the bedroom of the lady of the house. Wisteria curled around the columns of the pergola in purple pendants and climbed up the balustrade. In September, a vine burst forth with sweet muscat grapes. Under the pergola *Nonna* had placed pots filled with bright azaleas: white, pink, burgundy and red. The whole town talked about the Lady's potted flowers, because no one else dared grow azaleas in such a dry, hot region. She had stubbornly created a microclimate and she'd managed to maintain it: she watered the plants three times a week and conserved the earth's moisture by scattering over it pine-bark chips that she had delivered from the factory. She filled the pots with rusty bits of iron, too, adding minerals to the soil. *Nonna* was proud of the results, especially of the 'Queen of Bellorotondo,' a deeply-red azalea that was so lush and vast that not even three people in a circle could get their arms around it. When it bloomed in April, Angela would open up the garden to the entire town for a few days, inviting the women in to stroll through the ornamental borders of strongly scented flowers, which mingled with the rich perfume of the wisteria on the trellis above.

To the south, infront of the conservatory, there was a maze garden composed of neatly kept paths of box hedges. Further on, there was on close knife group of trees: two cedars, a willow, a palm, two limes, a plane tree, three orange trees and an enormous cherry street together—. Marking the boundary between the garden proper and the vegetable patch stood a shed, the clothersline, the main water tank that collected water from the roof of the house, and two almond trees that bloomed in mid-January long before the spring arrived.

A whitewashed wall protected the garden to the south from neighbours' prying eyes. It was covered in rose bushes that climbed up and hung over to the street side. On hot summer days, the neighbours passing in front of the palazzo looked up enviously at such exuberant greenery and couldn't help inventing all sorts of legends about the Convertinis' secret paradise.

The Month of Flowers

WHEN THE MONTH of flowers arrived, *Nonna* was transformed. She spent hours in the garden, planting geranium cuttings or transplanting marigolds and zinnias that she had grown in pots and old cans during the late-winter months, inside a small greenhouse behind the laundry. During those short weeks of May, her mood was transformed too. She relaxed the rules, especially in the garden area outside the palazzo, and allowed displays of affection that, at other times of the year, would have seemed quite immodest. The children couldn't help but notice the change in their grandmother, and they celebrated May's arrival as the glorious promise of imminent summer.

At the start of the month, *Nonna* organized the gathering of the white flowers, which she then distributed to decorate half the Virgin Marys of the town. She gave bouquets to all the churches, to her grandchildren's schools, to the asylum, to the nuns at the convent, to her friends and neighbours, also arranging them in all the main rooms of the palazzo. And sometimes she even had some sent as far away as the Franciscans in Martina Franca and the Sisters of

Charity of the Immaculate Conception of Ivrea in Massafra.

On the first of May, in the afternoon, she marched out into the garden like a general and gave strict orders to an army made up of the cook, two maids and a couple of workers from the sawmill, who had arrived after lunch armed with ladders and pruning shears of all sizes. Before beginning, they filled all the buckets and basins they could find around the house and placed them in a row, beneath the porch, to keep the flowers fresh until it was time to make up the bouquets. Then, they deployed themselves throughout the garden to carry out the Lady's orders with military precision, as she pointed to the flowers she wanted cut, one by one.

Nonna herself gathered the water lilies for the palazzo's chapel, and the lilies of the valley for the chapel of the Blessed Sacrament at the Immacolata. Then she ordered the sawmill workers, whose hands were calloused from carrying rough planks, to start cutting the best white roses from the bushes that covered the walls. These were reserved for the priests at the churches of Santa Anna and of the Madonna della Greca in town. Meanwhile, the maids fashioned bouquets of peonies, daisies and gladioli for the other parishes of the town and, when they'd finished those, busied themselves making arrangements of dogwood, viburnum, meadowsweet, lilac and the first baby's breath of the season for the schools and convents. And while Grandmother's small army marched out to deliver the bouquets all over town, she was still cutting the first Madonna lilies, so perfumed and laden with pollen that they stained everything they touched. She placed them in a very delicate green glass vase, at the feet of the Virgin Mary in the entryway, and for more than a week, the intense scent of the lilies reminded visitors that it was the month of flowers, and that Lady Angela Convertini was the indisputable queen of Bellorotondo.

On the first day of May of 1927, the activity around the gathering of the white flowers was unusually intense, both because the April rains had yielded an exuberant garden and because on the last Sunday of the month Giovanna, Vitantonio and their cousin Franco were to be confirmed at the Immacolata by the bishop. A week before their confirmation, they were also to receive their first communion, in accordance with the tradition of having the ceremonies over two consecutive sundays, when the children were seven or eight years old.

By the time *Nonna* had finished gathering the flowers and sent out her army to deliver the bouquets, the children had long since stopped paying attention to their work and were up in the cherry tree, laden with red, ripe fruit. They picked the darkest cherries, one by one, and they hung them over their ears, like earrings. As soon as they realized that *Nonna*'s helpers had left, they climbed down from the tree, gathered up the remaining flowers and petals that were strewn over the garden and started a flower fight. Giovanna had made a crown of dogwood, and still wore her red cherry ear-rings. Vitantonio threw handfuls of rose and peony petals at her. She responded in kind and they began a bizarre dance beneath a thick swirling veil of white petals that looked like a blizzard. Eventually, they dropped to the ground, on top of the carpet of flowers, and stretched out on their backs, panting.

When they got up they were still laughing. Franco, who had been the last to climb down from the cherry tree, crept up on the twins with a handful of flowers, threw them over Giovanna and kissed her on the cheek. She pulled away angrily. He tried to kiss her again.

'Get off me!' she shouted, as she pushed him away, growing more and more irritated with her cousin.

Franco threw himself at her again, pinned her down and brought his lips to her face. But he didn't see Vitantonio coming. The boy grabbed him hard, shook him and pushed him to the ground; Franco hit his nose on the terracotla bricks of the terrace and it started to bleed.

Their grandmother, hearing shouting, came through the conservatory's French doors and saw a trail of blood on the carpet of white flowers. At the foot of the garden stairs, Franco was crying hysterically, his shirt in tatters, his face a mess, his nose pouring blood . . .

An hour later, after the doctor had left, the adults called Vitantonio inside; he'd been waiting in the garden, frightened. As soon as he entered the living room, he knew that they weren't going to be very understanding. His *zia* was there, with Father Felice, and his *nonna*, who spoke to him in the harshest tone he'd ever heard.

'This year you won't be confirmed, nor will you receive your first communion.'

'Your behaviour this afternoon shows you aren't ready,' added Father Felice.

Vitantonio started to cry, but he didn't say a word.

'Do you have anything to say about what happened—' started to ask his aunt.

'There is nothing to say,' interrupted Grandmothers. 'Such violence is simply not allowed in this house.'

'We've only heard Franco's side. We should listen to his as well,' insisted Donata.

'You're spoiling him! His behaviour is unacceptable. And don't talk back to me in front of the children.'

'The boy might be prove to high spirits, but he always tells the truth. He's never lied before and he wouldn't now.'

Zia got up, held out her hand to Vitantonio, who was still sobbing, and called to Giovanna, who was waiting in the kitchen.

'Ggiuànnin!' This was the girl's name in the Matera dialect of Donata's own childhood, which she how used for the first time in many years.

Lady Angela silenced her with a furious look, but she didn't get up from her armchair. The serenity of the month of flowers had lasted a mere twenty-four hours.

On the day of the confirmations, Donata informed Lady Angela that she wouldn't be attending the solemn service at the Immacolata, and instead she went with Vitantonio to the first mass of the day at the church of

Santa Anna. The night before she had sent Giovanna to sleep at the palazzo so that in the morning, her *nonna*, who was also her godmother, could dress her in the princess dress she'd had made by a tailor in Bari. When Donata came out from mass, she found Lady Angela waiting for her, anxious, by the door to the courtyard, the one that opened on to the Piazza Santa Anna.

'Giovanna's disappeared. I dressed her first thing this morning and I left her in the kitchen having breakfast. When I came back from getting Franco ready she was no longer there. We've been looking for her all over the house for an hour. Has she come back here?'

She sounded desperate.

They both went into the house and called for her, but there was no sign of Giovanna.

Donata knew that the girl had been furious for days about Vitantonio's punishment and she was certain that running away was her way of making a protest. She'd surely turn up before too long, so she tried to reassure her grandmother.

'You go to the church. Don't make the bishop wait. I'll look for her and when I find her, I'll bring her there. She can't have gone far.'

As soon as her *nonna* had closed the door, Giovanna appeared at the top of the stairs, in full regalia. She'd been hiding on the first floor.

'If Vitantonio's not going to be confirmed, I won't be either!'

The Family Religion

ON THE NIGHT before St John's Day in late June, while they were packing to go to the house at Savelletri on the coast, one of the maids timidly asked Lady Angela why they weren't taking the twins with them that summer.

'If this is all about Franco's nose, you should know that he was really asking for it, Lady Angela. When I came back from taking the flowers to the church of the Immacolata, I went into the garden through the side door and I saw him really pestering Giovanna.'

That evening, *Nonna* came to Donata's house.

'I'm not here to apologize. But perhaps I was a bit hasty.'

'Vitantonio was only defending his sister, but you had no interest in listening to a seven-year-old boy. You've never truly accepted him . . .'

'I won't stand for this.' The grande dame of the Convertini family was highly offended. 'I consider him as much my grandchild as Giovanna and you can rest assured I treat them both equally. In fact, the only ones who have any right to complain are Matteo, Marco, Luca and Giovanni's children, who live far away, and particularly Margherita's, whom I only see in the summer and at Christmas.'

'The problem isn't how often you see them. It's about how you treat them, about being kind and fair to them.'

'Kindness is a sign of weakness. But you can be sure that I will always be fair with Vitantonio. I am fully aware that if my eldest son hadn't been so imprudent and impetuous in the war your husband would still be alive and the young boy would have a father. I know that I am in his, and your, debt. And I will never forget what you did for Francesca when she was ill . . .'

'You've always judged him more harshly than the others.'

'You haven't been listening to a word I've been saying! You want him to be a Convertini? Well, now he is! That is why I push him so hard. You are too lenient with the boy. A little punishment is good for him; it teaches him that, if he doesn't want to be passed over, he has to learn to stand up for himself. Vitantonio has to prepare himself for the future, he has to be able to act like a Convertini, which requires preparation and discipline. In this family we practise a religion that has its own rules and we are members of a church that never depends on others.'

'Don't you think that such boundless ambition is an offence to God?'

'Nonsense! If God had wanted us to all be equal he would have created us that way!'

'Well, I still think that it's a sin of pride.'

'Isn't it also a sin to renounce a child?' Lady Angela raised her eyebrows and stared straight at Donata. Then she smiled. 'Of course it's a sin! But you did it out of love, so God forgives you and I applaud you.'

The younger woman held her gaze. A few seconds passed and then Angela continued.

'The boy needs to learn to fight and be a leader like a Convertini and you have to help me to teach him. You certainly don't act like the daughter of a shepherd from Matera: you have the pride and drive of a Convertini – or, perhaps even more so, of an Orsini from Venice. That is the only reason I gave you custody of the children. God knows from where you get your strength, but they can learn more from you than from any of my sons.'

Angela was still looking straight at Donata; she admired, and envied, the serene strength she found in her. She tilted traight her chin haughtily, but this time in her gaze there was a plea. 'Tomorrow we are heading to the coast. By September, when we return, I hope that all this will have been forgotten.'

'You hurt him! You'll have to win his heart back,' said Donata. 'And you will also have to win back Giovanna's respect.'

'I'm not worried about the girl, she has the Convertini pride. But Vitantonio still has to learn that it's not easy being part of a family that bears so many responsibilities. Or have you not understood the price I pay for being the Lady of Bellorotondo?'

The Summer House

THEY SPENT THE last week of June in Bellorotondo and the children missed the sea and dunes of Savelletri, where their *nonna* had gone for the summer. On the coast, during the languorous hours of those first days of summer, everything had more flavour, colours were more vivid, smells stronger and every feeling more intense. By the sea, their lives were much freer; Vitantonio and Giovanna created adventures out of nothing: they stretched out on the beach, covered in sand, and told each other secrets or searched for worms to use as bait; spread out by the water, they let the waves caress their bodies.

Vitantonio also missed Cousin Franco, who had always been his summer playmate. They had learned to fish by dunking a glass jar covered with a white rag into the shallow water: the fish entered through a small slit in the middle of the rag to feed on the bread and cheese they put inside as bait. When the boys dived in and pulled up the jar with some fish trapped inside, they shrieked with glee and told everyone in town about it.

The seaside was paradise. Vitantonio and Giovanna didn't understand why their aunt wouldn't let them go there this summer to be with their cousins, the way they always had. On the feast day of Sts Peter and Paul, 29 June, by which time they had begun to resign themselves to the fact that this summer wasn't going to be like all the others, they left for the countryside, to the old Palmisano farmstead, and as soon as they set foot there they forgot about the sand, fish and friends in Savelletri.

Just on the outskirts of town, in the house where *Zia*'s sister-in-law Concetta now lived all by herself, the children discovered a life with even fewer rules than at the seaside. They took dips in the stone laundry trough, caught crickets in the garden, ran through the fields as the farmers cleared the dead leaves from the olive trees, and they ate dinner together at the kitchen table. In the evenings everyone gathered on the threshing floor and sat in the cool air: the grown-ups sang and told stories and the children played hide-and-seek until they were so worn out they fell asleep on their aunt's lap.

The old Palmisano farmhouse was at the centre of a *contrada*, a cluster of *trulli* huts with a cistern, an oven, a small windmill and a large threshing floor, all used by three families: the Palmisanos, the Vicinos and the Galassos. Concetta and Donata were the only Palmisano women who had stayed in Bellorotondo after their husbands' tragic deaths and they had inherited the shared property that included the house and three hectares of vineyards and olive groves. Since Donata had moved into town, Concetta took care of the land and the cow, pig and mare that they jointly owned with the Vicinos. The third family, the Galassos, never had enough even to have a share in an animal: they had six children, but only one hectare of land.

They called it the farmhouse, but it was just a modest square building around an old *trullo*, the traditional Apulian drystone hut. The conical stone roof that crowned the *trullo* was very elegant and on it the Palmisanos had painted in whitewash a large sun that gave off wavy rays of light. The house had two more *trulli* attached to it, which served as a pen for the animals and storage for the tools and the olives. Successive renovations had added two rooms originally intended as bedrooms for when the various branches of the family multiplied, but the Great War had rendered the additions unnecessary. Despite the tragedy, Concetta and Donata refused to give up and, to challenge men and gods alike, they painted a big 'P' for Palmisano in the middle of the sun that presided over the central *trullo*. And they agreed that Concetta should take in the four eldest Galasso children, because that entire poor family was crammed in together in their one-room *trullo*.

The day they arrived, Concetta's house smelled as good as the kitchen in the house on the Piazza Santa Anna whenever Guiseppe Skinny Vicino delivered the boxes of fruits and vegetables. The entrance to the house was covered with baskets and boxes of courgettes, onions and cucumbers, filling the whole space with their rich scent. The tomatoes brightened the entire house, especially the first Regina di Torre Cane variety, grown in vast quantities to hang up and conserve for wintertime. In one bucket nestled freshly picked fruits, the first plums and pears and some yellow hard-fleshed peaches, and on the kitchen sideboard sat a round tray filled with small apricots that gave off a deliciously sweet smell; of every conceivable shade of yellow and orange, they had burst in the heat and were covered in little black freckles. When the children went into the kitchen they saw also a couple of boxes of apricots on the floor, which Concetta was peeling to make jam.

The scent of the fruits and vegetables lingered long through the hot days; throughout the summer, more and more vegetables came into season, bringing new fragrances to vary slightly the perfume that infused the walls of the house. In late August they gathered boxes of aubergines to preserve in oil, they hung whole boughs of chilli peppers up to dry and let the ripest tomatoes occupy every room in the house. It was as if they had painted the house red and decorated it for a party: there were basins, baskets and buckets filled with plum tomatoes everywhere. Over the course of three days, Concetta, *Zia* and Skinny's wife filled up the glass jars that would mean tomato chutney and sauce for the rest of the year.

Giovanna helped them scald the tomatoes. For every two she peeled, she ate one, biting into it like into an apple, juice streaming down her whole face. Vitantonio was more attracted to the fruit, which he devoured in big bites straight from the trees. To escape the bees that chased after the bits of tomato and fruit stuck to their faces, hands and legs, Vitantonio and Giovanna would run and jump into the stone laundry basin. The day they had first discovered the rainwater reservoir in the middle of the garden, their dip had been a quick one; in fact they only went in so no one would know they were afraid to. They were scared of the slimy, half-rotted fig leaves that, along with the pond-skaters, floated on the surface, and of the toads that lived deep below. As soon as they stepped in, their feet sank into sludge and when Salvatore, Skinny's son, told them that sometimes there were snakes in there, they decided that they'd had enough: they declared they were too cold and leapt out of the water, frightened.

Four days later, they were swimming in the large stone basin fearlessly. Salvatore helped Giovanna to stay afloat, holding her up with one arm under her stomach; Vitantonio loved watching the pond-skaters and chasing the tadpoles, convinced that when they became frogs he would be able to keep them as pets. In mid-summer, the reservoir dried up and wouldn't be filled again until the late-August storms; but before it went dry, swimming rated second best on the list of his favourite things that Vitantonio made each evening with *Zia*. The first was always listening to the grown-ups tell stories after supper, as they waited for the sea breeze to come in before going to sleep.

When the level of rainwater in the reservoir was too low for swimming, they made their first trip to the Stagno di Mangiato, halfway between Martina Franca and Alberobello. They went in the cart driven by

Salvatore, travelling at the pace of mare's slow, measured gait, which she maintained even as she lifted her tail to take a long piss and Giovanna and Vitantonio burst out laughing. The children spent all morning running through the local forest and, before lunch, jumped into the dark, thick water of the *stagno*. After they'd eaten and lain in the shade, they dived back in the pond, to the shock of the farmers passing by on their way to Alberobello: they went to the *stagno* for a stroll, but they would never have thought to swim in it. Later they sang songs, stretched out on the meadow with the adults; and at mid-afternoon they started back and Vitantonio was allowed to hold the reins for a little while. After that first trip to the pond at Mangiato, the trips there were top of the list of the day's best moments that the boy recited to *Zia* each evening.

By the end of the summer, Vitantonio and Giovanna could reach the long-necked figs that grew beside the laundry, which never made it to the table because they ate them right off the tree. When the days grew shorter they had to come inside earlier and they used that extra time to shell green almonds and sort them by size. They rolled the green almonds back and forth along the kitchen table, pressing them with their hands to strip the husks, while laughing and telling stories.

On the last day of September a bit of rain fell and the fig trees were covered in fruit that had been split open by the drops, especially the Santa Croce and Dell'Abate varieties. They were no good when the water got into them like that, but the children gathered them anyway and laughed, because the figs showed their red pulpy flesh as if they had yawning mouths. At dusk they were all holed up in the kitchen and Concetta was bustling about the stove. When the children smelled the sweet scent of tomato sauce, their eyes grew wide as saucers as they tried to figure out what she was making; for days all they'd eaten was chickpeas and broadbean soup with chicory. Just then *Zia* came in, and when she saw the sauce she immediately guessed her sister-in-law's plans.

'Stuffed aubergine for Sunday lunch?'

'You know what they say: it's not Christmas without cream-filled apostle's fingers; it's not Easter without lamb and rice, and it's not Easter Monday without *sartú*; it's not a wedding banquet without sugared almonds and it's not summer without a nice big plate of stuffed aubergine.'

'And when have you ever eaten those things?'

'Never, but I've heard tell.'

'On special days we could also eat *orechiette* with thrush or hare stew,' pointed out Salvatore, who had just entered the kitchen with a bunch of onions. 'All we'd have to do was keep what we catch instead of offering it up to the aristocrats in town as a sign of our servitude.'

Donata and Concetta hid their smiles of approval and pretended they hadn't heard him.

It was the best summer the twins had ever had. Vitantonio spent all day running around freely, and when

Salvatore came back from working in the fields Vitantonio ran to meet him. Before dinner, Skinny's son would teach him to catch crickets and frogs and set up crossbows, and on some Sundays he even took him out hunting with a rifle. Donata watched on, thinking how Vitantonio, without realizing it, had spent those two months in the countryside discovering his own roots.

The Confirmation

ON THE FIRST Sunday in October, when they returned to Bellorotondo, they went over to the palazzo for lunch and put the incident in the garden behind them for good. Franco's broken nose and their grandmother's punishment, which had left the twins unconfirmed and without their usual summer holiday at the beach, were never mentioned again. *Nonna* gradually reintroduced her disciplinary routine but *Zia* rather suspected that, when there were no witnesses around, she lavished more attention on the twins in an attempt to win them over.

Three months later Donata's suspicions were confirmed. On the eve of the Feast of the Epiphany in 1928, Befana the Witch visited the palazzo, as she did in folklore throughout Italy, delivering gifts for the children. She brought the twins the clothes that their grandmother had ordered from the best shops in Bari on asked Margherita to send from stylish Venice. The following morning, 6 January, after trying on a wool sweater and some hiking boots, Vitantonio discovered one last gift with his name on it, wrapped in very striking paper, which Befana had left on the floor of the conservatory, beneath a sock hung from a doorknob. When he unwrapped it, he couldn't believe his eyes: it was a wind-up cable car that appeared to travel from a small town in the Alps to the very top of a mountain. Surrounded by fir trees and with their roofs dusted with snow, the model station and houses looked as if they were made of real wood, just like in the calendars sent by the Austrian timber merchants and just like the electric train set in the playroom that only the grown-ups were allowed to turn on.

At the other end of the conservatory, Giovanna was trying on some blue patent-leather shoes and she hadn't noticed that she had a special gift from Befana, too. Her grandmother pointed it out to her: the package wrapped in gold paper contained a lavishly produced edition of *Little Red Riding Hood*. It had a centrefold showing the woodcutter's house and all the characters in the story; when you opened it out, the big bad wolf appeared from behind the trees, on the trail of Little Red Riding Hood and her grandmother.

'That's me and that's you,' said her *nonna*.

When Giovanna saw that figure with long braids and a red cape she forgot all about the patent-leather shoes and gave her grandmother a huge hug. Angela turned redder than the hood itself.

The rest of the winter passed without incident and the following spring, when the palazzo's garden bloomed again and *Nonna*'s army distributed the white bouquets throughout town, Giovanna and Vitantonio were once again ready to be confirmed.

They were confirmed on the second Thursday in June 1928, on the Feast of Corpus Christi, in the illustrious surroundings of Bari cathedral, because *Nonna* wanted to compensate for the year-long delay by making the ceremony as solemn as possible. The night before the big day they both slept at the palazzo. Their grandmother wanted to have plenty of time to get them ready and to oversee personally their attire, which she'd had tailor-made, for the second time. When Donata left her house bright and early, the early-bird parishioners were already at eight o'clock mass at the church of Santa Anna and the streets of Bellorotondo were deserted. The *tramontana* – the northerly wind – had been blowing hard all week, leaving one of those clear skies she was so fond of. These were probably the last few mild days before the southern winds would bring in the unbearably hot summer.

Giovanna was waiting for Donata on the steps to Angela's house, wearing a white organdie dress. A gauzy veil covered her hair, which was black just like her mother's had been. A pink belt held the dress tightly around her waist and a pink rosary hung delicately from her white-gloved hands. Those were the only touches of colour, because her patent-leather shoes and her socks, which were pulled up over her calves, were also white.

'My little princess!' exclaimed Donata, as the girl threw her arms around her neck.

They went upstairs hand in hand and there they found *Nonna* knotting Vitantonio's tie. She had dressed him in a navy-blue suit jacket, shorts and sweater. His shirt was white in contrast, as were his gloves, socks, shoes and the handkerchief that peeked out of his jacket pocket. His *nonna* had parted his hair on the left. When the boy turned around, Donata struggled to stifle the cry that came from deep inside: '*Santo Dio,* Vito!'

Vitantonio was a perfect portrait, in miniature, of Vito Oronzo Palmisano. Dressed in jacket and tie, he was the spitting image of his father in the wedding photo they'd hurriedly had taken in Bari on the day he went off to war. Anyone who looked at the photo, which hung in a frame in Donata's living room, would have worked out Vitantonio's true parenthood immediately.

The Archbishop of Bari officiated at a long, tedious ceremony at the San Sabino cathedral, lasting almost three hours. More than three hundred children formed four lines – two of boys and two of girls – along the Romanesque nave flanked by columns. Archbishop Curi's right hand was half numb and his thumb was aching from anointing all the children's foreheads with the holy oils in the sign of the cross. Behind each child stood their godparent who, after the anointing, wiped off the oil with a handkerchief and then tied it around their godchild's forehead to remind them, for the rest of the day, that they had just been confirmed. *Nonna* stood for the entire ceremony behind Giovanna, her goddaughter. Father Felice was Vitantonio's godfather and also stood behind him, on the other side of the nave. Neither of them needed to hear the archbishop's warnings to the children and their godparents; they were inspired by the catechism of Pius X, which they knew by heart.

'Kings have their soldiers, who defend them and fight to make their kingdom larger and more powerful. The soldiers are always chosen from among the strongest and bravest young men. In the same way, our Lord wants his soldiers. Confirmation makes you perfect Christians and soldiers of Jesus. What an honour it is to serve the King of Heaven and Earth! Never forget that, as soldiers of Jesus, you must fight against the devil. Never listen to him, because he wants to rob you of your grace and banish Jesus from your hearts.'

When they left San Sabino at around one o'clock, they were starving, and they still had to stand for a group photo in the square outside the cathedral before heading to the hotel banquet. The feast was to be served at the Hotel Oriente, on the Corso Cavour in Bari, because Angela Convertini didn't want to have to wait the two hours it would have taken them to return to Bellorotondo to dine at the palazzo as was traditional.

Zia presided over the banquet to the right of *Nonna*, as if she were now definitively part of the family. She kept looking at Vitantonio with poorly concealed pride, and she also melted looking at Giovanna, who was growing more mature every day. She felt nostalgic for the days when she and Francesca had taken turns nursing them. *Nonna* looked at her out of the corner of her eye and smiled, and if *Zia* could have read her thoughts she would have been quite surprised: despite their differences, Lady Convertini was more pleased than ever that she had accepted her daughter-in-law's wishes and allowed Donata Palmisano to raise the twins they were both so very proud of.

Once the dessert had been served, Grandmother tapped her champagne flute with a knife to get the table's attention for her toast.

'Today you have taken a big step and we must begin to prepare you for your future: Donata and I have decided that next year you will go to boarding school in Bari.' She lifted her glass and cried out, 'To my grandchildren! To the children of my beloved Antonio, may he rest in peace!'

She brought the flute to her lips and drank. Everyone else did the same. Her eyes were glimmering just like Donata's were. The twins' uncles called them over and began to shower them with presents: medallions, catechisms bound in mother of pearl, illustrated books of sacred history, cufflinks for the boy, earrings and a necklace for the girl. The last one to call them over was their grandmother, who very solemnly placed a watch on each of their left wrists.

After lunch they left Bari for Bellorotondo along the coast road. When they reached Polignano a Mare, where they were expecting to take the inland route towards Castellana and Fasano, *Nonna*, who drove better than all the men in the family, stopped the car suddenly and shouted, 'Good lord!'

Everyone turned to look at her, frightened and wondering what was going on.

'My lord, what flowers!' she exclaimed, with a passion rarely seen in her. 'Jump over the fence and grab a couple of cuttings of those geraniums,' she ordered Vitantonio and Franco, who had been confirmed the previous year but had wanted to travel back to town in the same car as his cousins.

Nonna had stopped the car on the outskirts of the town, in front of a small house with a tiny garden, shaded by a dry, crooked eucalyptus tree. It was right next to a spa complex that had just been opened and was enjoying great success among the Bari bourgeoisie. Three steps led to an even tinier terrace, hemmed in by a white decorative railing. The façade was whitewashed, as were the two long, narrow planters beneath the windows. From one of the planters hung brightly coloured geraniums in pink, fuchsia and crimson. In the other there was an even more delicate geranium, which trailed down to the ground, covered in blood-red flowers, like a cardinal's cape. Angela had never seen anything like it on the entire Adriatic coast.

'What if they see us?' Donata tried to protest.

'We're not doing any harm. And besides, no one ever comes to these houses on the coast until the end of the month.'

Franco stayed in the car. Vitantonio was already out and over the fence. He still had his confirmation handkerchief tied around his forehead and the watch on his wrist, and he felt prouder than ever.

Zia watched him run over to the terrace and shouted, 'Be careful, don't catch your shorts.'

'Leave him be, he knows what he's doing. He'll be nine this summer.'

Donata gave Angela a puzzled look and saw that she was watching her grandson's movements with a gleam in her eye. She would never understand that woman. She had spent the whole lunch scolding the little ones, making sure they didn't spill anything on themselves or forget their manners. Now she'd sent Vitantonio over a dirty, dusty fence to steal geranium cuttings.

'Bravo!' said Lady Angela when the boy delivered a couple of crimson flower cuttings and a whole handful of tender shoots he'd chosen from the cardinal-red geranium that trailed all the way down to the ground; they would take pride of place in the finest pots in the palazzo. *Nonna* gave Franco, who hadn't budged from his seat the entire time, a reproving look, and then addressed Donata.

'You see, nothing happened. When you're strict with them, they shine,' she said as if deliberately to provoke her, and she grabbed hold of the steering wheel, turned on the engine and took the road to Bellorotondo at top speed.

'It was lucky no one saw us,' was all Donata replied.

'They would be thrilled to know that we liked their flowers,' retorted Angela.

That's how *Nonna* was: a blazing sun who took for granted that every planet revolved around her. And she wouldn't have had it any other way.

Red Earth

THAT SAME DAY, when they'd passed the Fasano mountains, the earth turned red and they saw the first terraced plots of land that heralded their arrival in the Itria valley. The peasant farmers in the valley wisely planted their crops at different heights: at the top were the trees with large boughs, the olive, fig, almond and cherry trees; on the second level grew the apricot, prune, pomegranate and other smaller fruit trees; beneath them were the local vines that would produce a wonderful Primitivo wine come September; further down were the beans, aubergines, peppers, cucumbers, onions, chick-peas and tomatoes. The lowest level was saved for the squashes, which crept all over the red earth.

Nonna's car had been driving alongside drystone walls for a while by then. Vitantonio had lowered the window and was enjoying looking out at the fertile fields scattered with *trulli* huts and tiny farmhouses. He'd been anxious to get home ever since *Nonna*'s toast.

They reached the palazzo by mid-afternoon and went straight to the garden. The town photographer was already there waiting for them; Grandmother had personally given him the task of immortalizing her two eldest grandchildren's confirmation day and he decided to photograph them on a wooden bench, surrounded by plants and bushes, convinced that the Lady of Bellorotondo would be pleased by the natural backdrop. *Nonna* was the first to sit down, on one end of the bench, with her left arm stretched out over its back and the other at a right angle over her thighs; in her right hand she held open a fan decorated with a black and gold pattern. She was dressed entirely in black. Around her neck she wore a small pearl necklace and she had coquettishly pulled her white hair back into a bun. A few wrinkles gathered around her bright, eagle eyes, but her figure was still slender and her face still showed how lovely she'd been as a young woman: she had simply exchanged youthful beauty for mature elegance.

At the other end of the bench, *Zia* wore a bright white dress. Her hands rested on her lap and in her right one she held the bouquet of flowers that Giovanna had carried that morning at the ceremony. Donata was still a very attractive woman.

The twins stood behind the bench between the two women, who looked straight at the camera with pride. Giovanna held the back of the bench with one hand and gave the lens a penetrating, defiant gaze. She looked happy. She was still thinking about what her grandmother had said earlier at the hotel restaurant, and she was pleased they were sending her to study in the city: she was anxious to grow up and she knew that in Bellorotondo she would always be seen as a little girl. Vitantonio, on the other hand, seemed upset and was looking to one side of the garden, with a heavy gaze. He was afraid of leaving Bellorotondo for school in Bari; something he couldn't put into words tied him to the valley and made him feel homesick whenever he left.

Everything was ready for the photo. The broad, fleshy leaves of one of *Nonna*'s alocasia plants peeked out from behind Vitantonio and woodbine climbed up the stone wall. Just to the right of the group hung cherry boughs, laden with fruit. Giovanna grabbed a couple and dangled them from her ear like earrings. It was the only moment when Vitantonio smiled. The photographer clicked the shutter, capturing the girl's and the two women's pride and satisfaction, but also the boy's anxious, half-smiling expression.

'Take one of Franco and Vitantonio together,' *Nonna* ordered the photographer when the group disbanded. 'Come on, over here.'

Franco sat on the bench and Vitantonio stood beside him, with his right foot resting on the dark green wood. Just as the photographer was about to take the picture, Franco turned to his cousin and said, 'Will you teach me how to fight?'

'What's got into you? You can't teach fighting. When you're in the right, you fight – and that's it.'

In Bed

Zia CAME IN with breakfast on a tray. A piece of toast sprinkled with oil and salt, and a glass of milk that she had sent up from Concetta's cow each day, which she mixed with an infusion of eucalyptus, as per Dr Ricciardi's orders.

'How's my little soldier doing today?'

The afternoon of the twins' confirmation, Vitantonio and Franco had stayed out in the palazzo garden until nightfall, playing soldiers of Jesus with the wooden swords Skinny had made for them at the factory. It had been a muggy day, but in the evening the temperature had dropped sharply and Vitantonio had come in for supper at the house on the Piazza Santa Anna shivering. The next day he'd woken up feverish and Donata had called the doctor, who had diagnosed tonsillitis and said he needed some bed rest. He had been in bed for three days and was fed up, but Dr Ricciardi, who came by to check on him every afternoon, wouldn't hear of him getting up.

'He needs to stay in bed for two more days, until his fever has completely gone down. And then he should spend two or three more days at home, without going outside at all.'

When *Zia* took away the breakfast tray, Vitantonio stretched out an arm and picked up an illustrated book, *The Battle for Grain*, that the school had given them that year as part of a government campaign to convince Italian farmers to plant more wheat and make the country self-sufficient. Mussolini had had more than six million copies distributed to schools throughout Italy. Vitantonio liked to look at the drawings of the wheat fields, and they reminded him of the men who had winnowed the wheat, the previous summer, on the threshing floor at Concetta's farmhouse.

When he put down the little book he understood he missed the July mornings when they had bathed in the laundry trough and the feast days when he'd been hunting in the olive groves with Salvatore. He closed his eyes for a moment and proudly imagined that he was already as brave and grown up as Skinny's son; he saw himself climbing trees and going out hunting all alone with the rifle, through the brushwood of Alta Murgia and the marshes of Torre Cane. Until he realized that his whole body was itchy and his daydream vanished as quickly as it had come: there were toast crumbs all over his bed and in his pyjamas. His aunt came to his rescue. 'Get up. I'll make the bed and air out your room.'

When he returned, the room was like a paradise. The air was fresh, morning sun bathed the entire room and the bed had clean starched sheets on it. He leaned back on to a pillow, and was captivated by the reflections of the sun on the leaves of the lemon tree's tallest branches, which reached his window. Giovanna appeared in the doorway.

'Are you still sick?'

She went over to the bed and put her lips to his forehead, as she had seen *Zia* do. Then she kissed him on the cheek, just as he was turning his head. Their lips brushed together.

'Yuck!' complained Vitantonio, laughing nervously. 'Sisters don't kiss their brothers.'

'I do,' she said, very earnestly. And she left the room.

PART THREE

Cherry Earrings

Sweet Sixteen

'HOW'S MY POORLY little brother?'

Giovanna made Vitantonio jump. He looked up from his book and saw his twin sister in the doorway. She was a vision; he hadn't seen her since Christmas. Since the winter holidays they hadn't both been in Bellorotondo at the same time once, because she'd spent Easter on a school trip to Rome. She looked very different, beautiful. She wore a close-fitting dress emblazoned with blue and red flowers, and she was beginning to bloom as her sixteenth birthday approached. It had been nearly seven years since he last lay ill in this bed and saw his sister in the bedroom doorway.

He looked her up and down curiously, unable to pinpoint what it was that was so different about her. She noticed him looking and let out a laugh, her mouth wide, revealing very white teeth and pink gums. Her long black hair was pulled back into a ponytail that hung past her waist; a couple of ringlets had escaped and danced playfully on her forehead. Giovanna teased him, striking poses like a fashion model. When she turned to one side, Vitantonio was surprised to see that his sister's chest was starting to look like a woman's. She wore two cherries hanging from her ear.

'What do you think?'

'You left here an ugly little sister and now you're an ugly big sister.'

Giovanna let out another loud laugh. Leaning one hand against the doorframe and lifting her skirt with the other, she revealed long legs in flesh coloured silk stockings.

'You can say what you like, but the boys all turn their heads.'

Vitantonio found her very attractive, but he kept his mouth shut. She was his sister! When he looked at her that way, he felt very confused. She came over to the bed, put her lips to his forehead and declared, 'You don't have a temperature, you're faking it.'

She put a cherry in his mouth and ate the other one. She spat the stone into her hand and turned to go, leaving behind a trail of perfume, roses perhaps. As he watched her go, he was ashamed to feel a strange sensation in his grain.

His aunt's entrance surprised him.

'Get up, I'll make the bed.'

Vitantonio loved her taking care of him as if he were still a little boy. He hadn't had a single day of illness since the soul of tonsillitis just after his confirmation, seven years ago. For the last five years he'd been at boarding school in Bari, and he could scarcely remember the pleasure of drifting off to sleep while his *zia* bustled about the house. In early April he'd been diagnosed with a double pneumonia and, since the nurse at school didn't inspire much confidence, it had been decided that he should recover at home.

Every time his aunt came in to air out his room, and shake the bread crumbs out of his sheets and remake his bed, he congratulated himself on having convinced the priests to let him come back home from Bari to Bellorotondo. That morning, though, when he saw Donata come in, he got up and tried his best to hide the strange reaction Giovanna had provoked in him. Then he went back to bed, pleased to find the linen fresh and starched, and dozed off. He was woken't by the calls of Dr Ricciardi, who was coming up the stairs.

'What is that boy reading today?'

Without waiting for an answer he placed two books on his bedside table: *The Charterhouse of Parma* and *The Gambler*. The doctor liked to talk to Vitantonio about books the young man had never heard of and then he would often bring them to him from his own library, not least because in their far-flung corner of the world the doctor had little opportunity to find a protégé who might be interested in Stendhal and Dostoyevsky, his favourite authors. Vitantonio thanked him with a smile and Ricciardi pulled another surprise out of his satchel, a recently published issue of a literary magazine. 'It's the first part of *The Red Carnation*, by Elio Vittorini,' the doctor announced dramatically, reading the title off the cover. He winked at him and hid the magazine under a pillow.

The word around town was that Gabriele Ricciardi

was not a big supporter of the fascists and that any day now they might deport him. But that would never happen because the wealthy old families of Bellorotondo didn't want to lose their doctor, so they encouraged the local authorities to turn a blind eye to his impertinent, but harmless, comments.

His visit lasted only two minutes. Just enough time for him to give Vitantonio the books and ask him to cough a couple of times. The young man heard him walk downstairs and he wondered if he was headed to the kitchen to talk to *Zia*. At first she had been alarmed by the rattling in his chest when he breathed, reminding her of Francesca's illness, but the doctor had convinced her that bronchitis was nothing like tuberculosis, and Vitantonio just needed warm compresses, a lot of eucalyptus-oil inhalations, fluids and plenty of rest. Hearing his motorcycle start off down the Via Cavour, Vitantonio knew that Ricciardi had left. He was sorry that it had been such a short visit; he was convinced that on the days when the doctor stayed to chat for a while in the kitchen, *Zia* was always in a better mood.

No one knew how Dr Ricciardi had got his bike to Bellorotondo. He was popular among the children in town, who liked to admire his motorcycle and his clothes: a leather jacket, and an airman's goggles and cap from the time of the Great War. When the sound of the doctor's bike faded as he left town, Vitantonio closed his eyes and listened to the silence, which was only occasionally broken by the children playing in the

square. He heard a dog barking in the distance, perhaps on the avenue that led to the cemetery, and donkeys braying in gardens in the lower part of town. Then he heard the neighbours' water wheel being set in motion to draw water from their cistern. He took the Elio Vittorini story out from under his pillow and tried to read it, but the memory of Giovanna in the doorway in her red and blue flowery dress with cherries hanging from her ear was too distracting. He put the magazine in the drawer of his bedside table and dozed off, trying to figure out what it was that was so different now about his sister.

During the summer holidays, Vitantonio liked to work at the family factory. The Convertinis called it the 'factory' or the 'warehouse', but in town it was referred to as the 'sawmill' or, simply, the 'mill'. Vitantonio was used to stopping by to say hello to his *nonna* in the office. He also liked to see Skinny Vicino, the thin, wiry worker who used to deliver oil and vegetables to their house on the Piazza Santa Anna; since that summer at the Palmisano farmstead he'd thought of him as an uncle.

As a boy, if they'd let him wander around, he would run to the back of the warehouse and climb up the piles of planks. The adults let him do it, trying not to think about how in Signore Antonio's time a poorly stacked pile had collapsed and killed two men. In the factory, Vitantonio also hunted for bits of wood to make swords with; Skinny would cut some long pieces to a point to make the blades, and some shorter ones that he then stuck together in the shape of a cross, for the hilts. The first time he brought a wooden sword to the palazzo, Franco wanted one too and from that day on his cousin always went with him to the factory.

When he was strong enough to wield a shovel, Vitantonio would help load the sacks of sawdust, which had to be kept wide open to get the entire shovelful inside. It wasn't a difficult job because the sawdust didn't weigh much and he could easily lift huge shovelfuls. And as he grew older, he would go to the factory to help do the inventory of the increasingly large fir shipments they imported from the Volga sawmills by boat, which they unloaded at the port of Taranto then to share with other timber importers throughout southern Italy.

Vitantonio wasn't afraid of hard work, like loading trucks with wood chips or manoeuvring the tree trunks through the saws. Hauling planks, however, was not his cup of tea. He could never find the right balance on his shoulder as he walked, the planks scraped his skin raw, causing a very painful wound. Skinny, on the other hand, lanky as he was, would carry four or five planks at once, holding them in place with just one finger as he walked.

By the last week of May, Vitantonio was over his pneumonia, and he showed up at the factory ready to work until his return to Bari for his end-of-term exams. On his last day at the factory, as he was unloading chestnut from the Gargano groves off of a truck and piling it up in a shed, Vitantonio surprised Skinny with a question. 'What was my father like? Was he brave?'

'He was certainly brave,' Vicino said after a pause in which he collected himself. 'And bold. Everyone in the company admired his courage. And we respected him too because with Lady Angela's money he could have got out of going to war and he didn't. Of course, he was my bosses' son and I was careful to keep a respectful distance, and because of that there isn't much more I can tell you.'

He looked into the boy's eyes and saw in them a need to know more. He was fond of him and regretted not being able to satisfy his curiosity.

'I spent more time with Palmisano, your father's friend, since we came from a similar background. Shortly before the war we both joined the Confederazione Generale del Lavoro, and whenever we read union pamphlets your father would poke fun at us, saying, "You changed your church when you became socialists, but you keep reading the catechism like all the women in town."'

They laughed as they recalled the silly things that Antonio Convertini and Vito Oronzo Palmisano had shared before dying, one right next to the other on the front, on the last day of the Great War. It was sticky and hot and Vitantonio undid a couple of buttons on his shirt, revealing a birthmark. It was heart-shaped and dark red, between his collarbone and his left shoulder. Skinny's expression suddenly changed.

'What's wrong?' the boy asked.

'Nothing, I'm fine,' he said, brushing it off. And he headed towards the factory exit, remembering the day

Vito Oronzo Palmisano died in his arms after a night of feverish delusions.

He had lied to Donata: the last Palmisano's death hadn't been quick and painless: he was still alive when he was rescued and died in agony. Vicino relived that night, 4 November 1918, remembering how his fellow soldiers were celebrating the ceasefire while he was cleaning Vito's wound. And in his mind's eye he again saw that perfect heart on Vito Oronzo Palmisano's left clavicle, as his friend begged him, 'If I don't make it, tell Donata that I died instantly.'

Franco, however, was jealous of Skinny's skill at his job and was always looking for a way to provoke him. One day, when they had loaded up an army truck with wood chips, Vitantonio caught his cousin screaming at Vicino, who couldn't understand what he had done to deserve such a rude dressing-down from his boss's son. On a break, while resting on a pile of wood, Skinny had lit a cigarette and explained to one of his co-workers why he didn't share Mussolini's imperialist vision: he'd had enough with the disastrous Great War, which he'd seen from the front line. Overhearing him, Franco decided to use it against him.

He went into the office, upset, and he demanded of his father Angelo, 'You have to fire Skinny Vicino!'

'Leave him be!' interjected Vitantonio, who had tried in vain to calm his cousin down. 'Skinny hasn't done anything wrong.'

'He's a unionist!'

'He's a worker! Probably the best one we have.'

'Vitantonio is right,' said Angelo, refusing to side with his son. 'He's the best worker at the factory and he's devoted to the Convertini family. He would give his life for your grandmother.'

Then he looked at Vitantonio and, with a jeer, proceeded to contradict his nephew as well.

'But Franco is right – we can't let anything compromise our loyalty to Mussolini, so Vicino will have to leave the factory until we send for him again. A couple of months without pay should make him rethink things, as well as setting an example to the others. Anyway, we don't have much work right now; when we need to unload a shipment of fir at Taranto, we'll have him come back.'

'He can't be out of work for two months. What will he live on?'

'He should have thought of that,' interjected Franco.

'Franco's right about that, too,' Angelo said to his nephew Vitantonio, making it abundantly clear that it was the end of the discussion.

Father Felice

ON THE FEAST of Corpus Christi at the end of May, *Nonna* summoned Donata and the children to the palazzo. The cook opened the door for them and quickly explained to them what was going on: Father Felice, Lady Angela's brother, had suffered a stroke. They found the family gathered in the living room, with the lights very low. They looked for their grandmother, but she wasn't there. The rector of the Immacolata, Father Constanzo, was leading the rosary. He nodded discreetly to them and continued reciting.

'*Stella matutina.*'

'*Ora pro nobis.*'

'*Salus infirmorum.*'

'*Ora pro nobis.*'

'*Refugium peccatorum.*'

'*Ora pro nobis.*'

Donata sat in an armchair, beneath the two paintings of white and red flowers that presided over the room. Vitantonio looked at his uncles and cousins, who were reciting by rote but seemed far away from the living room, and he remained standing, with his hands on the back of his *zia*'s chair. The litanies were the part of the rosary he had the most patience for; he found their musical rhythm calming. He recited them with conviction, in the hope that the prayers would help his godfather recover.

'*Regina Angelorum.*'

'*Ora pro nobis.*'

'*Regina Patriarcharum.*'

'*Ora pro nobis.*'

'*Regina Prophetaum.*'

'*Ora pro nobis . . .*'

Nonna entered the living room and whispered something to *Zia*, who got up from her chair and gestured for the tuins to follow her upstairs. They went straight to Father Felice's bedroom. Seated at the door was a nun, who was also reciting the rosary and who didn't look up at them. Dr Ricciardi was inside with another doctor, whom they didn't know because he'd come up from Bari.

When they approached the bed, Father Felice didn't move. His eyes were open, but he wasn't looking at them. He didn't say a word.

'Give him a kiss,' requested their grandmother.

Giovanna moved closer and kissed him on the forehead. Then Vitantonio kissed him on the cheek; the priest hadn't shaved and his check was scratchy. Before moving away from his bedside Vitantonio whispered, 'Get well, when you're better we'll go up to the Maggio festival in Accetura,' even though he knew he couldn't hear him.

'Pray for him,' insisted *Nonna* as they were leaving the room.

That morning, as Father Felice was heading to the San Sabino cathedral in Bari to celebrate the twelve o'clock mass with the bishop and assist him with the confirmation ceremonies, he had collapsed, and the stroke had left one side of his body paralysed. When the seminary had called to let Angela know, she had gone straight to Bari and insisted she wanted to take him home with her.

Father Felice didn't recover in time to go up to Accetura for the Maggio festival, which he'd been promising to take to the children to for years. Nor was he ever again able to make a trip like that, nor resume his music lessons. It was six months before he could even walk again, and in the months after the stroke he spent much more time in Bellorotondo than in the seminary in Bari.

Father Felice was a simple man, who lived in his own world. Had he been a peasant farmer they would have said he was a *poor man*, but since he was the Lady's brother they all called him a *good man*. He was such an innocent soul that everyone assumed he couldn't be happier, and that if anyone mentioned the poverty in Puglia or the horrors of fascism, he wouldn't have had any knowledge of them. In truth; he would have been unable to distinguish which of his parishioners were in his social class and which were dirt poor. He definitely was not of this world.

He had moved to Puglia from his native Venice, following in his sister's footsteps, and he had adapted without difficulty, despite all his relatives' pessimistic murmurings. At the Bari seminary, they entrusted him with the music classes and he also taught private piano lessons. Whenever he could, he liked to take his students up to the mountains hiking, and during the holidays he would make himself at home at the Convertini palazzo.

Angela adored him and refused to let anyone make fun of him. Not even when he burped at the dinner table and apologized with a smile. The children were also very fond of him; he would teach them songs, take them on long walks and he never scolded them. Angelo and the four evangelists, on the other hand, would laugh openly at him, as they had learned to do from their father, Signor Antonio, who had never missed a chance to mock his brother-in-law. Signor Antonio was a rural landowner with a hard heart, who simply found Father Felice too much of a nice chap.

Cockfight

AT THE BOYS' boarding school in Bari there were two cocks ruling the farmyard: Vitantonio and Giocavazzo. They were the strongest, bravest and most independent, and they competed for the other students' admiration. The other pupils were chicks and hens, who divided themselves into two opposing groups according to the staunchly adversarial plans of their two leaders.

Very few students didn't fall into one of the two factions, just the loners, who did their own thing: Argese, whom no one wanted on their side because he had a limp, and Sante Miccoli, who was horribly homesick and wandered around like a lost soul. Such loners made up a very small, peculiar group who had a terrible time of it, because, naturally, those who didn't belong to either gang were always picked on. Especially Miccoli, who was considered a sissy and awakened the others' bullying instincts. Vitantonio protected him from a distance and couldn't stand it when the others took advantage of him. His green eyes reminded him of Giovanna's.

The two gangs fought at the slightest provocation and soon no one even remembered what had started it. Not that it mattered, seeing as it was really just a means of burning off excess energy, which was stifled by the priests' overly rigorous discipline.

Vitantonio and Giocavazzo had learned to hate each other from a distance. Their rivalry went back to their earlier school days, at the Bellorotondo primary school and at the middle school in Martina Franca. In their previous institutions, they'd at least both always acknowledged the other's strengths and avoided any run-ins; at the boarding school in Bari, on the other hand, some contact was inevitable and, during that summer term of 1935, it seemed that conflict was imminent.

They almost came to blows one day when a group of boys went after poor Argese, who was trying to run away, dragging his bad leg. Vitantonio stood up for him and broke up the gang. Just when he had tripped up the last two of the pursuers and had them on the ground, Giocavazzo showed up, looking defiant.

'I see you think you're pretty tough dealing with these small Fry. But now let's see if you've got the guts to take me on.'

'Just tell me if you want a proper fight and we'll meet up on the football pitch, but tell your gang to leave Argese alone. He walks with a limp because he had polio when he was little, but he's smarter than the lot of you. By exam time you'll probably all be begging for his help.'

His rival stared into his eyes, but didn't say a word. The two gangs gathered, waiting for the punches to start flying any second, but Giocavazzo surprised everyone. He turned on his heels and shouted, 'Let's go. Nothing to see here.'

It had always been the same: the two leaders might fight with three or four other rivals at once, but no one had ever seen them fight each other directly. So, the afternoon they finally squared up to one another, the news spread like wildfire and half of the boarding school showed up to form a circle around the two contenders.

It was the day after Vitantonio had come back from Bellorotondo, having recovered from pneumonia and from seeing Father Felice lying half-dead from his stroke. He was feeling more sensitive than usual. Smoking on the sly in the toilets, he heard Giocavazzo making fun of his aunt's husband's family.

'The Palmisanos were cowards. Otherwise, how would everyone in the family have ended up dead? No doubt about it, there's only one explanation: in wartime, death sniffs out cowardile straight off.'

Vitantonio opened the cubicle door and pounced on him. He had the advantage of surprise and slammed his rival against the wall. Stunned, Giocavazzo took two punches to the face and fell to the ground. Vitantonio leapt on him again and they rolled on the floor towards the door to the corridor.

'Convertini and Giocavazzo are killing each other in the second-floor toilets!' The news spread through the whole school and pupils from every year started gathering.

Vitantonio was more agile and had an effective technique for pinning down his rivals. But Giocavazzo was stronger and threw a good punch. They were pretty evenly matched. When they had been going at it for quite some time, they could both taste blood in their mouths and were gasping for breath. Rolling around on the floor, Vitantonio managed to trap his rival's arm, twist it behind his back and immobilise him, face down. For the first time in the whole fight he had him where he wanted him. Just then he heard Franco cheering him on.

'Kill him! You've got him now. *Finish him off*!'

Vitantonio was disturbed to see Franco's eyes gleaming with rage. His cousin was his best friend and he hated that he always seemed to get caught up in violence; and right now he couldn't stand seeing him shouting like that, out of control. Suddenly, he could sense the bloodlust the fight had roused in boys from all the years; half of the boarding school was watching and urging them to beat the hell out of each other. He was unpleasantly surprised by their excitement. Seeing that they were all hoping to see one of them humiliated, to reaffirm their own pride, he lost all desire to go on. None of those boys deserved such a spectacle. If they wanted to experience strong emotions, they'd have to fight themselves.

He leaned over Giocavazzo's back and brought his lips close to his ear.

'Should we leave it as a draw? Pretend we've had enough and call it quits?'

The other boy didn't answer, but he stopped struggling to get free.

'Turn around and throw me to the ground,' insisted Vitantonio.

Soon they were both sitting up and brushing down their uniforms. When Vitantonio broke the silence, they were still looking at each other warily.

'You must have a guardian angel, I really had you there. Next time, you're a dead man!' he said, keeping up appearances.

'Next time, I'll hand you your own head on a plate. You just caught me off guard today,' retorted Giocavazzo, just to say something. He still didn't understand what had happened.

The other students didn't understand what was going on either. It was the second time in recent weeks that they'd been about to see a proper fight and were left wanting more.

'Why didn't you finish him off when you had him? If you'd broken his arm, he wouldn't have been able to carry on!' shouted Franco, who was the most disappointed of them all.

Vitantonio didn't answer. The other students looked at the two rivals, still expecting them to lay into each other again. Just then Father Pius, the master in charge of discipline, showed up.

'Who started it?'

The two rivals challenged Father Pius with proud gazes, making it clear that they wouldn't stoop so low as to accuse each other. They were surprised by Franco's voice: 'It was all Giocavazzo's fault.'

Vitantonio glared at him but felt forced to admit

that it had really been him. 'That's not true, Father. I was the one who started it.'

They both ended up in the master's office, which had been named after Pope Leo XIII but was known as 'the torture chamber' among the boys. As punishment, you could be made to stand there for hours with some weighty tome in your hands, preferably the lives of the saints or some sacred history, without being allowed a break or to go to the toilet. The record was held by one boy who'd stood there for twenty-four hours straight. Father Pius didn't care so much about the content of the books he forced them to read as he did about their weight, and the heavier they were, the more memorable the punishment.

'Convertini, you really are a nutter!' shouted Giocavazzo from the other end of the room when the master had left them standing with two hefty tomes in their hands.

When they'd been in the torture chamber for four hours, Giocavazzo asked Vitantonio, 'Tell me if anyone's coming.'

He slipped out into the hallway that led to the classrooms, which were empty at that time of day. He went into the first one and wrote on the blackboard: 'Father Pius is doing it with Sister Lucia.'

Just hours later, the entire boarding school was abuzz with the slander. One pupil claimed that he had gone into Father Pius' room one morning to sweep it out, and found the nun in the master's arms. Others said that they had seen them in the garden 'doing stuff', and there were even those who swore they had caught them feeling each other up in a classroom and kissing in the priest's office.

The next day, Vitantonio questioned Giocavazzo in their dormitory. 'And how did you know about the father and Sister Lucia?'

'I didn't, I made it up. But you see, it turns out everyone's seen them kissing . . .'

Vitantonio made a disapproving face. 'Father Pius is a bastard, but not even he deserves to have a lie like that made up about him. Our reputations are the most sacred thing we have.'

'It's his fault. Father Pius himself gave me the idea. Do you know who Prior Giovanni Montero was?'

Vitantonio didn't know what on earth he was talking about. He shrugged his shoulders and listened.

'Monsignor Giovanni Montero was the prior of the San Nicola basilica in Bari. In 1662 they accused him of having it off with a nun, and the viceroy sent the archbishop of Brindisi to Bari to find out the truth behind the rumour that had been spreading through the city for months. When the process was made public, the list of sins supposedly committed by the prior got much longer; halfway through the investigation he was said to have fathered two children – it wasn't clear if it was with a married woman, a single woman or a servant – and towards the end they accused him of raping a coachman's wife and even buggering the coachman in the same incident. The investigation concluded that it had all been invented by the wicked wagging tongues of a society hell-bent on destroying people's reputations. But the damage had been done. In the eyes of the population of Bari, the prior of San Nicola was guilty. Just like our Father Pius prefect.'

Vitantonio was staring at him, increasingly incredulous. Everyone thought that Giocavazzo was one of the dimmest students in the whole boarding school.

'And how the hell do you know all that?'

'Father Pius dug his own grave when he punished us. You know which book he gave me to hold in the torture chamber? *The History of the Church of Bari through the Centuries*: in it there's a whole chapter devoted to the life of Monsignor Montero.' He looked at him with a malicious gleam in his eye and added, 'Every lie I spread about the father came straight from the book he gave me.'

And he let out a laugh, giving the other pupils in the room a light. They couldn't understand why, instead of pummelling each other, these two were now sharing secrets.

And from that day on, they were inseparable. One morning, as they were leaving class, Giocavazzo came over to Vitantonio. 'I have a brother who also had polio: my little brother Raffaele.' He swallowed hard and added, 'My parents are ashamed of him and won't let him go to school. He lives with my grandparents.'

They walked alongside each other for a while, without speaking. Giocavazzo looked at the ground. Suddenly, he asked, 'Will you get cross if I teach that bastard Franco a lesson for grassing on me?'

'All right, but don't hurt him. He's my cousin and I'd have to stick up for him.'

The next day, two masked boys surprised Franco in the bathroom, held him down and stripped him. He spent the whole afternoon naked, huddled up sobbing in one corner of the room, with his face buried between his knees and his arms wrapped around them. Before dinner, a priest heard him crying, found him in that pathetic position and took him away wrapped in a blanket.

On Sunday, at home in the palazzo, he described a less humiliating version of the events and said a couple of masked boys had beaten him to a pulp.

'Tell me their names and I'll have them expelled!' was his father's furious response.

But Franco didn't know what to say. It could have been anyone. Despite being under Vitantonio's protection, he wasn't very popular at school. The priests promised to investigate it thoroughly and make an example of those responsible. But with only two weeks to go until the summer holidays, the incident was never properly resolved.

The Second Summer at the Farmstead

THAT JULY THE twins world turn sixteen and Giovanna surprised everyone by insisting that they spend the summer at the old Palmisano house in the countryside. *Nonna* tried to dissuade her, saying that in the country they'd be too hot and bored, but Giovanna insisted, repeating over and over that she hadn't seen her aunt Concetta in a long time.

'Or the Vicinos,' said Donata, interrupting her with a teasing smile. She had noticed the girl's interest in Salvatore Vicino, Skinny's son, some time back.

Giovanna ignored her and tried to involve her brother in her unusual request. 'Vitantonio's always saying he misses going out hunting with Salvatore . . .'

Finally they reached a compromise: they would spend July in the countryside and at the end of the month they would go to the coast, to meet up with their *nonna* and the Convertini cousins at the house in Savelletri.

In late June they went to the farmstead. They no longer bathed in the laundry though, that was for children play, but even if they'd wanted to cool off that way they wouldn't have been able to: for months now not one drop of water had fallen and the usual sludge on the bottom was as dry and hard as stone; instead of pond skaters and tadpoles, there were now lizards. There hadn't been a single day of rain that spring and for weeks the families there had endured sweltering temperatures brought on by a sirocco that came at all the wrong times. Usually the southerly winds didn't arrive before July, but that year they'd had weeks of desert sand blowing through all of Puglia, sending the farmers mad. The only ones who didn't seem bothered by the heatwave were Giovanna and Salvatore Vicino.

That July, Vitantonio found that Skinny's son didn't have as much energy as before, plus he was easily distracted. He no longer put out traps for the birds or invited him to go hunting. He only seemed to want to stroll through the olive groves with Giovanna, and looked for any excuse to go on even longer walks with her. He seemed to have a lot to talk about with Giovanna, and she encouraged him at every opportunity.

Whenever they went out in the cart, the adults sat in the back; Salvatore and Giovanna sat on the bench up front, with Vitantonio, who held the reins. He liked to be lulled by the cart's slow rhythm and the steady swaying of the mare's hindquarters. If a wheel came out of the rut in the track, the cart wobbled madly from side to side until the wheel found its way back; Giovanna and Salvatore took advantage of this to grab on to each other and laugh like fools, under Vitantonio's scornful scrutiny.

When Vitantonio grew weary of their laughter, he

put down the reins and jumped into the back with the adults. Stretched out on a bed of sacks and horse blankets, he put his hands behind his neck and let himself be carried off by all sorts of dreams, as he watched the slow motion of the clouds and the whimsical shapes they made.

Giovanna and Salvatore's walks were too leisurely for Vitantonio, and he got bored. So instead he'd go up to the olive groves with Skinny's father and the other local men. Or he'd walk up the mountain with Mastega, the Vicino grandfather's dog, who was ugly and stout, but the best hunter in the house. Vitantonio liked to spend the day out in the open and not come home until the evening, exhausted, just in time to eat a big plate of grilled aubergine. Or green peppers, which Concetta made just for him, fried over a low flame with oil and Regina di Torre Cane tomatoes.

After dinner they would go out on to the threshing floor to wait for the cool of the night, which hardly every came that year, and there they would listen to the stories of the Great War that Skinny told them when he returned from his day's work in the sawmil. Sitting among the men, Giovanna would place little Michele Galasso on her lap. He was the youngest of the now seven Galasso children, and he followed her around all day. He had just turned six and she was intent on teaching him to read and write.

Every morning, when the men went off to work, Michele turned up at the farmhouse and, from the doorway, watched Giovanna washing the breakfast dishes while she pretended not to have seen him. When she'd finished, she turned her back to the sink and dramatically opened her arms to him, and scooped him up in a big hug. With the boy in her arms, she ran a rag over the red oilcloth on the kitchen table and went over to the sideboard to grab the notebook and pencil she stored inside a biscuit tin. Then she sat Michele down on the bench, took a knife from the cutlery drawer, sharpened the pencil, opened the notebook, drew some vowels with all sorts of flourishes and asked him to copy them over the whole page. As he filled up the notebook, Giovanna finished tidying up the kitchen. Then she opened up the bread bin and pulled out a loaf, which Concetta always marked with an enormous 'P' on the crust to distinguish her breads from the other local families', since they were all baked together in the same oven. Giovanna made the traditional Catholic 'X' in that huge loaf with a serrated knife, cut off a slice and put it in front of the boy, because she knew that breakfast was meagre in the Galasso home. Michele pounced on the bread and devoured it, his gaze distracted by the flies stuck to the sticky tape hanging from the kitchen's light bulb.

After he'd had breakfast, he knelt on the bench, leaned forward, stuck out his tongue in concentration and started to fill another page with letters. Giovanna would occasionally look over his shoulder and correct the position of his hand or teach him to hold the pencil less awkwardly. After just a few days, the little boy was already able to identify his vowels. Giovanna was thrilled.

'If he had the chance to study, Michele could go far,' she said solemnly one evening as they were telling stories on the threshing floor.

That evening, the heat was even more suffocating than on the previous nights. The air smelled of hay and was filled with husks that scratched at your throat and made it hard to breathe.

'You said it yourself: if he had the chance. But he doesn't . . .' said the father of the Galasso family, cutting her off brusquely.

The man avoided Giovanna's angry glare. He fixed his eyes on the ground and then everyone began to wander off, knowing that they wouldn't be able to sleep in this heat.

They had barely slept in several nights: when they stretched out in bed, the cicadas were still scratching their bellies noisily, confused by temperatures that defied all logic. Sometimes a cricket would get inside the *trulli*, searching for some cool, and then the crickets' concert met with the cicadas' reply, taking on symphonic dimensions. It was impossible to get a wink of sleep the whole night, and in the morning, when it would miraculously grow silent, both the men and women would have to get up, because they needed those first hours of the cool dawn to work in the olive groves. By mid-morning the temperatures would reach forty degrees and staying out in the fields would have been suicidal, so they would go back home and stretch out in the shade, careful not to waste the little energy they had.

That night, Giovanna was the last to fall asleep. She was tossing and turning in bed, imagining ways to kidnap little Michele and take him with her to Bellorotondo so he could study with Father Sinisi at the primary school.

July flew by. On the twenty-first they celebrated Salvatore's saint's day with dancing on the threshing floor to the sounds of an accordion. Feeling that their time together was already running out, Giovanna and Salvatore didn't leave each other's side the entire evening. The others laughed and nudged each other at the couple's most obvious displays of affection. Giovanna only left Salvatore's side once, to go over to Vitantonio, who was sitting on the steps of the *trullo* that was used as a shed; she took him by the hands and tried to pull him out on to the threshing floor to dance.

'Brothers and sisters don't dance together!' He shook her off and went to play in a corner with Mastega the dog, far from the music, trying to banish thoughts of Giovanna's hips as they moved to the rhythm of her contagious laugh.

When the adults had already gone to bed, Salvatore took Giovanna behind the laundry and tried to kiss her. She rebuffed him and he was surprised by her curt response. Her frankness usually amused him, but this time he found it unnerving. 'I dance with you because I like to hear you talk and I know you're involved in an anti-fascist group. I like you, but I won't let you kiss me, because you're uglier ever than your grandpa's dog.'

'That's not what the girls in town say,' he protested, aware of his popularity among them. 'You won't let me kiss you because you think like a girl from a rich family; if you were as revolutionary as you claim to be, you'd know how to make a man like me happy.'

'Well, then it looks like you're clear on what you have to do: find a girl who's revolutionary enough,' she retorted before leaving, laughing like crazy and keeping a tight rein on her desire to kiss him.

The Altamura Market

IN AUGUST, VITANTONIO and Giovanna settled into their *nonna*'s house in Savelletri on the coast, along with Franco and his family. There, they met up with their other cousins, who were staying in their own house. Donata was invited for a fortnight, but after that she left the twins in Savelletri with their grandmother and their aunt Carmelina and went back to Bellorotondo and the *trulli* with Concetta. The twins dreaded the moment their *zia* left, because their aunt Carmelina Ferrante, Angelo's wife and Franco's mother, was a nervous, anxious woman who wasn't particularly easy to deal with.

Their aunt worried about everything. She always saw the negative side of things and she usually predicted that they would only get worse. If someone had a cold, she diagnosed them with pneumonia. If someone was having trouble breathing, she was sure it was tuberculosis. If a friend got pregnant, she wondered if the baby would be deformed. And if a few of the Convertini cousins came down with the same illness, she would immediately suggest bringing a half to the summer holiday by the coast as the only way to avoid the spread of the epidemic that threatened all the youngest members of the family.

If they took a trip by car, Carmelina imagined all sorts of accidents. If they travelled by train, she feared a derailment. If they went out sailing, she didn't let anyone move an inch, so they wouldn't capsize the boat. If Angelo suggested having a coffee out in the garden in the summertime, she refused, because she found that time of the year exceedingly treacherous, and the weather could shift unexpectedly at any moment. If the temperature continued to climb and belied her prediction that it would cool down, she got nervous about the heat and obsessed over the possibility of sunstroke. In September, if she discovered a single cloud in the midst of a radiant blue sky, she would point to it and shout, 'Good lord, here we go again!'

'What's wrong? What's wrong?' Angelo would shout, confused. He always seemed to be just waking up from a nap.

'That cloud, over there. We're going to have a terrible storm again!'

'One cloud? My God, I've married a lunatic.'

'Late-summer storms always creep up on you,' she insisted before ordering the servants to collect the cushions from beneath the pergola. 'Just in case.'

Franco grew up to be just as obsessive as his mother. Vitantonio and Giovanna, on the other hand, could never get used to the crazier side of their family. When the children were hot and sweaty, their aunt wouldn't let them drink anything, because she had heard that a

Spanish king had died from drinking cold water after playing a game of pelota. If they went to the beach, they had to wear a hat and a T-shirt, to protect them from sunburn. If there were any waves at all, they couldn't go in the water. And they had to steer clear of the rocks because she claimed the whirlpools would suck them down, that they'd drown and their bodies would never be found. If they ate the smallest snack, they had to wait at least three hours before they could go in the water, because she would panic over stomach cramps. And they weren't allowed to dive in, because they could break their neck or have a heart attack from the shock.

If life ever corroborated her fears to the slightest extent and something actually happened, she would announce that they were on the brink of an irreversible catastrophe. Her pessimistic obsession earned her the nickname *Auntie Calamity*, which Giovanna came up with. When *Zia* and *Nonna* heard it for the first time they played it cool in front of the children, but when they were alone together they fell about laughing, impressed by the girl's imagination, and decided to adopt the nickname for their own use.

When things took a real downturn, Carmelina suffered attacks of religious fanaticism and wanted to confess her imagined sins all the time: she was convinced that was the only way she could appease God's desire to punish the impiety of the summer holiday-makers. Father Felice avoided her, claiming that it didn't seem prudent or proper for him to hear the confession of a family member, but the rector of Savelletri had no excuse. He was afraid of her in the confessional: if he judged her too harshly, she would go into hysterical shows of repentance; if he forgave her sins too quickly, she would get angry and demand more rigorous penance.

'Sometimes she confesses, while sobbing, that she ate chocolate between meals or that she served herself the largest helping, and she wants me to give her a penance as severe as if she'd committed murder. If it were up to me, I'd condemn her to eternal hellfire for being so annoying and neurotic. May God forgive me,' the rector complained to Father Felice, completely beside himself, one day when Carmelina's insistence had nearly brought on in him a crisis of faith.

For the Feast of the Assumption of the Virgin Mary in mid-August, family tradition dictated that they leave the house on the coast for a couple days and drive inland to the scorched town of Altamura, where Aunt Carmelina's family had a palazzo. They travelled there the day before Assumption, in Uncle Angelo and *Nonna*'s cars, and the children moaned the whole trip, because they were scared of Aunt Carmelina's two Ferrante brothers, who lived in Naples most of the year and were even crazier than their sister. But as soon as they arrived, their worries dissipated and they were happily caught up in the flurry of activity around the big summer market.

The fifteenth of August marked the end of the

farming year and was the day all agricultural and rental contracts ended. Everyone from landowners to administrators, tenant farmers and temporary and permanent labourers gathered in the capital of Alta Murgia on the day of the feast to buy, sell and negotiate. Offers of work were made – or not – and new rental contracts were signed for apartments, farmsteads and land, valid through to mid-August of the following year.

All the deals were made in the market square in front of the cathedral: from the biggest businesses to the smallest concerns. But first everyone had to attend High Mass, which was the farmers' chance to see the landowners in their stylish urban clothes up close. Walking from the palazzo to the cathedral, Vitantonio, who was accustomed to Itria valley farmers living in *trulli* right out in the fields, was surprised to see that in Altamura the farmers lived in the city itself; every day they had to get up at four in the morning to make the long trip to the land they worked. On the day of the feast they left their carts lined up on the streets outside the city walls, in front of their three-storey homes: a half-basement with a pen for the mule; a kitchen and one bedroom on the ground floor; and a granary upstairs.

When the cousins were little, the Altamura cathedral had frightened them because its façade was dominated by two stone lions just as fierce as the ones at Bellorotondo's church of the Immacolata. But now they laughed at their childish fears and, as they left mass they'd stop and put their hands into the lions' mouths. Giovanna always dragged this own, because she had realized – with a combination of annoyance and pride – that all the boys looked her up and down as she performed the ritual. Vitantonio, on the other hand, invariably tried to rush ahead, but he had to wait while his uncles greeted their fellow rural landowners gathered on the Corso Federico II. Only after the family had paid their respects to the regional aristocrats did they begin to make their way through the market. Uncle Angelo led the procession; he was the administrator of Carmelina's family's six hundred hectares because his Neapolitan brothers-in-law were both remarkably useless.

They crossed the square diagonally, following Angelo, who wanted to say hello to the administrator and the head of the tenant farmers, who had been closing livestock deals all morning. Giovanna was surprised to see, on the other side of the square, Signor Galasso – Aunt Concetta and Skinny Vicino's neighbour – talking to the *capo* of the farmers. He had little Michele, who was crying inconsolably, by the hand. In fact, it was only his sobbing that had caught Giovanna's eye, because his father had dressed Michele in a hat, jacket and tie, and she wouldn't have recognized him in a million years.

'Michele! What are you doing here?' she called out, taken aback.

The little boy ran into Giovanna's arms. She met his father's eyes with a questioning gaze.

'I brought him here to rent him out as a hired hand. We got lucky, the *capo* thinks he's clever and has taken him on as a shepherd.'

'For God's sake, he's only six years old!'

'I have six more mouths at home and I can't feed them all! At the Ferrante farm they'll at least give him enough to eat.'

When Giovanna heard the name Ferrante, she was devastated: that was Aunt Carmelina's brothers' farm. On her one visit there she'd seen enough to make her ashamed of how they treated their workers: they made them sleep in haylofts that were less inviting than the stables. She imagined Michele in one of those unbearable haylofts, away from his family, more than a day's walk from his home, surrounded by strangers who were just trying to survive in subhuman conditions, and she felt faint. The boy clung to her legs and she didn't know how to console him. All she could do was cry.

When they left the market, Giovanna approached her uncle Angelo and begged him to order the men at the farm to treat little Michele well.

'It's best if you don't get involved. There are sometimes more than a hundred labourers at one time there, and if we want the farm to do well we can't waste time on any special treatment.'

'He's just a boy, he's only six!'

'And you're not doing him any favours by spoiling him. They wanted a job for the boy and now they have one. They should be thanking God for their luck.'

Giovanna turned her back on her uncle, refusing to speak to anyone for the rest of the day. Nor did she say a word the next morning on the way back to the coast. She broke her silence only to vent her fury to

Vitantonio. 'Salvatore is right. The farm owners in Alta Murgia are soulless bastards —'

Her grandmother cut her off. 'Such language! I don't want to hear you speak like that again. Lately, your rebellious streak has been making me very uncomfortable, but your rudeness is simply unforgivable.'

Then, as if she were talking to herself, *Nonna* continued, 'Actually, that presumptuous bunch in Alta Murgia have proved themselves utterly useless, completely incapable of turning over the land to olive groves and vineyards. They'll still be planting wheat there in a hundred years' time, waiting for divine providence to send them rain or for the government to offer some compensation for their barren land.'

Summer's End

THE SUMMER FELT like it was stretching on for ever, and Giovanna realized that she missed Salvatore. Vitantonio, Franco and the gang at the beach seemed like children to her and she couldn't stand her aunt Carmelina. *Nonna* was the only one whose company she sought. She accompanied her every time Grandmother took the car out to visit her female friends from Bari and Naples who'd had *casini* built in which to spend their summers at the coast; Lady Angela Convertini got on best with the wives of the more modern landowners, the ones who had replaced their traditional wheat and oat fields with large olive groves and vineyards, making their farms flourish. And when *Nonna* received visitors on the terrace of the house in Savelletri, Giovanna would spend all afternoon in a deck chair, pretending to read, while she listened to them gossip.

Whenever hot winds blew in from the south, Aunt Carmelina would begin to predict new calamities. She'd say that, if they were so reckless as to swim, the abominable wind would blow them out to sea and they'd only be found days later on the Dalmatian coast. The first of

September was one of those windy days when Aunt Carmelina wouldn't let them anywhere near the water, and so Vitantonio went looking for the usual gang. Giovanna decided to go with him because, if she couldn't swim, she might as well kill some time with the gang rather than sitting around at home waiting for the sirocco to bring the temperature up to forty degrees. When Vitantonio and Giovanna headed out that day they found Salvatore waiting for them on the corner.

'What are you doing here?' she asked, as surprised as she was concerned to hide her excitement.

'The whole of Bellorotondo is here. There are people scattered all over the beaches, from Savelletri to Torre Cane. The whole town has come to the seaside, and I've come to see you. Don't you know what day it is today?'

That morning they'd been woken by the rattle of the first carts and horses arriving from the Itria valley, along the Fasano road. It was the first of September, the day the valley's farmers all came down to the coast to bid farewell to the summer. They did so every year, on horseback, by bicycle, by cart or on foot, and they spent the whole day on the beach. It was the only day in the entire summer that they even got close to the sand. The children splashed in the water while the adults stretched out on the beach to relax. After lunch, the women drank mineral water and watched the children take another dip, while the men shoozed. Come mid-afternoon they leisurely started to make their way home.

Giovanna and Vitantonio had always enjoyed the day when their neighbours from Bellorotondo came down to the coast and they had always run from beach to beach until they found their friends. But this year, enraged by Aunt Carmelina's swimming ban, they had completely forgotten about the end-of-summer celebration. Until they ran into Salvatore.

Skinny's son had come down on his motorcycle the evening before and spent the night with some cousins who were fishermen in Torre Cane. Salvatore had friends and cousins throughout the entire region and Giovanna never knew whether they were actually relatives or if that was just his way of referring to his comrades in the Party.

The three of them left Savelletri's small fishing dock and walked along the seafront, beyond the last houses in town. Heading south, they followed a sandy path that wound through thistles and balsam plants blooming with white and pink flowers. The first storm of the summer had broken the evening before and it was still relatively cool that morning. The rain had left the scent of fennel hanging in the air, their stalks laden with hundreds of small snails. At a certain point, the path climbed up behind the rocks, through a thicket of mastic and tamarisk trees, which the wind was tossing to and fro. It also lifted little eddies of sand that got in their eyes. Then the path split into three or four trails that twisted through the scrub and met up again further on.

'Where are we going?' asked Giovanna.

'To the shelter,' answered Salvatore, pointing at the rock pools just past the sand dunes, where a tarpaulin held up by four sticks was flapping in the wind.

Vitantonio often rowed out to the rock pools, and he would also put up wood and canvas shelters to store his tools in the shade as he fished for octopus. Using a catgut line tied with a white rag, he would lure the octopus in, which was drawn to the white colour and then trap it. He would yank it from the pool with a hand-held net, grab it by the head and bite down hard right between its eyes to kill it in one go. Giovanna preferred the dark, calm nights when *Nonna* let them row out to sea to fish by gas lamp, as long as they promised not to stray too far from the port. They had named the boat *Principessa* at *Zia*'s suggestion, and they always shared the rowing; while one of them hold the oars, the other used a mirror to look over the side down to the sea bottom, spearing any fish that were blinded by the reflected gaslight. This primitive technique allowed them to catch cuttlefish, scorpion-fish, gilt-head bream and sea urchins with a rudimentary weapon made by splitting a pole at one end.

When they reached the awning, Salvatore's cousin was already there. Once introductions had been made, both the Vicino young men took off their shirts and rolled up their trousers, tied a bag to their waists and went down to the rocks. They each carried a screwdriver and when they reached the water's edge, they bent over the rocks and started scraping. Vitantonio imitated them, finding an old scrap of iron among the tools under the canvas and leaping from rock to rock until he reached the sea.

The three boys' bodies were tanned dark brown by

the Puglia sun. After half an hour they came back up with bags full of limpets and spread them out on the wooden crate they used as a table. Salvatore's cousin grabbed a shell, put it in his mouth and pulled out the snail with his teeth. Vitantonio followed suit. Taking another that was bright orange, Salvatore squeezed a few drops of lemon on to it and, when the snail shrank into its shell, he pulled it out with a knife, held it up on the steel blade with his thumb and brought it to Giovanna's lips. She chewed it slowly, letting the intense flavour of the sea spread throughout her whole mouth. Vitantonio didn't know anyone who was fonder of limpets than Giovanna, and Salvatore found that out when he saw the satisfied look on her face. She never ceased to surprise him. He smiled and prepared another for her.

They had lit a campfire with the driftwood the storm had washed up on the beach and put the limpets in a pan with seawater to blanch them. Giovanna watched the three young men curiously: their tanned bodies were dusted white with dried salt from the water. She noticed that her brother had had a growth spurt over the last few months and that all his muscles were getting firmer. Then she looked at Salvatore, savouring him with her gaze. Skinny's son put another pan on the fire and sautéed three garlic cloves and a hot pepper. When they turned golden he tossed in four ripe tomatoes and half a cup of water to soften them up a little and then he let them simmer. After taking the pan off the flame he added finely chopped parsley. Giovanna came up behind him. 'If you do all the housework this well, you'd make the perfect husband,' she teased.

Salvatore paid her no head, caught up in his cooking. He strained the spaghetti his cousin had cooked separately, mixed in the sauce and the limpets and put them over the fire again for just a few seconds. He stepped back a few paces, looked at the dish, tossed in a pinch of black pepper, then bowed and invited them to eat.

'Will you have supper with us?'

'No. We have to get going or we'll be late for dinner and it'll be hard to convince them to let us go out later,' said Giovanna, stopping him in his tracks.

She grabbed the fork, stabbed a limpet, curled some spaghetti strands around it and brought it all to her mouth. 'Though we'd probably enjoy your meal more than the one waiting for us at home,' she conceded as she left.

As they started down the path, she suddenly stopped, asked Vitantonio to wait and turned back to the shelter. She walked straight over to Salvatore, who was just sticking his fork into his spaghetti. He looked up, surprised.

Pouncing on him, she gave him a kiss on the mouth. 'You're still as ugly as your grandad's dog, but all tanned like this, you're worth a second look,' she said. Then, laughing heartily, she left, as quickly as she'd walked in.

When she caught up with Vitantonio, she saw that he had filled up a jar with little land snails to use as bait when they went out fishing. The last storm clouds had disappeared. The sky was dazzling and there was no longer any trace of the morning cool. The heat was starting to bear down again, as if not a single drop of rain had fallen, and they hastened their pace.

At the Cinema Comunale

When the lights went out, Primo Carnera appeared at the doors to Madison Square Garden, amid the photographers' popping flashes and surrounded by fans trying to leap over the journalists to touch him. The giant's presence on the screen at the Cinema Comunale was greeted by a huge uproar. He wore a fedora, which floated above the other heads, because the Italian boxer was six foot six inches tall. The entire audience stood up and applauded the recently crowned heavyweight world champion.

The titles for the newsreel suddenly came up, at the top of the screen, and scrolled downwards as a prelude to the change in scene; the new location thrilled the audience equally: the boxer reappeared on a Long Island beach jabbing at a punch bag with his left fist. Every once in a while, when you least expected it, he switched arms for a right hook.

'A right uppercut,' explained Vitantonio to Giocavazzo, who was sitting beside him.

Next, the boxer was skipping on the same beach, surrounded by girls in bathing suits, and the cinema crowd again erupted in cheers. They sat back down when the camera focused on his legs jumping to the rope's rhythm before it made its way up to a close-up of his face, scarred by his matches and marked by very thick black eyebrows. Despite his rough air, he seemed like a good kid; Primo Carnera was the *gentle giant*.

Soon the images showed him getting into the ring at Madison Square Garden, wearing a shiny silver silk robe. Vitantonio threw himself forward and exchanged a smile with Franco, who was sitting two seats away. Carnera was their idol and they howled like madmen when poor Jack Sharkey went down for the count in the sixth round and didn't get back up again. The whole cinema was reliving 29 June 1933, the feast of Sts. Peter and Paul, when the hero of Mussolini's Italy had won the gleaming belt that proclaimed him world champion.

The film sped up. The fights flickered over the screen so quickly that the spectators could barely follow the events: a title announced a match a year later with America's Max Baer, but they weren't shown the footage of Carnera's defeat, which Mussolini himself had censored. Next up was a very equal exchange with the American Joe Louis in June 1935, but the report still omitted the Italian boxer's fall to the canvas at the end of the sixth round. It had been only three months since Carnera's latest defeat, which Italy's fascist leaders were trying to downplay, and Vitantonio expressed his firm conviction to Giocavazzo: 'When he gets another chance, he'll win back the world title. He's the strongest.'

The end of the newsreel repeated the images of the Italian boxer's glory days. The cinema again burst into applause and calm didn't return until Vittorio De Sica appeared on the screen, pedaling along with a charming smile, and the film *What Scoundrels Men Arc!* began. The first few frames acted to tame the savage beasts at Bellorotondo's Cinema Comunale. Vitantonio again leaned forward to give Franco a sign of approval, but he found him halfway to his feet and staring to one side of the theatre. Scanning the hall to see what had caught his cousin's eye, three rows further on he saw that Salvatore had just put his arm around Giovanna's shoulder.

As they were leaving the Comunale, Franco berated him. 'If she was my sister, I wouldn't stand for that. His father is a communist and he probably is too.'

'Don't start with that again,' said Vitantonio, frustrated. 'Skinny Vicino is a good man and a good worker. They'd be lucky to have more like him at the factory.'

Giovanna and Vitantonio had been at secondary school in Bari for six years now, she at the Istituto Margherita and he at the Liceo classico Quinto Orazio Flacco, but their boarding schools were two different worlds and their paths rarely crossed in the city. They saw each other only at Christmas, Easter and special family occasions at the palazzo in Bellorotondo. But every time they did manage to meet up, they hugged each other tighter than ever. During this summer's holidays, Giovanna had often been seen at the Cinema Comunale with Salvatore's gang, all of them five or six years older than Vitantonio's friends. The first time he saw Giovanna and Salvatore together he felt a very unpleasant stab of jealousy, but he soon shrugged the feeling off. If it had been someone other that Skinny's son, he might not have been able to stand it; but in fact, it was Franco who couldn't bear seeing her with Salvatore.

The Beating

ONE AFTERNOON SEVERAL months later, Vitantonio saw Salvatore on the other side of the street and was about to cross over to greet him, when two men intercepted skinny's son. A third grabbed him from behind without warning, and put him in an armlock. Once Vitantonio had recovered from his initial shock, he ran to help Salvatore, but a car came to an abrupt stop and blocked his path. The assailants pushed Salvatore into the back. Were they arresting him? Both of the men were dressed in normal clothes and the car, a Fiat model he'd never seen before, didn't look like it belonged to the secret police. Two of the men sat in the back, one on either side of Salvatore. The third man shot a threatening look over the hood at Vitantonio, who had frozen in the middle of the street, then he too jumped in and the car sped off.

Vitantonio stood there for a little while longer, dazed. He kept running the scene over in his mind, searching for an explanation, but the only things he could think of were very dark indeed. Then he thought he caught sight of Franco, who looked as if he had been watching the scene from behind a carob tree on the other side of the street. He ran over to him, but by the time he reached the middle of the square, his cousin had vanished.

Inside the car, Salvatore watched in terror as they left town and took the Alberobello road. He was struggling to stay calm; he still had no idea what was going on. The car turned off towards the clearing where they burned the town's rubbish and screeched to a halt. All four men got out and made him get out as well. Salvatore didn't know any of them, they must have all been from out of town, maybe from Bari. When he registered that they hadn't bothered to cover their faces, he figured that meant they had no fear of being identified later. In other words, he was a dead man. He was overcome by panic. Just then a punch broke his nose and for a moment everything went black. Another fist was rammed into his liver and his knees folded under him as if they were made of rubber. When he fell to the ground, he felt a foot stamping on his face and he thought his head was coming off his body.

He lay out on the ground and gasped desperately for breath, inhaling smoke from the burning rubbish deep into his lungs. He gagged and then shook violently. He took another series of kicks to the head and stomach and lost consciousness.

When he came to, one of the men was peeing on his face and the others were laughing. It took him a while to grasp that he was still at the dump, but he fixed his gaze on the black, rotting teeth of one of the perpetrators, the biggest one. His teeth looked like the dark caves in the Sassi di Matera he'd seen the day he'd been to visit Giovanna and Vitantonio's *zia*'s father. He swallowed piss and started to retch. When he tried to sit up so he could vomit, he found that neither his arms nor his legs were responding. The man whose mouth was filled with dark caves kicked him in the face and he lost consciousness again.

The rubbish men found him the next morning. When Skinny and Vitantonio arrived, his hands were still tied and his mouth was still filled with fifth. The rubbish men hadn't touched him because they were afraid he was dead. They took him home and called for Dr Ricciardi.

Months later, the doctor would confess, 'When I got to your father's house and saw how badly you were breathing I thought that your broken ribs had punctured your lungs. I didn't think you'd last more than twenty-four hours.'

'The role of all-powerful god suits you, Doctor. I like you better than the real one!' laughed Salvatore.

'God?' he asked, confused.

'Yeah. You're God because you brought me back to life. And, by saving me, you're taking life away from that bastard with the rotted teeth. Because I swear that when I find him, he's a dead man.'

That autumn of 1936, Franco went off to Rome to university and a year later surprised everyone when he left to fight for General Franco in Spain. The evening they all bade him farewell, *Nonna* confessed to

Giovanna, 'Wars are never good, not even for your poor cousin. He's a coward and everyone knows it, but he's trying to make a man of himself so he can be like Vitantonio; that's why he wanted to go to Rome to study, and now he's heading off to fight in Spain. I don't know what he'll do there, with the volunteers; I suppose he'll cling to some captain and end up as his batman. Just so he doesn't have to go anywhere near the front. I still don't understand how Vitantonio stands him: your brother might be the only one who gets angry with him, but he always forgives him in the end.'

The Gentlemen's Circle

THE GENTLEMEN'S CULTURAL Circle was a prestigious institution that, oblivious to the pompous adjective affixed to the building's façade, promoted card playing and long talks over after-dinner coffee instead of 'culture'. Its members were rural landowners and merchants; the card games were legendary, as were the discussions, which focused on the local economic situation and the difficulties the circle's members had in finding amenable and loyal workers. On the other hand, its aficionados tended to avoid politics except to consider international conflicts, which naturally made them feel more cosmopolitan. The gentlemen were divided: some supported the Pact of Steel that Mussolini had just signed with Nazi Germany, and others would have preferred to repair relations with England, but they all agreed on Il Duce's expansionist plans for the south of France, the Mediterranean and, of course, east Africa.

The conversations went on simultaneously in the salon and the library, which was used for reading only the newspapers. If a member ever approached the shelves to pull out a book it was to check a fact that could help him win an argument at stalemate. After lunch, the gentlemen separated off into two or three card games, which were played in closed rooms prepared especially for that purpose, particularly since the level of betting had been raised a notch when an old landowner had thrown his farm into the pot.

When the games were over, they gathered again in the salon to discuss them with a glass of cognac in one hand and a large cigar in the other. Finally, some of them would slip off discreetly to the garden, which was very pleasant, particularly in the summertime. Two lime trees and an enormous laurel afforded wonderful shade, but it wasn't so much the coolness that the members appreciated as the back door that unobtrusively connected the courtyard with the neighbouring property. The other garden was smaller, more feminine, with miniature roses in pots and hydrangeas in the window boxes. The walls were covered in five-leafed ivy and in one corner there was a fountain where water gushed from a mermaid's mouth into a pool filled with red and black fish.

Later in the evening, after dinner, the gentlemen would quickly cross the two gardens and slip into the house of 'La Bella' Antonella, "the attractive widow of a bankrupt fabric merchant, who ran the most famous brothel in the city. The main entrance was on a side street, but no one used it until the night was deepest black and the neighbours were fast asleep. If the girls only had the customers who came in through the street entrance, the widowed madam would have had to shut her establishment down; luckily, the Circle's garden gave 'La Bella' Antonella the best clientele in all of Puglia.

Most of Vitantonio's classmates at the boarding school in Bari had all their lessons at the Liceo Orazio Flacco. They slept, ate and studied at the religious institution, under the stern regime of the priests, but a number of them also took classes at the secondary school on the main road of Bari's seafront, the Lungomare. There They were seated in alphabetical order, so Aurelio Cavalli shared a desk with Vitantonio. Cavalli was from Bari; in fact, his mother's house was right next door to La Bella Antonella's premises. His mother was a seamstress and from the house's work room there was a wonderful view of the Circle's garden and the smaller, secret one belonging to the brothel. The boy had good business instincts and soon saw that, when his mother went out to take clients' measurements, he could make some money by charging his friends to spy on the whores from the window of his house.

On their way from the boarding school to the school on the Lungomare, Vitantonio and his fellow pupils had no choice but to walk past Cavalli's house, and they soon became his best customers. They would spy on the girls, who took their breaks in the garden, wearing only petticoats, and they would laugh watching them untangle and brush each other's hair. When the lights behind the windows were turned on, the boys would all become tense, trying to glimpse the moment when the girls took off their clothes. The results were usually very meagre, but their imaginations made up for that and they became as aroused as if they were in the room with the whores, and might just reach out and touch them or gaze directly upon their nudity. Especially when it was Isabella Dardicce changing; she was the youngest of them all, and so sweet that she seemed to the boys a tasty fruit ripe for the plucking.

The most active members of the sewing-room club soon discovered a new source of entertainment: from the same window they could keep track of the comings and goings and then they would laugh about their schoolmates whose fathers were among the brother's regular clients. One day, as they were surveying the customers, Vitantonio was surprised to see his uncle Angelo emerge from the Circle, walk through the garden gate and greet the girls very familiarly.

'Bloody hell, my uncle Angelo!' slipped out of his mouth.

Pasquale Raguseo was beside him, watching the scene. He was the son of one of the few farming families in the Itria valley whose vineyards had prospered. Pasquale quickly stuck his head out of the sewing-room window and shouted, 'Uncle Angelo! Vitantonio's uncle Angelo!'

Vitantonio crouched down, horribly embarrassed.

'How could you! Now he'll know I was spying on him.'

The incident had immediate consequences, the very first of which occurred the next day when Cavalli's mother received a visit from the president of the Gentlemen's Circle, who urged her to be discreet if she wished to maintain her reputation and job.

'A seamstress who is invited into all the city's best homes must never look or listen. And in any case she's sworn to professional secrecy, like a priest,' he threatened the poor woman, who cried and promised, over and over, that it wouldn't happen again.

That same day, her son, much to his dismay, had to close up his business.

The second consequence revealed itself the following Sunday at the palazzo. After lunch Uncle Angelo got up from the table, put his arm around Vitantonio's shoulder and invited him to smoke a cigar with him in his office.

Vitantonio thought he was dead. He had never been fond of his uncle and he imagined it was mutual. They sat down, face to face, and Angelo lit his cigar. The boy started sweating profusely, wondering how long this display of friendliness would last, and at what point it would give way to angry recriminations. But these never came. Instead, his uncle offered him a glass of the cognac that had been a gift from his French timber suppliers. Then he began to speak to Vitantonio in a persuasive tone.

'You've grown up, Vitantonio, and you must miss having a father figure. There are things he probably would have talked to you about and perhaps the time has come for someone else in the family to discuss them with you. How's your luck with girls?'

Vitantonio couldn't hide his shock. He didn't know whether he should confess that he'd visited a bordello on the outskirts of Bellorotondo a few times with Salvatore. He stammered, hoping to buy himself some time in which to work out where his uncle was headed; he decided it was more prudent to act the innocent.

'Well, Uncle . . . You see . . .'

'I see that you've never been with a woman. Perhaps it's time I introduced you to someone; I'll give you an address and you can tell them I sent you. But don't mention it to your cousin; there are some things better not shared between father and son.'

Was his uncle inviting him to a brother? He couldn't believe it. His mind was spinning and he had a sudden flash of inspiration.

'I really appreciate it, Uncle, but I could never do that in Bellorotondo. I wouldn't want my *zia* to find out, she wouldn't like it at all.'

'Well, you have to start somewhere . . . Is there some place you would feel more comfortable?'

'Maybe in Bari. There is a place behind the Corso Vittorio Emmanuele that seems to be very discreet, especially if you enter through the Gentlemen's Cultural Circle garden . . .'

If he was surprised, Angelo didn't let it show. He just nodded and two days later Vitantonio went with his uncle to the Gentlemen's Cultural Circle.

'This boy is a good student and he's earned this show of confidence. I've made him a member of the Circle and advised him to come occasionally and study here in the library,' announced Angelo to his card-playing companions. 'That way he can listen in to our conversations and complete his education.'

Vitantonio had a look around on the library shelves and after a little while he went discreetly out into the garden. When he went through the small gate that joined the two courtyards, on his way to a rendezvous with Isabella Dardicce at his uncle's expense, he turned towards the second floor of the neighbouring house and waved to the seamstress's son who was spying on him from the work-room window.

The next day the whole school had heard about it. When Vitantonio went out into the schoolyard, after his first two morning classes, he was received with applause and many envious looks.

When Uncle Angelo said that he was going to the city, no one knew if he meant Bari, Brindisi or Taranto. He would have business lunches, or spend some time at the Circle or attend a political meeting, but no one ever asked about it or went with him, so they didn't really know what he did there – until Vitantonio saw him walking through the garden of the Circle. That day marked the start of his uncle's unexpected interest in him, as he desperately searched for a good influence on his son Franco, who had inexplicably first gone off to Rome to university and than had ended up in the civil war in Spain. Franco would be sure to come back to Bellorotondo at some point.

Since the incident, whenever he went to Bari on

business, Angelo would take Vitantonio with him and they'd go to the best restaurants. The priests were happy for Angelo to take Vitantonio out, because they considered that strong relationships between different generations of men in a family were most advantageous for the future heads of the region's industry. Sometimes, he also took his nephew with him to visit clients and representatives from foreign timber companies.

Vitantonio, on the other hand, was wary. They had never got on particularly well. At the offices of Convertini Timber, Uncle Angelo knew how to maintain the discipline that *Nonna* had introduced, but he was capricious and fickle in his decision-making. And he was particularly arbitrary in his treatment of the workers, unlike Lady Angela, who may have kept them at a distance but took good care of them, considering them the factory's most valuable asset.

On their trips to the city over several months, Angelo got so used to Vitantonio's presence that one day he asked him to accompany him to the doctor. As they left, he seemed confused: the nurse had given him a packet of powder to dissolve in water and take before going to the radiologist for a stomach X-ray. Despite playing the role of the demanding despot at the sawmill, Angelo was useless at making decisions outside of the office, no matter how small. His uncle didn't know how to take the powder and he said to Vitantonio, 'Let's go to the Albergo delle Nazioni.'

Twenty minutes later they were seated in the dining room of Bari's finest restaurant, which was completely empty at that time of day. A waiter wearing white gloves brought over a silver pitcher of water and dissolved in it the contents of the packet Angelo gave him. Then he served him the liquid in a glass, which he refilled three times, until his uncle had finished the entire dose prescribed by the specialist.

The X-ray didn't reveal anything serious and to celebrate, a few days later, Uncle Angelo took Vitantonio back to the Albergo delle Nazioni. This time they went at lunchtime and, halfway through the meal, he opened up to his nephew. Worried that Angelo was going to ask him again about his love life, Vitantonio was surprised when he began talking about Franco and the factory.

'I want you to stop studying and start working at the factory. It's the only way I've come up with to get Franco to want to work there. It's high time he packed in running around with soldiers, he's been in Spain for months; he should take his rightful place as the heir to Convertini Timber. You two get along and he feels safe with you. One day he'll be the boss and then you'll be his right-hand man, and with a good salary too.'

His uncle picked up his cutlery with all the delicacy of the scion of a good family and turned his attention to his mouth-watering dish of partridge and cabbage. But when he put the fork in his mouth the table manners of the palazzo lunches vanished: he ate so quickly that he didn't have time to lift his elbows from the table, all the while chewing ferociously. Vitantonio found him unpleasant. He screwed up his courage and replied, 'But . . . I want to study law. I want to defend the farmers of Puglia.'

'Law? Defend the farmers? Are you *crazy*? What kind of a job is that?'

'The kind I want to have. I'd like to help the small farmers achieve better conditions and defend themselves from the abuses of absent landlords who just wash their hands of any problems.'

'I won't hear of it! You are a Convertini and you can't turn your back on the family business, or work for some poor wretch who'll never amount to anything.'

'I've made up my mind, I'm not giving up my studies. Franco is old enough to run the mill himself and he's more capable than you think. If you'd paid more attention to him, and showed him that you were proud of him, he wouldn't have felt he had to volunteer in Spain.'

Since Salvatore had been attacked, Vitantonio had become more sure of himself; he'd lost his innocence but even he was surprised at his own words. He lifted his head and openly challenged his uncle with a glare. In his anger, his uncle had puffed himself up like a boar: his cheeks were round and pink and his double chin hung down so far that it looked like he had no neck; his eyes and mouth were ridiculously small in the middle of his bloated face.

'You will make a lot of money at the factory—' Angelo huffed, trying to redirect the course of the conversation.

'You can keep it!' replied Vitantonio, cutting him off.

Uncle Angelo seemed daunted. He made a strange face and his right eye started twitching. He had never been spoken to with such insolence. And much less from a nineteen-year-old kid. But he needed to convince Vitantonio, so he pretended he wasn't offended.

'Being the right-hand man to the owner of Convertini Timber is no joke. In time you can make your own investments and you will build up your own fortune. One day you'll have family obligations of your own and you'll have to be up to the job. You have to learn the business quickly and when Franco comes back from the war in Spain you'll train him and teach him everything you've learned.'

'*Nonna* and *Zia* want me to finish my studies, too. I've made up my mind to become a lawyer.'

'They will do as *I* say. And you will too! Members of this family have to have more pride than that.'

'And wouldn't that same pride keep me from wanting to be just my cousin's employee?'

Southern Winds

FOR TWO YEARS, a drought had plagued the land, and hot southern winds blew in from North Africa. Every morning, the valley's olive groves turned their leaves towards the ground, to conserve what little dampness they still had, and at dusk they looked back up towards the stars, begging for a few drops of dew. From the large terrace in Bellorotondo, it was an extraordinary sight: in the midday sun, the leaves appeared to be almost silvered, glimmering like the Adriatic Sea. Yet, up close, they were a leaden green. The olive trees had shed their flowers from lack of water and the farmers knew that the harvest would be meagre for the second year running. Their nerves were frayed, fully aware that any stray spark could set off a tragedy.

Such sticky heat also affected everyone's mood at the palazzo. Every morning *Nonna* went out on the terrace and surveyed the horizon, searching for a change in the weather that failed to materialize. The water in the tanks had come out murky all spring long and finally, one day in June, it dried up altogether. Lady Angela considered it a disgrace and, from then on, she had the garden and the square swept continuously, in the hope that when the storms finally arrived, not a single drop of water would be lost. Every morning she went up to the terrace, clutching the balustrade with tense hands, and from her privileged position, directed the maids and made sure that the channels were well cleaned. When she retired to her room, the terrace floor was scattered with dried flowers that Lady Angela had compulsively, unthinkingly, pulled off the wisteria; they too were suffering from lack of water.

At midday, she went out into the garden, through the kitchen door, looking for even the faintest of breezes to ease the oppressive heat. On one of the hotter mornings they had emptied the fish pond to save water. The next day, when Lady Angela found it filled with dry leaves and instinctively pumped the iron handle, the tap emitted a hoarse metallic sound, like an animal's cry. Frightened, *Nonna* beat a hasty retreat to the terrace.

When she reached the azaleas she let out a shriek that echoed through the narrow, twisting streets of the old quarter: the 'Queen of Bellorotondo' had begun to lose its flowers and even its leaves were turning yellow. Her most prized azalea had a withered, sickly look and she allowed herself a few private moments of worrying that this damn drought would be the death of it, before the servants responded to her cry. The cook and the maid ran out of the house in a terrible state, and found their mistress standing stock-still in front of the azaleas. With her arms in the air and her fists tightly clenched, the Lady of Bellorotondo looked up towards the heavens and defied her creator. 'What have I done to deserve this? What is my crime?' she cried. 'Am I guilty of circumventing every obstacle in order to grow the freshest flowers for your churches? Was it a sin of pride to refuse to accept the fate of this miserable region? Was it vanity to create a paradise here in the midst of this parched land? Must I give up like all those farmers you've left resigned and dispirited?'

Seeing her trembling, the maids rushed to her side to make sure she didn't collapse. She pushed them away and ordered, 'Have them prepare the car. I'm going to the factory.'

A few minutes later, she burst into Angelo's office and demanded that he have the palazzo's water tanks filled.

'Bring water from the Bradano river or the spring in Torre Cano. If that's not enough, have some brought from Abruzzo. Have the cistons filled with water from the Po, if necessary, or from the very heart of the Alps. I don't care how you do it, but I want them brimming. *Tomorrow!* Before my entire garden dies of thirst!'

While the Lady of Bellorotondo argued with God and recriminated with him for sentencing her azaleas to death, the farmers in the *trulli* were growing desperate as they watched their olive trees start to turn yellow and their flowers drop to the ground. They too anticipated a weak harvest, but they lacked a direct line to their creator, or enough familiarity to reproach him for their unfair punishment. Nor did they trust intermediaries such as Father Constanzo: for weeks, the rector of the Immacolata had been celebrating masses with the other priests in the valley and praying for rain, invoking every saint on the calendar. The men of Puglia just looked up at the sky in resignation and cursed their bad luck to be born in that parched part of the world.

The next morning, when the water from the Bradano river reached the palazzo, *Nonna* drenched the garden. Meanwhile, on the other side of town, Donata and Giovanna were shelling fava beans in the kitchen of their house on the Piazza Santa Anna. As they were pricking one side of the pods with a knife and dividing them in half to dry them, Dr Ricciardi came in wearing a serious expression, unable to conceal that he was the bearer of bad news.

'Little Michele has killed himself.'

The women cried out in distress. Donata brought her hands to her face. Giovanna dropped the knife, which fell on its point and stuck in the table. When she stood up, her face was distorted in agony.

'What do you mean, he killed himself?' she cried out. 'You mean he's dead? Little Michele? *My* Michele?'

'It seems for weeks now they'd been hearing him cry all night long,' Dr Ricciardi tried to explain. 'Yesterday morning, when he went out with the sheep, he ran away and flung himself into the ravine. When they found him at the bottom, he was crushed against the dry riverbed, and there was nothing they could do to save him.'

Giovanna felt a sudden stabbing pain and grabbed

her belly with her hands; all at once, a thousand blades jabbed at her stomach, one after the other. She twisted in agony, and brought one hand up to her mouth as she began to vomit. Donata got up to support her forehead; Ricciardi wetted a rag and ran it over her face. They hugged her. She cried inconsolably and they cried with her.

'I don't understand how he managed to last over a year there. Didn't they see that he was just a child and needed his mother? He was only six when they took him away, he didn't even make it to eight. We should have stopped them!'

Ricciardi acknowledged that she was right. 'They treated him no better than a dog.'

When they reached the Galassos' *trullo* to give their condolences, the women were sobbing and shrieking over the body that had just been brought from Altamura. Giovanna didn't dare go in; she stayed in one corner of the threshing floor, far from the local men, who sat looking at the ground in silence. Salvatore, standing in the centre of the group, addressed those shamefaced men with harsh words. He blamed them for the tragedy and condemned their fatalism, which had them always bowing their heads.

The Galasso father seemed the most resigned of all. 'We couldn't do anything about it: poor Michele was born so tiny; he was always clinging to his mother's skirt.'

Inside the women screamed, more and more hysterically. Convinced their cries would end up scaring poor Michele's soul, Giovanna decided to go inside. She stood over the little boy's lifeless body and asked for his forgiveness. 'I promised you that you would go far and you didn't even make it to the age of eight.'

She walked out to the threshing floor, grabbed Salvatore by the arm, pulled him away from the group and asked him, 'I want join the Party, take me to a meeting. I'll do whatever it takes, but from now on I want to devote myself to fighting the bastards who are destroying this land.'

The Indiscretion

DURING THE FIRST days of December 1938, Father Felice fell ill again, with one side of his body succumbing to paralysis once more. That Christmas, Donata and the twins moved into the palazzo to help *Nonna*, who insisted on taking care of her brother in person. After the holiday, *Zia* returned home and Vitantonio went back to university in Bari; it was his first year studying law there. Giovanna, on the other hand, stayed on in Bellorotondo a few more days to keep her grandmother company and help her out with her uncle, who was rapidly fading away. It seemed the end was near.

Giovanna and her grandmother took pleasure in the closeness they'd always cultivated. After breakfast, Giovanna would settle into the conservatory and read, basking in the January sun that warmed the garden, which had been cleverly designed to face south. She covered the books in coloured paper to conceal the titles of the banned literature she'd brought from Bari. She wanted to put off the moment when her grandmother would discover that she was no longer reading D'Annunzio, but rather Baudelaire, Pavese and other authors that could land her in trouble. At midday, she would head out for a walk and go over to the house in the Piazza Santa Anna for lunch with her *zia*. She was back at the palazzo soon after, reading again while her *nonna* visited friends.

When it started to grow dark, they both retired to the study and dealt with the letters that had come for Father Felice; since the news of his relapse had spread, he received many. Giovanna would read the longer ones out loud to him, because her grandmother's sight was failing. And then *Nonna* would dictate the answers to her granddaughter, because her own hand was too shaky to write as elegantly as she felt was proper.

On the feast of Epiphany, 6 January, Father Felice died. The two women were swamped by messages of condolence: there were parishioners from his former churches who wrote only a few lines in a card, but family friends sent very long letters, as did his old students from the seminary, and it took them two weeks to answer them all.

Seated in the palazzo's office, Giovanna and *Nonna* shared those intense but gratifying hours of work. Until the afternoon, when they had finished replying to almost all of the letters, that an oversight on the part of her grandmother threw Giovanna's whole world off balance. That day, when Giovanna returned from lunch with her *zia*, she found that Lady Angela had gone to the parish church. In the entryway she had left her a letter to copy out neatly, along with a note:

Cara Giovanna,

Please write out this letter neatly and, if you finish it in time, take it in person to the post office. I have to go to the rectory at the Immacolata to arrange the masses for Father Felice's soul and, while I'm out, I'll also visit Maria, who has been laid up with pneumonia for a few days now. I'll be home before seven for supper.

Nonna Angela

Giovanna sat in the office, turned on the desk lamp and began to copy the letter, which was addressed to the Bishop of Otranto, a personal friend of Father Felice since their youth, when they had studied together at the Padua seminary. And in the text of this letter was *Nonna's* unforgivable slip:

Bellorotondo, 18 January 1939

Most Reverend Bishop of Otranto,

Please forgive my delay in replying; under normal circumstances I never would have made you wait so long. I am writing to explain the details of the death of our beloved Father Felice (may he rest in peace), who as you know left us on Epiphany to find the peace of our Lord Jesus Christ, whom he always served with enthusiasm and loyalty. You yourself saw that over many years of friendship and collaboration. Before Christmas he had a relapse and was, unfortunately, unable to get out of bed, although he still maintained his mental clarity and memory, both of which which stayed with him until his last breath. His body, however, had become a useless burden some time earlier.

Father Felice died shortly after reading your letter, which was of great comfort to him and which he sincerely appreciated. I also want to thank you for your kind wishes at Christmas, which we were still able to spend together. I can assure you that up until his last day he remembered you very clearly and entrusted you to the Most High.

Again, please excuse this delayed reply, but I've had my granddaughter and my adopted grandson here these last few days; a real pleasure that, since they began studying in Bari—

Giovanna felt an enormous pressure on her chest, and struggled for breath. She went back to the text and again read 'adopted grandson'. The two words hammered at her skull. The office began to spin, leaving her half faint. When she finally recovered a little, she continued reading the letter, in the hopes of finding some sort of an explanation.

Again, please excuse this delayed reply, but I've had my granddaughter and my adopted grandson here these last few days; a real pleasure that, since

they began studying in Bari, I am able to enjoy
less often, so I have devoted myself fully to them.
Please accept my apologies and my best wishes
for this new year, 1939.

Faithfully yours,
Angela Convertini

Giovanna remained glued to the armchair in the office, breathing with difficulty, unable to understand what was happening. Then she stood up and started running. She didn't stop until she reached the door of her aunt's house. She entered shouting, 'What does 'adopted grandson' mean? Why did *Nonna* write that Vitantonio is her adopted grandson?'

She pounced on *Zia* and started to beat her chest with both fists, repeating louder and louder, 'What does it mean that Vitantonio is her adopted grandson? What are you hiding from us?'

Donata was alarmed. What in the world had Angela Convertini said? This couldn't be happening. She hugged Giovanna tightly and led her over to the kitchen table, like when she was a little girl.

They talked all night long, as Donata explained every last detail of their family history, and the Palmisano curse. Twelve hours later, when they finally got up from the table, the sun was beginning to peek out from behind the Cisternino olive groves.

Giovanna let out a nervous giggle. 'You know what? Sometimes when Vitantonio would look at me and

I didn't see him as a brother. I've always wondered why . . .'

'He *is* your brother! Never forget that!'

They stood there, face to face, staring at each other for a long while. Finally, Giovanna broke the silence.

'I don't know if I hate you for lying to me or if I love you more for everything you've been through. You're like that mother who asked King Solomon to give her son to another woman, rather than see him cut in two . . . But how could you give up your son? How could you bear the pain?'

'All the men in the family were dead. Vitantonio was the only survivor and he was doomed.'

'The curse of the Palmisanos . . . To think that the rumours around town were true—'

'It's no rumour. All twenty-one of them died, one after the other.'

Donata's eyes were again filled with tears and again she begged Giovanna, 'Swear that you won't say a word of this to Vitantonio. He can never know, he *has* to be a Convertini for ever. His life depends on our secret.'

A Letter from Spain

Signora Angela Convertini
Palazzo Convertini
Bellorotondo – Puglia
Italy

Girona, 5 February 1939

Dear Grandmother,

It won't be long now. Today we liberated the city of Girona, the last Spanish provincial capital before the French border. The Republican revolutionaries and bandits are fleeing as fast as they can and there is scarcely any resistance to the advance of the glorious Francoist troops we are fighting with as part of the Corps of Volunteer Troops. Today we will witness a memorable victory for fascism, which will be admired throughout Europe.

I think of you all often. We entered Girona following a wall along a path used to depict the stations of the cross. We walked the stations in the wrong direction and then found ourselves in a city of narrow, steep streets, which often end in impossibly steep steps. The city centre has a group of very old churches, none as lovely as ours in Lecce or Trani on Barletta, but taken together it is very impressive. It feels as if time stopped in the era of the Crusades, awaiting liberation by us. When we ousted the last Reds from the city, we discovered on the outskirts a small chapel surrounded by tree trunks and planks. It was dedicated to our St Nicholas and when we went inside there were . . . saws!

They belong to a family that imports wood like us, but their business had been collectivized by the revolutionaries and they barely had anything left in the warehouse, which is in the garden. I decided to settle in the house, which is as big as the palazzo but a bit more run-down. Fabrizio, the unit's doctor, came with me. The soldiers, exhausted by the march from Barcelona, are sleeping in the sheds; some have buried themselves deep in sawdust, because it is very cold and they say that tonight it will freeze over again. The commander took lodgings in a neighbouring house, with the other officers and the cook, who had dinner brought to us. We shared it with these good people, who had never tasted spaghetti with garlic, oil and chilli. I don't know if they enjoyed it, but they were half starved and gulped it down.

In the evening, by which time we had liberated the whole city, we strolled through the streets of the old town, and they were covered in the bodies of boys that couldn't have been more than seventeen or eighteen years old. Is Giovanna with you? Tell her that that's what the revolutionaries do: send children to war, burn down churches and steal factories from their owners. And Vitantonio? If you're there, you should know I've missed you; if you'd joined us, you'd be our leader by now.

I pray every day for you all, and for Il Duce. Now we are marching toward Figueres, further north, and they say that we'll reach the French border in less than a month and then it will all be over. God willing.

Until then, I love you and entrust you to God in all my prayers.

Your grandson,
Franco

P. S. This morning, when we said goodbye to the owners of the house, the warehouse supervisor came in shouting that the saw belts were missing. It seems the soldiers steal any rubber they can find and use it to make soles for their boots. I ordered a sergeant to find out who had done it and make them return the belts. As deputy commander I couldn't allow low-ranking soldiers to steal from people who are almost like us.

At the French Border

No, Giovanna wasn't around in the palazzo to read Franco's invectives; she too was mired in the same Spanish hell, more than seventeen hundred kilometres from Bellorotondo. While Franco and the Italian volunteers were heading north from Girona, following General Franco's elite Navarra division, she was hastily leaving the city of Figueres and beginning an arduous journey towards the French border, amid heavy aerial bombardments. On 6 6 February 1939, only forty kilometres separated the two cousins, but they had never been further apart. Giovanna had always thought little of her cousin Franco, but now they were divided by a huge, gaping rift. He was advancing with the fascist volunteers; she was retreating with the International Brigades. He would have killed to make himself a man; she would kill only to save a life. He would have given anything to gain his cousin's affection; she found consolation only in her hatred of those responsible for the cruel wave of fascism that was washing over Europe.

Deeply unsettled by her *zia*'s revelations, she had bid a cold farewell to her *nonna* and left Bellorotondo almost immediately. It had taken her four days to travel through Italy and southern France by train and then four more to cross the Spanish border and reach Barcelona. Only two weeks earlier she had met up with Salvatore and, since then, she'd been on the run. They were taking the route in reverse now, to the north, in the midst of a heartrending procession of starving, freezing men and women trying to reach the Pyrenees. They walked mechanically, in columns that only broke when enemy planes started bombing.

'*Maledetti sparvieri!*' shouted Giovanna when she identified Savoia-Marchetti SM.79s, the Italian 'Sparrowhawks', among the attacking planes.

The refugees carried all sorts of things with them, like mattresses and kitchen utensils. Giovanna walked behind an old woman with a hollow gaze who was holding on to an empty cage: her instinctive compassion had led her to free the birds when she saw that the war was lost. Those poor lost souls walked with their few remaining possessions, which preserved in them the hope of a fresh start.

Salvatore and Giovanna had only been fleeing for two weeks, but each day felt like an entire year and those fourteen together were an eternity. The past had become completely unreal. They'd dissociated themselves from normality so quickly. What had Europe been doing these last three years, while in Spain they were killing each other? Where were the authors of those banned books that she had read wrapped in coloured paper so that her grandmother would be none the wiser? Where were the students she had met up with secretly at university? Where was she? Three weeks ago she was writing letters from the palazzo and now she was in another time, another place, and her worries were no longer her own. She was living in a mirage of extreme cruelty. And she barely recognized herself.

After meeting up with Salvatore, they had left Barcelona behind on the first day; on the next, Mataro; then Arenys, Blanes, Tossa, Girona . . . Now they were fleeing Figueres and Giovanna wondered how many of the refugees around her would die before reaching the border. She went from one column to the next, trying to dress wounds, helping the exhausted elderly, giving a last caress to the dying. One day, someone called to her, 'Nurse!', and she assumed the role quite naturally. That was how, without even realizing it, she became someone who tended to the desperate, she became a nurse.

It was only in the evenings that she was able to spend a few hours with Salvatore. She still hadn't found the right moment to tell him what she had read about her brother in her *nonna*'s letter to the Bishop of Otranto. They embraced and it felt good to be in his arms, but she fell asleep thinking of Vitantonio. She wanted to tell him that they weren't siblings, that she missed him terribly. But she had sworn to *Zia* that she would keep the secret to protect Vitantonio. That was why she had run away to Spain.

Rumours of War

VITANTONIO WASN'T IN Bellorotondo either, so he too missed the chance to read Franco's letter. He would have liked to have news of his cousin, even though he hadn't forgiven him for volunteering for the fascists, and how that had led to Giovanna running away as well. He assumed his sister had joined the International Brigades to make up for Franco fighting against the Spanish Republic. But what the hell was wrong with them? What business did Giovanna, Salvatore and Franco have fighting amongst themselves, in a country far from home? What could they possibly hope to find there in Spain, a place even poorer than their own country? Vitantonio was no fascist, but nor was he an anti-fascist. Not even an anti-fascist in the style of many of his friends, who had no fondness for the regime but considered the dissidents a pain in the arse. All he knew was that he supported the small farmers of Puglia against the large landowners, but he found the whole larger political struggle exasperating.

At university in Bari, far from Bellorotondo, he had become a man. He had very southern looks, dark skin and black hair, with a curl that fell over his forehead, and a strong jaw. Yet his gaze was deep and tender, and drew you in. His warm smile softened his hard face. His back was broad. He was both strong and sweet at once. That was his appeal: he turned heads, but the young women didn't just label him 'handsome', they called him 'adorable'.

He had just returned to Bari, to his law course, not wanting to miss a single day in his mission to defend the interests of the *trulli* peasants. He had spent the last few days of January at the Palmisano farmstead, helping the Vicinos and Concetta with the olives; they had come in very late that year and ever since Salvatore had gone off to Spain, Skinny and his aunt were overwhelmed. He had also gone hunting for a few days and rediscovered the pleasure of knowing he could take care of himself in the mountains. Something told him that it would soon come in handy.

Rumours of war were spreading throughout Europe, and Vitantonio had started to wonder whether Italy would get involved. During Easter Week, Mussolini had given the government in Tirana an ultimatum and was preparing to invade Albania. Vitantonio shared his fears with his *zia*, who urged him to make his escape.

'If we go to war you have to hide in the mountains. You can't fight on the side of the Germans, who killed your father, but you can't stand against your homeland, either!'

PART FOUR

Rain of Stars over Matera

The Unwilling Conscript

GUARNERI, MARINOSCI, RAFFAELE, Carmelo Pizzigallo, Giocavazzo, Sante Miccoli, Cavalli . . . entire former classes of the schools in Martina Franca and Bari had gone off to the war. Even Argese had managed to conceal his limp and get himself sent to the Greek island of Cephalonia, in the same battalion as Pasquale Raguseo. That list was missing only one student: 'Vitantonio Convertini, *figlio di* Antonio *e di* Francesca, *della classe de* 1919, *del comune di* Belloro-tondo, *distretto di* Taranto, *provincia di* Bari.' To avoid conscription, since June 1940 Vitantonio had been hiding in a cave in Matera.

It had been a huge surprise to others. His friends had always supposed that he would be the one best prepared to survive at the front and, as the rumours of an imminent declaration of war intensified, they all predicted that he would be the first to enlist. Not only had he become the best hunter in the county, but whenever a fight broke out he was also the first to jump in, especially to protect others, so everyone in town was convinced he would rush to the defence of their home-land. His refusal to enlist came as a real shock. What had happened? What had turned the bravest young man in town into a coward? Did it have something to do with Giovanna's disappearance? Had he become a Marxist like Salvatore Vicino?

No one thought to look for the explanation in Donata's extreme fear of war. They didn't realize the terror that had been struck in to her heart by Italy's entrance into a conflict that threatened to turn Europe once again into a vast cemetery. Panicked that the war would awaken the curse of the Palmisanos, *Zia* begged her son to flee to the mountains. His *nonna* agreed. All her other grandsons were at war: the ones in Bari, the ones in Otranto and the ones in Venice; twelve in total. Vitantonio's uncles Marco, Luca and Giovanni had also been called up. Only Angelo, because of his age, and Matteo, who walked with a limp, had been spared. Franco, since his return from Spain, was rapidly rising through the ranks of Mussolini's secret police. The homeland couldn't complain about the Convertini family's sacrifice; the army could make do without Vitantonio.

In June of 1940, Mussolini simultaneously declared war on France and the United Kingdom, and the Italian army began to call up those born in 1919. That was when Vitantonio heeded the two women's pleas and went into hiding; he was a few weeks away from turning twenty-one. He had never liked Mussolini's blackshirts and he liked the Germans even less: in fact, they'd been on the same side as the Austrians who had killed his father and his aunt's husband, somewhere north of Trento, on the last day of the last war. Why the hell should I help them, he asked himself when he received the conscription notice. And he fled to Matera.

With close to fifty thousand inhabitants, Matera was a good place to disappear: a city the world had forgotten, with homes dug out of the rock and occupied by generations of the same families since the Bronze Age. Two adjacent natural amphitheatres, perched over a rocky ravine – the Gravina di Matera – held the Sasso Caveoso and the Sasso Barisano, the two largest cave networks in the world, which formed Matera's old town. More than twenty thousand people, most of them peasant farmers and shepherds, lived in primitive conditions in the caves, alongside animals and all sorts of diseases. In the cities of the south, and certainly in Rome, they had forgotten all about Matera; Vitantonio was safe.

He took refuge in the home of Grandpa 'Nzìgnalèt, Donata's father, in a dwelling hewn from the rock, at one end of the Sasso Caveoso, the more southern of the two cave networks. Vitantonio didn't know it, but he had returned to his roots: he was in the very same cave that, over twenty years earlier, had been Donata's haven during the months of her clandestine pregnancy.

For three years, no one heard anything from the young man. He lived between the cave and some shepherds' huts in the Alta Murgia, the region of Mediterranean evergreens and thickets that gave him shelter when he took the animals out to graze with his neighbours in the Sassi. It was his way of thanking them for their hospitality and for the pact of silence they had taken on to protect him from prying eyes. In three long years, Vitantonio only went against prudence the once, when he slipped down in secret to visit Bellorotondo.

Bells for the Dead

ONE EVENING AS the sun was setting, Skinny appeared at the cave with the news that Vitantonio's *nonna* was fading fast and that, according to Dr Ricciardi, it was only a matter of hours before she died. They left immediately and walked all night long and through the next day, keeping to forest trails that were frequented only by boars and the most experienced woodcutters. By mid-afternoon, just as they were reaching Bellorotondo, the news of her passing found them in a patch of holm oaks where they stopped to rest; Signora Galasso, Michele's mother, was waiting there to confirm that the Lady had died earlier that day. Later, while Vitantonio lingered by the holm oaks until nightfall before entering the town, he heard the bells ringing out for her death and he knew that his *nonna* was gone for ever.

Six months earlier, the Lady of Bellorotondo had fallen ill with rheumatic fever that a Hected has badly and left her with a weak heart. She grew tired just walking through the rooms of the palazzo. The slightest effort left her short of breath and when she took to her bed her breathing only worsened and she had to sit up to recover. Her condition deteriorated further as time went on. Her ankles swelled up and she grew worryingly thin, but she wouldn't allow the heart and lung specialist from the regional capital to treat her. To everyone's surprise, she called instead for Dr Ricciardi, whose political ideas she had always been wary of, and asked him for a diagnosis.

'My doctor wants to send me to Bari for a bloodletting he says will revive me, but I refuse to be pressured in any way. I won't put myself in the hands of some inept medical students practising on the poor patients at the local hospital. I won't leave my home. You agree, don't you, doctor?'

Ricciardi held Lady Angela in high regard, but he had never been scared of her. In fact, he had enjoyed some of the particularly intense arguments over Italian politics they'd engaged in the past, where they'd aired their diametrically opposed views.

'It's not a question of whether you are better off being treated here or there, Lady Angela, but your illness requires an urgent intervention. I would never order you to have bloodletting, but maybe you should order it yourself.'

Without any further complaints, Angela placed herself entirely in the doctor's hands and followed the treatment he prescribed to the letter. He didn't force anything on her, he merely reminded her that it was the same treatment followed by patients in the best families of the great European capitals. Unwilling to be felled by some common disease, the Lady of Bellorotondo patiently allowed her doctor in Bari to perform the bloodlettings, always with Dr Ricciardi overseeing the procedure from a distance, and she began to improve rapidly.

She spent her daytime hours in the conservatory, from the first light of dawn to sunset, and sometimes she even stayed there once it was dark, because when she was lying in bed, she felt she couldn't breathe. Sitting in an armchair, facing the garden, she found comfort in the quiet contemplation of the small changes in the plants, and in Donata's visits each afternoon. When Angela was alone, she talked to herself and conducted long discussions with God, accusing him of having abandoned her in that palazzo that was falling to pieces around her and filled her with such nostalgia. She missed Giovanna, her favourite granddaughter, who was still far from Italy and gave no sign of wanting to return, and she also missed Vitantonio, whom she had ended up loving more than her own grandsons.

Her spirits revived slowly, but still she never left the house. She continued to spend her days warming herself in the sun in the conservatory. Sitting in that armchair, facing the bare autumn trees, she received the news of her sons Marco and Giovanni's deaths on the Russian front, in the siege of Stalingrad, and she couldn't bear it: suddenly tired of living, she stopped her treatment. She had always judged her sons harshly; she found them pretentious and lacking in personality, but she wasn't sure that it was entirely their fault. The Convertini family had been too demanding of its young, who were never able to meet their elders' expectations. As children, their father barely listened to them; he let them speak but, preoccupied with business matters, paid them little attention. Eventually they grew used to his indifference and accepted their insignificant role: they could have been prepared better for expanding the family empire, but it was enough for them to marry well and exploit the poor peasant farmers on the lands they'd inherited in their own right or later acquired through their brother Antonio's death. None of them showed any remorse for having accepted those assets in exchange for agreeing to Francesca's whim of leaving Vitantonio and Giovanna in the charge of a poor peasant woman from Matera. They'd found her decision eccentric, but it had suited them just fine.

For Angela, Antonio had been different. The eldest Convertini boy had always grown up in her shadow, and as a mother she was very demanding, but she also favoured him from a very young age – until Antonio decided to volunteer for the war and she stopped speaking to him. Angela Convertini regretted it for the rest of her days; she was sorry she'd wasted the last four years of her eldest son's life, the only one of her children who'd really mattered to her. That had been more than twenty years ago but she hadn't recovered and now she didn't have the strength to face her other sons' deaths. Perhaps she hadn't loved them as much as Antonio, but they were hers and she couldn't bear the thought of them freezing to death at the other end of Europe. It brought her immense pain.

She also couldn't get over the deaths of her grandsons. In just the first two years of war five had died: one in the invasion of the French Alps; another in the siege of the port of Tobruk, in North Africa; two more near Ioannina, in northern Greece, and the last one aboard the *Bartolomeo Colleoni*, a warship sunk by an Australian cruiser and British destroyers as it was providing cover for the German landing on north-eastern Crete. The incompetence of the top brass played a part in all these disasters. Princes, counts and marquises with no military merit shared command of the troops with the fascist leaders promoted thanks to their lack of scruples. Most of them had as much personal ambition as they had disdain for the lives of their men: they had been promised an easy victory and now fronts were collapsing and filling up with dead bodies.

When in late 1942 she received word of her sons Marco and Giovanni's deaths in Russia, Angela decided that she had lived through enough. She allowed herself a few weeks to implore divine providence to grant her the opportunity to say goodbye to Giovanna and ask for her forgiveness, but her favourite granddaughter was nowhere to be found; when she convinced herself that no miracle was forthcoming, she stopped fighting. Her breathing grew weaker and her face grew pale. The Lady began to fade like a lantern on its last few drops of oil. Two months later, on 23 February 1943, she died.

Approaching Bellorotondo from the south, the cemetery is at the far end of town. A whitewashed stone wall encircles the whole graveyard and also divider off the rows of more modest graves from the monumental mausoleums of the county's important families. From a distance, amid the wild shrub oak, all that can be seen is the main gate and the dome of the funeral chapel, surrounded by a group of cypress trees as tall as the ones on the avenue that leads to town. Vitantonio jumped over the wall and searched for a hiding place with a good view of the Convertini mausoleum. He waited for the burial, kneeling on the ground of the Raguseo crypt, convinced that that family's ancestors would forgive his intrusion, because he was a good friend of their grandson Pasquale.

When the time came, he was surprised to see a huge procession, with so many women, accompanying the coffin. Everyone who wasn't away at the war had attended the funeral at the Immacolata and now they filed into the cemetery to bid the Lady of Bellorotondo farewell. From his hiding place, between the Curri and Pentasuglia family graves, Vitantonio saw the upright figures and serious faces of the mourners slowing making their way over the ground sown with crosses of every size. He wondered if any of those present actually loved his grandmother, and the only answer he came up with was that surely some of them respected her, but that most feared her, even in death. That was why they were at the burial. Angelo and Matteo, the two uncles who had avoided being called up, presided over the mourning, and Cousin Franco was also there, strutting proudly with the unmistakable demeanour of a member of the secret police.

Vitantonio couldn't help but shed a tear when he saw his *zia* enter the graveyard, walking behind the coffin, beside his aunts from Bari and Otranto. He could also make out Aunt Margherita, who had come down from Venice with her oldest daughter. He was surprised not to see Aunt Margherita's other daughter there and he searched for her in vain: no one had told him that his little cousin has just buried her husband, who had been killed on the island of Cephalonia in an ambush by Greek guerrilla fighters, and she hadn't had it in her to make the trip for yet another funeral. Among the few men in the procession he recognized Dr Ricciardi as well as Fini and his son, who was now the head of the lawyer's office and had been exempted from the call-up because he claimed he was asthmatic, although no doctor had ever confirmed that. At the end of the funeral retinue he saw Skinny Vicino, accompanied by the other senior workers from the sawmill.

He followed the burial as if he were watching a film, the live action intercut with distant memories: he relived his earliest holidays and all the flower wars with Giovanna; he recalled the Sunday lunches, the solemn masses at the Immacolata and the summers on the coast of at Savelletri; he pictured his *nonna* writing in her office at the palazzo and he could again see her walking tall and proud through the streets of Bellorotondo on her way to the factory. He saw the characters that moved in the background, by the Convertini crypt, and he imagined them years earlier on the streets of town, lowering their heads in deference whenever the Lady of Bellorotondo passed.

He watched the crowd filing past his two surviving uncles to offer their condolences and he waited a little while longer, to make sure they had all left. Hidden among the remains of the Raguseos, he could hear snatches of the mourners' conversations, and he desperately wanted to show himself and greet everyone, but he couldn't take the risk. His world and the world of his former neighbours ran parallel, but could never meet; it felt like when, as a boy, he was ill and stuck at home and could hear the other children playing in the Santa Anna square. It had always been a strange feeling for him.

The mourners started to head off down the avenue and Vitantonio passed the time by counting the cypress trees in his head. When they had all left, he took one last look at the Convertini mausoleum and he found it was right where imaginary lines projecting from the wings of the angel presiding over the Curri family met those emerging from the cherub's trumpet on the tomb of the Pentasuglias. The entrance to the mausoleum was now almost buried under flowers, because the bouquets for his *nonna* had been added to the dried wreaths still remaining from his uncles Marco and Giovanni's funerals. He concentrated and prayed for his father, Antonio, and mother, Francesca, as his *zia* had taught him when they had used to visit their graves on All Saints' Day.

When he was quite sure that there was no one left in the cemetery, he slipped out of the mausoleum and went over to the Palmisano tumbs. He plucked a red winter rose from a lone bush and placed it by Vito Oronzo's grave stone. As he was heading back to his hiding place to wait for night to fall, he ran into Ricciardi.

'I knew I'd find you here.'

With Lady Angela dead, the doctor was the only one left who knew Donata's secret. Not a day had passed without him thinking of those dramatic hours at the widows' house; especially when he visited Vitantonio as a boy and saw that he had the same heart-shaped birthmark he'd also seen on Vito Oronzo Palmisano's left collarbone, many years earlier, when he had just finished medical school and was beginning to practise in Bellorotondo.

The first time he'd seen the red heart on Vitantonio's collarbone, Ricciardi couldn't believe his eyes. 'I don't understand . . . birthmarks aren't hereditary.'

'Maybe it's the mark of the curse,' said Donata, crossing herself.

As he now extended his hand to the young man, Ricciardi smiled to himself as he remembered Donata's words.

'I can't give you any more books; I'm being sent away to Lipari,' he said in greeting to Vitantonio. 'Tomorrow they'll drive me to Taranto and from there on to Reggio, Messina, Milazzo and the islands . . . If I were younger, I'd treat it as a sightseeing tour.'

'I'm sorry to hear that, but I suppose it's better to be sent into internal exile than to prison.'

'I suppose I've also learned to look at it that way. Do you need anything? I can get it to you before I leave: books, medicine? They're letting me take barely anything with me.'

'Quinine?' asked Vitantonio.

When he returned to Matera, the quinine made him very popular for a few months, to the point that when he took the flocks out to graze on the Murgia plateau he had to change his hiding place often. In those days, in the mountains of Basilicata, whoever had quinine was god and became the object of pilgrimages that could end up attracting the attention of the military police.

The Confession

WHEN HE SAW his *zia* enter the shepherd's but, exhausted by the long walk, he hugged her, brought her a glass of water and waited for her to catch her breath. For days he had been rehearsing how to confess to her that he had decided to fight on the side of the Allies, against Mussolini. But seeing her so tired, he hesitated and asked instead about Giovanna.

'Have you heard anything from Uannin?'

Since hiding out in the caves, he had started to call his sister Ggiuànnin, in the dialect of the people of Matera, and he sometimes used the short form, Uannin. He'd now grown accustomed to speaking the language he'd heard growing up. In Bellorotondo, *Zia* used it only when she'd got angry with them as children or when she'd wanted to mark her territory in the face of one of *Nonna*'s attacks.

'She is still a nurse in the refugee camps in southern France, but she wrote a few days ago to tell us that she is planning to return to Italy,' answered Donata, with that hint of uneasiness she felt every time she spoke about Giovanna. 'She says that very soon Italy will stand up to the fascists and that when that moment comes her place is here, with us, like Salvatore. Her letter arrived on Monday, but it was dated over a month ago, because what with the war the post is a disaster. Who knows, she may already be on her way and I'll find her waiting for me when I get back to Bellorotondo.'

Giovanna was coming home: that was the best news that Vitantonio could hope for; he had never liked the idea of his sister risking her life in German-occupied territory. She was protected by her Italian passport, but he knew that Giovanna was unable to control her hatred for the Nazis. Hiding his concern, he asked after Skinny's son.

'Salvatore is back in Italy?'

'We just found out that he came back six months ago, but he was arrested as soon as he landed in Bari. No one has seen him since. We think he is most likely being held somewhere in Puglia, in a jail under the control of the fascist party.'

Standing there with Vitantonio, Donata wavered between contradictory emotions. She was worried about Giovanna, because she feared that she might meet the same fate as Salvatore. But at the same time she was very pleased to see that Vitantonio was becoming more rooted in his origins with each passing day. He had even started speaking the dialect, on his own initiative.

Seeing her smile, Vitantonio decided that the time for his confession had come. He had been hiding in the Matera caves for three years. Three long years that had convinced him that his original choice to turn his back on the fascists had been the right one, and three long years that now convinced him he had to take sides: the misery suffered by the peasants of that region had made his decision clear. It was the summer of 1943 and the time had come to take up arms and show that he was not a coward. He had waited for that third Sunday in July impatiently, his mind made up to reveal his intentions to his *zia*. Despite his worries, his need to make a stand on the side of justice and freedom could be fulfilled without betraying his country. He was determined to fight with the Allies for an Italy free of Nazis and fascists.

'*Zia*, I'll be going to war soon,' he said suddenly, taking the bull by the horns. 'The Allies are about to land on the peninsula. In Matera we are preparing a group of anti-fascists and internal exiles to help them when they arrive.'

Donata didn't say a word.

She covered her face with her hands and began to sob. Vitantonio tried to console her, hugging her and trying to wipe away her tears.

'You can't—' she finally managed to get out.

'Nothing's going to happen to me. We will fight against the fascists and the Germans that killed my father; we'll soon drive them out of Italy. Hitler and Mussolini will be disgraced, the war will end, Ggiuànnin will come back home and before Christmas everything will be the way it once was.'

'You can't—' Donata tried to reply, but again she didn't finish her sentence. She was horrified to realize that the promise Vitantonio was making her was the same one her husband had made twenty-five years earlier. She began to tremble, her eyes unfoucsed, as she repeated, 'No, no, no,' and shook her head. Vitantonio calmed her, clicking his tongue softly by her ear, as if trying to lull her to sleep, but she only grew more agitated. Knowing that she wouldn't be able to talk her son out of it, she started to tremble more violently.

'You can't,' she repeated once more, between sobs.

'I've made up my mind. I have to go.'

'No!' she shouted, beside herself. She dropped to the ground and beat her hands and head against the rock floor of the cabin. Vitantonio had never heard such a desperate cry before. It frightened him. What could cause her such pain? He tried to pick her up and felt sticky blood streaming through her hair.

'Nothing's going to happen to me,' he said, again, but with little conviction, knowing that his words would not calm her.

She was still shaking. When she lifted her face, he saw in it a gaze as terrified as the one on the animals he killed when out hunting with Salvatore. Blood was dripping on to her lips and she had trouble opening them when she tried to speak again. She got on to her knees and started to beg him. 'You don't understand, you can't go! You are my son! I'm your mother! *You are a Palmisano!*'

Time stopped in the hut. Outside the dogs left off barking and the cicadas ceased their monotone concert. The seconds ticked by and neither of them dared say a word. All that could be heard was Vitantonio's panting and Donata's ragged sobbing. She was having more and more trouble breathing. A donkey brayed in the distance, on the other side of the *gravina*. The animal's mournful lament brought Vitantonio back to reality.

Finally, he spoke. 'I always knew it! Mama!' He threw himself at her and began to kiss her forehead, cheeks and hands.

She hugged him with all her might. After a little while they pulled apart and she looked him up and down. Vitantonio was the spitting image of his father and she felt as proud as she had on his confirmation day, when *Nonna* had dressed him all in navy blue.

'What do you mean you knew? Since when? You couldn't have known.'

'I think I always knew, without knowing that I knew . . . I'm not sure when or why. One day I started to feel that you were my mother and ever since then I just assumed it was true. I've felt this way for years and just accepted it, I suppose.'

For some time Vitantonio himself had wondered how he'd arrived at that conclusion. He was never totally sure, since he had no proof. In fact, he didn't have the slightest sign. He just longed for it with all his heart. Nor could he explain where that intense longing came from. Maybe out of his desire to not be Giovanna's brother?

Donata looked up at her son, insisting, 'If you go to war you'll never come back! When the time comes, you don't choose sides, the side has already chosen you, long before. And you are a Palmisano ... the *last* Palmisano!'

'It's precisely because I'm a Palmisano that I have to go. You are right, Mother: long before I was born, you tied my fate to the Palmisanos. I can't break away from that. Even if I hated them with all my might I couldn't get away. If I chose not to take sides, I would still be shackled to them. But am I condemned to death by this curse? Aren't I a free man? Don't I control my actions? Can't I rebel and fight against destiny?'

'You can't escape it.'

'That was in the past. A man must face his future and not hide from it. You don't flee from curses, you fight against them. My duty now is to fight the fascists and the Nazis, according to my own moral convictions. Uannin has always seen things clearly; that's why she went to Spain to stand up to them.'

'She also found out the truth: she's known you're a Palmisano for some time now. That's why she left.'

Vitantonio paused. 'Uannin knows?' he said eventually.

'She read it in a letter written by your grandmother, when she was helping her answer the condolence cards for Father Felice. I don't know if it was a mistake or something *Nonna* did on purpose; she had been saying for a while that we should explain things. Anyway, Giovanna took it very badly. That's why she left, to make us pay for the betrayal.'

They spent the rest of their time talking through the revelations together. Donata knew that she wouldn't be able to change his mind. Finally, she screwed up her courage and asked, 'Did you say you're going with the Matera exiles? Have you become a communist?'

'No! You know I don't care for the socialists or the communists, but I want to be on the side of those who speak for justice and freedom, like Doctor Ricciardi. Surely you wouldn't want me to join the fascists? I'm a deserter in their eyes and they would execute me. Besides, you know I've never supported them.'

'I had the feeling you weren't going to be in hiding much longer,' she answered. And she burst into tears again.

Roosevelt

As Vitantonio watched his mother hurry down the path through the thicket, he found that he was already missing her. The trail wound out into the open, zigzagging amid the Murgia rocks, like a gigantic serpent. Every once in a while she would stop and turn and wave, until the path disappeared into the forest and she vanished among the trees. She reappeared further down, at the entrance to the ravine, but from that point on, the path was swallowed up by a copse of taller trees and he couldn't see her any more. They had spent the whole afternoon crying and had also cried when they parted; now he could feel his eyes welling up again. It was the first time in three years that he had allowed himself to be carried away by his feelings, something he hadn't been able to do during his time in hiding; he had never before cried when they said goodbye. But today his emotions had got the better of him.

He stood there for a little while longer, looking out over the Gravina di Laterza towards Bellorotondo. The sky had grown overcast and thunder rumbled on the horizon, towards Matera. The darkness spread rapidly and in a matter of minutes had swallowed up the hills. Suddenly, a voice appeared behind him.

'Goodness gracious!'

It was Roosevelt. He was just a few steps away from him, leaning against the wall of the sheep pen and looking at him indifferently. Vitantonio wondered how long he had been there, watching him. He would never understand how he could move about so silently.

Roosevelt had returned from America four years earlier and now lived all alone with his flock in a shepherd's hut on a hillside, a two-hour walk from Matera. He spent entire days without seeing a soul, herding his livestock on horse between Puglia and Basilicata. Alone, with just his dogs and sheep.

The log cabin comprised a single large room presided over by an image of the Virgin Mary and a portrait of President Franklin Delano Roosevelt. The shepherd's devotion to both the holy mother and the US president was shared by many homes in Matera and all the little villages throughout the mountains, but his case was an exceptional one. He talked about the American president all the time: that Italy needed someone like Roosevelt; that only Roosevelt took care of the poor; that Roosevelt was the best leader on the planet; that Roosevelt would soon liberate Italy; that Roosevelt would send the Germans running for the border. The shepherds of Alta Murgia had heard him go on about it for so long that they re-christened him: Mario Moncluso became plain Roosevelt from then on.

While Vitantonio had been in hiding, Donata had visited him every two months, always on the second or third Sunday of the month, and the shepherd let them use his hut to make sure their meetings took place away from prying eyes. The young fugitive would arrive at the cabin early in the morning to avoid running into anyone, and would wait there for his *zia*, who had spent the night halfway from Bellorotondo, in a farmhouse in Laterza where her cousin lived. When they went inside the hut that first sunday, Vitantonio couldn't believe what he saw: in addition to the two main images, the walls were covered with dozens of postcards and posters of Manhattan.

'Why did you come back from New York?' Vitantonio asked him.

'New York is a desert,' the shepherd answered without hesitation.

'A desert? But millions of people live there . . .' The young man looked at him in confusion.

'*Seven!* Seven million people live there, but it's a desert. I was there for ten years. Every day on the way to work I was in the subway with thousands of people; in the evening, coming home, I ran into them again. But in all that time I never spoke to a single one. I felt lonely in America, and that loneliness was killing me.'

'Then here in this forgotten corner of the world you must be really desperate!'

'Not in the least. I haven't felt loneliness like that since I came to Murgia.'

Roosevelt said those kinds of things. He thought

like a philosopher and talked like a poet. A flash of lightning on the horizon brought them back to reality, but Vitantonio still decided to walk back the two hours to Matera. Even if he got caught by the storm, by nightfall he would be back at the Sassi caves.

The Englishman

Vitantonio's cave refuge in Matera was dug vertically out of the rock and was more than likely an old cistern. A tiny opening led to both the space he used as a kitchen and to the stairs that dropped steeply down into the lower cave, which was in permanent darkness. At the top of the wall there was a tiny window always kept closed, which led directly to the cliff face. It was his emergency exit, only to be used in a life-or-death situation. Jumping through it would mean dropping on to the rocks and climbing down into the *gravina* along a vertiginous trail that was passable only for deer or very, very desperate fugitives.

When it was dark, Vitantonio would go outside to stretch his legs and smoke on the roof of the neighbouring cave house. From that vantage point, one year earlier, on a muggy night lit by a full moon, he had noticed a shadow zigzagging through the rocks. A man was wandering lost through the labyrinth of the Sasso Caveoso, trying to get as far away as possible from the Italian authorities, who unbeknownst to him were close behind. From the cave roofs, Vitantonio had watched the stranger moving from one side to the other, illogically, unaware that a group of *carabinieri* were climbing up from the ravine and were about to come face to face-with him.

The sudden appearance of the national police had caught Vitantonio by surprise; the *carabinieri* in Matera were afraid of the *gravina* and usually left the locals to watch over the two sets of steps that led to the city from the ravine. When Vitantonio grasped that the fugitive was in danger, he leapt from the roofs and dropped down right behind him. He didn't give him time to react: with one hand he rammed a gun into his temple and with the other he covered his mouth; another quick motion dragged him back into a dark corner. He could feel the man sweating and sensed that he was weighing his chances of taking on his assailant. Vitantonio pressed the gun barrel harder against his temple to discourage him and make him understand he had to keep still. Then they heard the patrolmen's steps drawing closer. They saw them pass by half a metre away and he felt the fugitive's heart beating like mad. The two men remained motionless for a little while, until the patrol had rounded a corner, and then he lowered the pistol and they relaxed. The fugitive turned and saw Vitantonio's face for the first time, and watched as his rescuer's eyes grew wide when he took in his military uniform.

'Well, this is a surprise. American?'

'British.'

They let some time pass and then he led him up the same steps the police had just taken. They went into the cave, dark as a stormy night. When they were down below Vitantonio invited him to sit.

'You'll get used to the dark soon.'

Hearing a deep grunt from inside the cave, the Englishman leapt up, knocking Vitantonio to the floor.

'Relax, it's the pig,' he told him as they got back up.

'A pig? Here in the cave?'

'Usually there are donkeys and goats too, but now all we have left is the pig.'

They heard another grunt, even closer, and the Englishman shouted, 'It's sniffing me! Get it off me, for the love of God! It's going to bite my leg!'

'Relax, that's not the pig. It's *Tatònn*, welcoming us.'

'*Tatònn*?'

'Yes, Grandpa, 'Nzìgnalèt. This is his cave.'

They hid out in the cave for a couple of hours and then Vitantonio took the Englishman out for some air and got him up to speed on the situation in that part of the country. It had been a sweltering day and when they sat down on the neighbours' roof, the cave rock was still burning.

'Luckily there's a bit of a breeze now. These hot rocks could fry our balls.'

The Englishman laughed for the first time.

'Can you hide me until they give up looking for me?' he asked.

'We're safe in the cave. In a few days I'll take you out of here and to my other hiding place in Murgia, on the other side of the ravine. It's a shepherd's hut. There you'll have more freedom to move about during the day. I'm a fugitive, too.'

'Can I trust the old . . . what did you call him before?'

'Here grandfathers are called *tatònns*. 'Nzìgnalèt is his nickname. You don't need to worry: after the defeat at Caporetto, in the Great War, the Germans killed his three sons. I've never met anyone who hates them so much. All he had left was Donata, his daughter.'

'Where am I exactly?' asked the Englishman, now that he was a bit calmer.

'In the Sassi of Matera. Cave neighbourhoods where the same families have lived for thousands of years. Right now, we're sitting on the roof of a house, which is also a street and a square. And sometimes a cemetery, because before the dead used to be buried in tombs carved out of the rock that forms the roofs of the homes. The whole thing is a dangerous labyrinth and the *carabinieri* don't like to get too close. What happened today is very rare. You must be a big fish.'

'I'm a lieutenant in the RAF, a cartography expert. A week ago we were on a reconnaissance mission over Taranto. I know the port because I took part in a bombing raid there two years ago; back then, we really gave them a good pounding, but last week we had problems and had to bail out. The others landed in the sea. I didn't have any choice but to climb up the mountain to hide.'

'If you are keeping an eye on the port of Taranto, that must mean that you are planning an invasion. That's good: we just have to wait and kill time until it happens.'

More than a year had passed since that first hopeful conversation with his new cave mate and the prediction hadn't come to pass yet: the English had been fighting all year in North Africa and, finally, that summer they had attacked Sicily, but there was still no news of a landing on the Italian mainland.

Vitantonio didn't want to get mired in negative thoughts; all he could think of was the moment he would join the action. Those three years of war had claimed half of his schoolmates and some of his closest friends from boarding school. Most of the Convertini men had also died; their names would be carved on the next war memorial in Bellorotondo. He knew now that they weren't his own blood, but he had grown up with them and still considered them his family. In September 1942, Uncle Luca had disappeared into the waters of the Atlantic along with most of the other fifteen hundred Italian POWs aboard the *Laconia*, a British ship torpedoed by a German U-boat, an Allied aircraft had bombed the German submarine when it had surfaced to try to save the shipwrecked men, sending the lifeboats to the bottom of the sea, along with women, children, British soldiers on leave and Italian prisoners. Uncle Luca Convertini was one of them.

In a short period of time three of his cousins had died as well, on the Dalmatian coast, in Greece and North Africa, and two more had disappeared in Russia. Meanwhile, Giovanna, who had long been taking excessive risks in southern France under the very noses of French collaborators and the Gestapo, was preparing to return to fight fascism within Italy. With every passing minute Vitantonio reaffirmed that he could no longer watch from a distance: desire for the freedom that Roosevelt and his new friends in Matera talked about compelled him to commit himself to the struggle.

The Announcement

At the Gentlemen's Circle in Bari on the evening of Sunday 25 July 1943, the atmosphere was very festive. The glasses were filled to the brim, the cigars were good, the card games went on long into the night and there was more than the usual traffic in the garden. That night, the brother couldn't keep up with all the demand. July was almost over, as were the days of freedom for the club's members: in August the men headed off to towns on the coast or farmhouses inland to spend the holding with their families.

In the large salon there was a contagious euphoria that seemed ready to spill over into a real ruckus because everyone was shouting, alternating political conversations with nervous giggles that followed salacious comments. The hilarity affected all the armchairs when a short, chubby man came running in and tripped on the rug; he was the most important forestry owner in the region. When he'd managed to regain his composure, he started waving his arms to get everyone's attention.

'Turn on the radio! They've just said that the king is going to make an important announcement to the nation.'

The conversations stopped and were replaced by

general murmuring. The exclamations of surprise and nervous questions spread from table to table.

'The king? What's going on? This doesn't sound good!'

The bolder ones moved closer to the radio, which the bartender kept in the drinks cabinet, and waited in expectant silence. A tall man with white skin and red hair, a lock manufacturer, started to turn the dial. He stopped when he heard the last few notes of 'the Royal March'. The others drew near and formed a circle around the radio.

A deep, serious voice read the king's announcement very slowly: 'His Majesty the King and Emperor has accepted the resignation of His Excellency Cavaliere Benito Mussolini from his duties as the head of the government, prime minister and secretary of state, and has appointed Cavaliere and Marshal of Italy Pietro Badoglio to be head of the government, prime minister and secretary of state.'

The broadcast ended before they had had time to process the statement. 'The Royal March' played again. The gentlemen looked at each other, confused. None of them had predicted Il Duce's end and none of them were expecting it. Angelo Convertini tiptoed over to his wingchair and dropped into it, dejected.

After a long silence, he was one of the first to speak. 'What did the king mean? He hasn't removed Mussolini from office, has he?'

'Shit, Angelo! Sometimes you just don't get it. The announcement couldn't have been clearer. The king has removed Mussolini and put Badoglio in his place,' explained the forestry owner.

'*Removed?* It can't be right. It was Il Duce who made us great,' stammered Angelo, disheartened.

'Great? Nonsense! What have we got out of this war?' said the lock manufacturer, who had been months without a sizeable order. 'Our economy is full of holes, just like our army. The Allies will end up winning the war and when that day comes, we'll be on the losing side. I don't know where you see greatness.'

'How can the Allies win the war?'

'They are advancing on every front. Now they are preparing to land somewhere on continental Europe and it won't be long before they conquer all of Italy if they put their minds to it; the Americans have an exceptional army, much better than twenty years ago. Don't you read the newspapers?' the lock man again challenged him.

'Maybe with Mussolini out of the picture Italy will leave the war before Germany drags us into an even bigger disaster,' pointed out the forestry owner, who had a nose for politics, seeing as he didn't have to work for a living and could devote all his time to reading the international press.

'You are completely right, fascism was a mistake,' Scarafile nervously interjected. He was a vintner who had used the wheat-campaign incentives to sow seed in hundreds of barren, worthless acres. He had made more money in three or four years that way than in an entire life making the finest Primitivo wine in the region.

Angelo gave him an incredulous look because he clearly remembered standing beside him on the Lungomare in Bari the day that Mussolini had come to review one of the Alpine divisions. They had been among the special guests, right in front of the Albergo delle Nazione, and he recalled Fiorenzo Scarafile applauding with exaggerated enthusiasm and elbowing everyone out of the way to get to shake the dictator's hand.

'Poor Il Duce. I think we should be more appreciative of the man who brought us prosperity,' insisted Angelo, thinking of what could happen to his son Franco if the fascists crumbled.

'You said it: "*brought* prosperity". Past tense. When was the last time you sold a fir plank? In fact you couldn't sell one even if you found a buyer, because there have been no shipments of timber from Russia for the last three years. And our best workers are at the front. How do they expect us to do anything without labour?' concluded the lock manufacturer. And that was the end of the discussion, because the club had emptied around them.

Feeling nervous, the members were suddenly in a rush to get home. Or perhaps they were still planning to go to the coast for the summer. The gentlemen of Bari could go up to the towns of Gargano; nothing bad could happen up on that craggy outcrop. Angelo could still gather with his family in Savelletri and wait out Rome's power struggle; its proximity to Bellorotondo would allow him to return to the factory when needed and from there he could also control the farms.

When they left the Gentlemen's Circle, they saw that the girls from the bordello had also turned off the lights and closed the doors and windows. With her customers so frightened, La Bella Antonella had little to celebrate.

The disquiet at the Bari's Gentlemen's Circle was inversely proportional to the euphoria the cave-dwellers were feeling in Matera. Without access to a radio, they weren't able to listen to King Victor Emmanuel III's announcement, but at midnight Roosevelt had brought them news of Mussolini's fall from grace. That was all they needed to know: it had been three long years since they'd had such good news.

The Demonstration

GIOVANNA HAD BEGUN the final stage of her journey back to Bellorotondo, but she still hadn't made it home as her *zia* was hoping. She had just got off the train in Bari and was searching for news of Salvatore. The last she'd heard was that he had been arrested after arriving in the city by sea and that he'd been held at the Alberobello political prison; that was already six months ago. As she was leaving the station, Giovanna found out about the king's announcement a day late; every front page of every newspaper was filled with it. In the following hours she contacted her old Party colleagues and was surprised at the naive euphoria Il Duce's fall had awakened in the anti-fascists. Later, when she found out that some activists were preparing a demonstration to demand the release of political prisoners, she decided to stay in Bari: she sent her aunt a telegram saying she'd arrive a couple of days later.

Giovanna's next forty-eight hours were frenetic. That morning of 26 July, she met up with some former classmates from the Istituto and a former university professor, Fabrizio Canfora, who had taught her philosophy. And she also took part in a meeting of teachers involved in the Liberal Socialism Movement. The contagious happiness of her former classmates excited her, but she soon realized that she was watching them as if from a distance, as if they were actors on a stage while she remained in the audience. Her flight from Barcelona and her time in the refugee camps in southern France had made her wary. *Freedom*, *justice* and *peace* were pretty words, but in real life the only things that were valuable were the ones that allowed you to survive; sometimes, it was enough to fall asleep in the hope of being able to open your eyes to a new day.

The next morning she marched through the streets of Bari with her fellow demonstrators, setting aside her scepticism to shout, '*Viva la libertá!*' More than two hundred people had gathered, including university students, professors and workers. They marched down the Via Sparano chanting slogans in support of the political prisoners but when they had passed the Piazzo Umberto and were approaching the Via Niccolò dell'Arca, near the cinema, they were cut off by an army detachment, forcing them to stop just below the local headquarters of the Partito Nazionale Fascista. When the officer shouted, 'Prepare arms!', Giovanna thought he was crazy, but she soon grasped that the soldiers were obeying and loading their weapons. They were getting ready to shoot. Giovanna couldn't believe what was happening.

In the four years she had spent in southern France, Giovanna had developed a sixth sense to alert her to any unexpected danger. A fleeting movement drew her eye to the fascist headquarters: she looked up and saw armed men hiding behind the windows. But just as she was about to warn the other demonstrators and shout for them to flee from that fatal trap, a familiar figure brought her attention back to the building: her cousin Franco was peeking out from behind one of the shutters and giving instructions to another man, who was leaning out over the street with a rifle in his hands. She stared at him, so frozen in shock that she didn't react until the army officer shouted, 'Fire!'

The first round hit the front line of demonstrators. It was the sign the men hidden in the fascist headquarters had been waiting for, and they too began to shoot from the windows. The demonstrators were trapped between the two sets of gunmen and many fell helplessly in the crossfire. The soldiers didn't hold back; in fact, just a few metres from the head of the demonstration, they put their all into shooting the anti-fascists.

Giovanna was trapped beneath the corpse of a boy who couldn't have been more than eighteen. Playing dead, she didn't move until she saw the fascists disappear from the windows. When she was sure that the military had also retreated, she started running and didn't stop until she had reached the safe house she'd agreed on with her old Party comrades. There, she learned that many had died, maybe more than twenty, and that more than fifty had been injured in the crossfire. At midnight, she had a premonition and moved to another apartment. She got away by the skin of her teeth; that night, the army and the secret police combed the city. Franco was the most thorough: he had many apartments searched and arrested the most prominent demonstrators.

A mere forty-eight hours after Mussolini's removal, the anti-fascist euphoria was subdued. The dictator had fallen from grace, but the king and the army, led by Marshal Badoglio, had too many things to hide and were unwilling to open the doors to freedom. Italy had touched the end of the war with its fingertips, but a few miserable leaders had condemned the Italians to continue fighting. The country was about to become the scene of even more violent combat.

A Never-Ending August

That August of 1943 was sweltering. The Englishman and Vitantonio had abandoned the shepherd's hut in Murgia and no longer left the Matera caves while they waited for the Allied landing. Roosevelt had entrusted his herds to the care of a nephew and had joined them in the cave, which wasn't made for so many people. Year round, the temperature inside remained stable at fourteen degrees, but that summer, with three men inside, it grew unbearable. Outside, the heat was horrific and only the cicadas seemed to be comfortable in the scorched air. The chirping that emerged from the *gravina* was so obsessive that it drove the men, trapped in their own refuge, crazy. If they went out to stretch their legs, it was even worse: a couple of minutes of exposure to the sun left them so stupefied that they had to come running back to the monotony of the cave.

Every evening, Giuseppe 'the Professor', a teacher from the north exiled to Basilicata, would come by the cave and tell them the latest. He got the news from the mayor of Matera and the more tolerant military men, particularly Francesco Paolo Nitti, a cultured officer who always sought out his conversation. That was how Giuseppe confirmed Mussolini's arrest and exile, first to the island of Ponza and then to La Maddalena on Sardinia; later they learned that Il Duce had been sent to Abruzzo.

But the good news didn't continue. When it came down to it, Marshal Badoglio's new government turned out to be just as reactionary and afraid of freedom as all the fascist governments before it had been. The Allies, meanwhile, were advancing rapidly in Sicily, but showed no signs of landing on the mainland. Closed up in the cave, Vitantonio and his friends were growing desperate and soon their euphoria turned to disenchantment. The month of August seemed to drag on for ever.

A Disconcerting Ceremony

THE NINTH OF September 1943 became a legendary day in Bellorotondo. When the official ceremony for the unveiling of the restored memorial to the victims of the Great War began, the temperature had already exceeded forty-two degrees and two newly recruited *carabinieri* who couldn't stand the sun had already fainted. The *carabinieri* had filed into the square at ten, half an hour before the agreed arrival time of the Bishop of Bari and the regional governor, who were to inaugurate the new monument. By then, the local authorities and church officials had filled the dignitaries' dais and the veterans, musicians and general public had also taken their places, anxious for the conculsion of the official pomp; most of them were only thinking about the celebratory concert and lunch.

The mayor had ordered everything to be ready to start just as the regional officials arrived but, inexplicably, an hour and a half later they still hadn't shown up and the event was on hold. Then, just as the bells of the Immacolata rang out noon, the first policeman fainted and the ceremony started to spiral out of control.

At that point, the *carabinieri* were still lined up under the midday sun; the dignitaries and clerics had already broken rank and taken shelter at the entrance to the square in the shadow of a generous holm oak. The musicians and veterans had rushed to follow suit, seeking the protection of the two carob trees in the middle of the pizza; the public, on the other hand, chose to gather on the side that was protected from the sun by trees and the Convertini-palazzo wall. The green of the Convertinis' garden was a welcome marvel in that suffocating heat.

Signor Maurizio, the former mayor, was sitting in a chair that he'd had placed in the shade and was admonishing the new mayor, his son Maurizio Junior, for losing control of the event. The crowd was growing impatient, but just when it seemed disaster was imminent they heard the deep rumble of a motorcycle coming up the Corso XX Settembre. When the diabolical machine came to a half in the square, a messenger dismounted and gazed around for those in charge.

'My God! They'd better get here and get started or we are going to melt like a block of ice,' complained the mayor, who didn't understand what was going on.

'It'll be a miracle if no one dies,' declared Father Constanzo, echoing the mayor's pessimism. His cassock was sticking to his back and two long white stains that began at his armpits revealed that he was sweating like a pig.

Just then, the second policeman fainted and everything started unravelling. The dispatch video handed a telegram to the young mayor. The poor man read it and felt his legs buckle beneath him.

'No one is coming. The king fled from Rome last night, to Brindisi,' he managed to explain. 'All the regional officials, headed up by the bishop and the governor, have gone there to welcome him instead.'

'The king and the bishop are in Brindisi and we're here, in this hellish heat and surrounded by this group of savages who are just waiting for us to leave so the dancing can start,' bemoaned the rector of the parish. Another big white sweat stain had just appeared on his cassock, right in the middle of his back.

All eyes turned to the mayor, awaiting his instructions; but young Maurizio seemed totally lost and incapable of regaining the initiative.

'Come on, let's wrap this up,' said Father Constanzo, who just wanted to go back to his house to turn on the radio.

The rector of the Immacolata signalied for the band to start playing a military march and grabbed the arm of the mayor, who was in a daze. Calling the other officials over, they formed a chaotic column, filing hastily towards the centre of the square to sit back down and mark the start of the ceremony.

Following the scheduled programme, a local poet went up to the dais and began to read some horrible verse. His delivery was equally terrible and suddenly the temperature in the square went up three or four degrees. Father Constanzo wore his cassock unbuttoned to his belly and ran a handkerchief over his sweaty chest. The commander of the *carabinieri* did the same, undoing his clammy tunic. Sitting in his chair, the former mayor grabbed his wife's fan out of her hands and started compulsively fanning himself. Three or four of the *carabinieri* in formation began to sway and it looked like they too might faint at any moment.

The mayor looked dazed. He had taken off his jacket, then loosened his tie and slung it over his shoulder. His hair was stuck to his damp forehead and his shirt to his stomach, which was also dripping. He was gripped by an intense panic attack, but unexpectedly, when everyone was expecting the worst, he had a moment of lucidity that saved the event: the mayor started to clap to put an end to the poetry recital and the audience, who couldn't stand another minute of it, joined in. The poet thought they were applauding his verse and, after a pause, tried to resume his reading with even more enthusiasm. At that point, the horrified mayor pounced on him, hugged him and led him off the stage. The square burst into another round of applause, the sincerest one the mayor had received since replacing his father in the post.

The love affair between the mayor and his constituents was short-lived, however: when he walked back up to the stage he pulled a bundle of pages out of his jacket pocket, which was still slung over one shoulder, and began to prepare to read the speech he'd written for the bishop and the governor. A murmur of disapproval spread through the square.

'This idiot is capable of droning on until there isn't a

single *carabiniere* left standing,' one of the veterans said out loud. He was standing beside Skinny in the shade of the carob trees.

The mayor must have heard him, or perhaps he was still flushed with the applause he'd received, because suddenly he felt sorry for that poor crowd on the brink of sunstroke and decided to spare them. He put the pages back in his pocket, stepped down from the dais, approached the monument, and whipped out the Italian flag to lay it on the new stone with the names of the forty-two victims of the Great War. Then he went back to the dais and shouted, 'The monument is inaugurated! Long live Bellorotondo! Long live Italy!'

The square responded with another enthusiastic ovation and surprising shouts of 'Long live the mayor!' It was the mayor himself who was the most surprised. The townspeople were just happy that they'd been spared the rest of the scheduled programme. The festivities were about to begin.

'What about The Royal March?' pleaded the *carabinieri* commander, addressing the mayor.

'You can give the band the order. But please, for the love of God, don't let them go on too long. Let's get this over with.'

The band launched into the first few bars of 'The Royal March'. Suddenly, from the square, some of the veterans, egged on by Skinny, responded with the first verse of the Republican anthem '*Fratelli d'Italia*', which for them was the true national anthem. They caught the commander by surprise, who responded by demanding more verve from the players, but the musicians' interpretation grew increasingly apathetic while they waited to see which song the crowd would favour. Everyone in the shade of the carob trees, mostly veterans, had enthusiastically started in on the Republican anthem and soon the town's fascists added their voices; they too loathed the royalist song.

'Brothers of Italy
Italy has awoken,
Strapped Scipio's helmet
To her head.
Where is Victory?
Let her bow down
For God made her
Slave to Rome . . .'

The whole square was shouting, infected by the enthusiasm of Skinny and his gang. In fact, the commemoration was in honour of him and his former brothers-in-arms, the soldiers who had died in the trenches twenty-five years earlier, between 1915 and 1918. That was why Donata had politely refused the invitation to sit on the stage and was now singing passionately among the peasants and veterans. This event was also in honour of her Vito Oronzo. And Francesca's Antonio.

The musicians had come to play at a party so, taking stock of the mood in the square, they didn't think twice before siding with of the popular insurrection. They turned their backs on the *carabinieri* commander, who was still exhorting them to play 'The Royal March' with more conviction, and they started up with the first notes of *Fratelli d'Italia* at a lively pace and the crowd burst into applause.

Angelo was following the scene from the palazzo garden, on the other side of the wall, and when he heard the resounding victory of the Republican anthem over 'The Royal March', he crossed himself twice. He had inherited the house when his mother, Angela, died, and less than a month later he had moved in, a clear sign of his aspiration to be recognized as the new Lord of Bellorotondo.

Just as he was crossing himself the second time, Carmelina arrived. His wife considered the event a huge disaster and, taking advantage of the conflict between the *carabinieri* commander and the band over the anthem, she had left the official entourage and slipped in through the side door from the square. She was anxious to seek her husband's opinion. He had stayed in the garden awaiting the arrival of the bishop and the governor. And even then only to be polite, because after the ceremony the dignitaries were invited to lunch at the palazzo and he was in no rush to see them.

'What a disaster! It seems the king has moved the court to Brindisi and everyone's gone there to welcome him instead.'

Carmelina's disquiet was painted clearly on her face

and she sought comfort in her husband. She scrutinized his gaze, but found that he too seemed upset.

'Don't you think you should have made an appearance in the square?' she asked him.

'This whole event is a mistake, but in any case the mayor and Father Constanzo were there to represent me. What was all that clapping for earlier on?'

'They were applauding the mayor.'

'That's hard to believe. What on earth did he say to them?'

'Nothing! That was what they liked! He put his speech back in his pocket and just unveiled the monument.'

'For the love of God, I don't understand a thing: the king moves the court to Brindisi; Il Duce is in prison; the people applaud leaders who don't speak; the peasants insist on the Republican anthem, and the stupid priest and mayor let themselves be convinced by the veterans to throw a big party for the inauguration of the new memorial to the Great War. Can't they see it's a slap in the face to the Germans?'

'It hadn't occurred to me that the Germans might be offended by such a modest little monument . . .'

'Well, they could be. In the last war they were the enemies!' He took a deep breath and continued in an increasingly frightened tone. 'And as if that weren't enough, our idiot of a son goes from being a soldier to being a policeman, and starts chasing anti-fascists in every town in the county; our niece Giovanna is coming home to conspire after parading around half of Europe with the International Brigades; and our nephew Vitantonio is a fugitive hiding in the mountains. Both of them are probably communists by now. If the communists come to power they'll string us up by our balls in the town square!'

Carmelina crossed herself and invoked the Virgin Mary. 'Holy Mother of God, don't say such things!' She went quickly into the house and came back out a little while later with two rosaries.

'What are you doing?' asked Angelo with an irritated expression.

'Let's say a rosary for our son. And one for the king.'

'A rosary at the Angelus hour? For the love of God, you're not right in the head. Our world is falling apart and you bring me a rosary!' shouted Angelo nervously. He had stood up and was pushing her towards the house.

She had never seen him like that and she went back to the stairs by the conservatory. When she got to the door, preparing to take refuge in the living room, she heard her husband calling her.

'Come back! Maybe we should invoke divine providence: Franco's fighting with the fascists, Vitantonio and Giovanna have turned anti-fascist and the imbeciles in town are provoking the Germans. We're lost. Whoever wins will have something against us. This can only turn out badly.'

He stretched out a trembling hand towards the rosary that Carmelina was offering him and shrank back into the wicker armchair.

'You start . . .' he said.

'Which prayer do you want? The Angelus or the rosary?'

'Let's do both,' said Angelo. He crossed himself and began to recite; 'By the sign of the Holy Cross, deliver us, Lord our God, from our enemies. In the name of the Father, the Son and the Holy Spirit. Amen . . .'

Then they said an Our Father, a Hail Mary, a Glory Be and an Apostles' Creed. When they started in on the Hail, Holy Queen, Angelo stopped short. With his voice choked by a sob he was struggling to contain, he announced, 'Let's go to Venice, to my sister's house. The south is no longer safe for us.' Then he returned to his praying.

Frightened by her husband's demeanour, Carmelina kept her hand firmly in her pocket and she kept touching, one by one, all the scapulars and saints' images she had hidden there.

They were both surprised by the cook and the maid entering the garden: they wanted to know what they were supposed to do with the lunch they'd prepared in honour of the bishop and the governor.

'Forget about lunch and pray with us,' ordered the head of the house, about to begin the Angelus. Then, even though it didn't follow naturally, he recited the Act of Contrition in a trembling voice. 'O my God, I am heartily sorry for having offended Thee, who art all-good and deserving of all my love . . .'

By this point Angelo was openly sobbing and when he heard himself saying, 'I detest all my sins because of

Thy just punishments . . .' he started to snivel and had to wipe his nose on his jacket sleeve. He led, one by one, the four Mysteries of the Rosary: Joyful, Luminous, Sorrowful and Glorious. And then he introduced the prayer to St Michael and a few others that the servants had never heard before.

When it was time for coffee after lunch, the mayor and Father Constanzo appeared, trusting that despite the absence of the regional officials, Angelo's invitation still stood. But as soon as they came in they looked at each other, puzzled: Angelo and his wife were in the garden, sitting beneath the trellis with the servants, reciting psalms from Father Felice's old breviary.

'Sit down. Sit and pray with us. You've really made a hash of things by offending our German friends.'

'To raise the morale of the troops fighting this war we had to properly commemorate those killed in the last one. The old memorial was crumbling . . .' the mayor said in his defence, emboldened by the acclaim he'd just received in the square.

The priest, overwhelmed by the excessive display of religious fervour before him, chose to remain silent.

'Well, you've really put your foot in it. You could have waited to see how the war played out . . . Now, whatever happens, we're totally screwed!'

And since they didn't know what was happening nor what could happen in the future, and they didn't understand what Angelo Convertini was talking about, the mayor and the priest joined the group and began to repeat the psalms in the magnificent shade of the bougainvillea and jasmine that Lady Angela had planted with her own hands fifty years earlier.

The next day, Angelo and Carmelina hastily shut up the palazzo, left Bellorotondo and fled far from the south. No one understood what safety they could possibly find in the north, nor why they moved to Venice, which, given to its geographical location, was far more likely to suffer the vicissitudes of war for far longer. But Angelo had made up his mind: for some time he'd felt that the townspeople of Bellorotondo were too familiar with him. Venice, on the other hand, was a noble city and he trusted that there everyone would know their place.

The Landing of the British at Taranto

ON THE SECOND Sunday of September, Vitantonio waited in vain all day long for Donata to appear for their usual meeting at the shepherd's hut. He finally gave up at midnight, left Roosevelt's cabin with an aching heart and took the road back to Matera, having made up his mind to remain in hiding in the Sassi caves, where he would wait for news of his mother. His arrival back at the cave woke everyone up. They still hadn't gone back to sleep when another commotion had everyone on their guard.

'The British have landed at Taranto!' shouted Roosevelt from the stairs, coming in all wound up, forgetting all the safety rules and risking a bullet. 'It sounds like they met with no resistance and they're heading east and north, towards Brindisi and Bari. They might even have already occupied them,' he added as he climbed down into the hideout, in an unprecedented state of euphoria.

Vitantonio and the Englishman might have felt safe in their cave, but with each passing day they also felt more and more trapped and desperate to see action.

Roosevelt, the only one of them who could move about freely, regularly went out in search of news. Giuseppe 'the Professor' only came by when he could get past the increased supervision that the mayor of Matera had imposed on those in internal exile. They had all been spending their waking hours dreaming that the war would come to Italy and they could finally take part, and the continuing tension had begun to have a dangerous effect on the group's morale. Until the morning that Roosevelt had come running from Montescaglioso to bring them the good news of the landing.

'The British are chasing the Germans towards the mountains. In less than a week they'll be up here to liberate Matera,' he explained. 'They say that Australians, Canadians, South Africans and New Zealanders have landed too; everyone except the Americans, who they say will land at Naples. I'm really irritated by that,' he added. And he laughed in that strange way he had of laughing at his own witticisms.

'Americans? English? Who cares who comes to liberate this miserable country! The only thing we care about is seeing some action and finishing off that bunch of bastards for once and for all,' interjected Giuseppe. Before being exiled to Basilicata, the Professor had endured both Mussolini's torture and prisons. 'We need to get moving and warn everyone. Let's meet this evening at the church.'

'You might not care, but *I* would have liked to fight alongside the *Americans*,' insisted Roosevelt.

He liked to imagine that in New York he had forged a secret bond with the many strangers that he had travelled to work with, and that the moment would come when they would recognize him as a real American citizen and fellow combatant.

'Fighting shoulder to shoulder with the Yanks against the Germans would have given meaning to the ten years I suffered living in America.'

'Stop daydreaming! With Mussolini out of the picture, this is going to happen fast,' insisted the Professor. 'The liberation of Italy is going to be a piece of cake and we'd better get moving if we don't want to miss it!'

'Don't you have anything to say?' asked the Englishman, surprised by Vitantonio's silence.

'*Zia* hasn't missed one of our meetings in three years,' was Vitantonio's response. He still hadn't found the right moment to reveal to his fellow cave dwellers that his aunt was actually his mother. 'Today is the first time she hasn't shown up. Something's not right.'

'If the British are making their way to Bari, the roads will be cut off by the fighting. When the front stabilizes, you'll have news from your *zia*,' said Roosevelt, trying to reassure him.

'We need to collect up our weapons and hide out in the forest. When the Germans attack the British, we'll attack their rearguard . . .' the Englishman said, as he began to plan.

The imminence of action finally got Vitantonio's attention.

'We might be more useful here, in Matera. The British won't have an easy time finding their way around the Sassi if the fighting turns into a house-to-house scrap.'

The Reunion

THE SOUND OF hurried footsteps that suddenly stopped when they reached the top of the stairs had the group in the cave immediately on their guard. They hadn't dared move since receiving the news from Roosevelt, afraid they would miss the Allies' arrival in Matera. They'd been inside the cave all week and it was only their conviction that the British were on their way up to the town that kept them going and prepared for action.

'Vitantonio?' came a stranger's whisper.

They all leapt from their beds and grabbed their guns. They aimed them at the cave's entrance, trying to identify the figure that was coming down the stairs. Only Vitantonio ran straight over, recognizing the voice he'd been longing to hear all though those years of confinement.

'Giovanna!'

They hadn't seen each other for four years.

Rushing into each other's arms, they embraced tightly. They touched each other's faces, backs and hair. And they kissed each other on the forehead and cheeks.

They repeated each other's names out loud, as if chanting a spell.

'Vitantonio!'

'Giovanna!'

Suddenly, Vitantonio remembered that he had forgotten to ask about his mother. 'And *Zia*? Why didn't she meet me at the hut on Sunday?'

Giovanna burst out laughing.

'She's working as a nurse in Bari. Doctor Ricciardi came back from his exile on Lipari and convinced her to go with him and help out in a military hospital. She is living in an apartment on the Borgo Antico, in one of those streets near the cathedral. Before she left she asked me to give you a message: "Tell your blockhead of a brother that I've gone off to war, too."'

Vitantonio hugged Giovanna again, lifted her in the air and twirled her around. When he put her back down he held her tightly about the waist and kissed her all over. Giovanna was crying and he couldn't hold back his tears either.

Then he remembered the others' presence and said, 'Let's go outside, down to the river.'

'Are you crazy?' spat out the Englishman and the Professor at once. The Germans had been patrolling the city's perimeter for a weak.

Giovanna hadn't seen the others in the cave and she jumped.

'Who are they?'

'Friends,' he reassured her. Then he addressed the group. 'We won't run into anyone at this time of day.

And the patrols don't like going down to the river: they're afraid of the peasants and the cliffs.'

'You can't risk it. Not today!'

'I'll be back by dusk.'

'Don't let him go,' the Professor begged the Englishman.

'*A ddo tres usol' nà'n tres u nidch*,' added Tatònn.

Recognizing his voice, Giovanna ran to hug Grandpa, 'Nzìgnalèt. She had always liked the grumpy old man who was willing to pour scorn equally on the fascists and the Germans.

'What's he saying?' complained the Englishman. He hated when Vitantonio and his grandfather spoke in the Matera dialect.

'Where there's sun, there's no need for the doctor!' translated Roosevelt. 'He means that a bit of fun will be good for this young man who's in love with his little sister.'

'Shut up!' Vitantonio laughed, pushing Giovanna towards the stairs.

'I don't know how you can claim she's your sister!' the Professor kept teasing him. 'A beauty like that can't be related to an ugly monster like you.'

'She's your sister?' asked the Englishman, completely mystified. Up until that point he'd assumed they were lovers. 'This country's filled with degenerates!' he shouted in indignation.

Giovanna and Vitantonio gave each other a look and went up towards the surface, still laughing. They had both just realized that it was the first time they had seen each other since discovering that they weren't siblings.

'*Bell i brìtt s'spòs'ntítt*,' declared *Tatònn* from the depths of the cave as they were leaving.

Roosevelt quickly translated. 'He says that everybody gets married, pretty and ugly alike.'

Beside The River

VITANTONIO WAS RIGHT: they didn't run into anyone. As usual, the Sassi peasants had woken up while it was still dark so as to reach the fields by dawn; the *carabinieri* were still asleep. The sky was clear, but the sun rising beyond the Murgia plateau heralded a muggy day, unless a breeze were to come in off the sea. That year, the summer had seemed to stretch on and on. They made their way down to the ravine along the right side, the more difficult trail, and just when they were almost down to the main path, Vitantonio had a strange feeling and he stopped short. He wasn't willing to wait to find out what it was; something simply wasn't right. He moved like lightning, grabbed Giovanna by the waist, and pulled her back roughly, covering her mouth with his hand. A second later they heard voices.

'Germans – don't move,' he whispered in her ear.

Peering around the rock, they saw a German patrol follow the road parallel to the ravine and stop when it reached the path. They held their breath, overwhelmed by panic: the Gravina di Matera had hardly any vegetation and there was nowhere to hide except for the rocks. The Germans had halted to discuss something; then they resumed their patrol northward along the path and disappeared behind some brambles. Crouched down, Giovanna was leaning on Vitantonio, and he was now breathing heavily near her ear. They remained still for a while and she finally turned her face towards him. Their lips were almost touching. When she opened them, it was to confess: 'I'm glad you're not my brother.'

He looked into her green eyes, which had hypnotized him even as a child, and trembled slightly. He softly touched her lips, as if tasting her. Then everything happened very fast. He moved his right arm, which was still around her waist, slid it decisively down to her hips, turned her to face him and kissed her with all the passion that had been pent up inside him, without him even noticing, since the day when he was ill and she had appeared up in the doorway in that flowery dress, with cherries for earrings.

They continued down to the bottom of the ravine, holding hands, and followed the course of the water towards the south; every so often they looked at each other and laughed, as if they had only just met. They were walking among stinging nettles and brambles. Downriver, the vegetation was more diverse; thyme, rosemary and wild roses tumbled down the slope to the water's edge and mixed with bindweed, mallows and lavender; mastic and jujube trees grew there as well as the more occasional tamarisk. The brambles were plump with blackberries and Vitantonio picked a handful. He put them in his mouth, one by one; they were ripe and very sweet. For more than an hour, they walked along the riverbed, towards Montescaglioso, and when they reached a pool they stretched out on the wild grasses, in the shadow of the rushes and reeds.

They lay there for hours, nestled in the fresh, lush grass that was nourished by the dampness of the natural grey-rock pools. It felt like a different world, far from the war and the miseries of men. The song of the cicadas mixed with the buzzing of bees and, wasps, and there were locusts, ladybirds and an army of vivid dragonflies. Brightly coloured butterflies flew in zigzags, as if curious about everything, until finally landing delicately on the thistles, clover and thyme. Two swallowtail butterflies with black and white markings circled some fennel bushes and then flew off over Giovanna's naked body. Vitantonio drank in her image as if he needed to memorize it. His left arm rested on the ground and supported his face. With his right hand he very slowly caressed her dark hair and breasts.

'Ggiuànnin,' he sighed.

'Ggiuànnin? I haven't been called that since that summer when *Zia* got mad at *Nonna* because she wouldn't let you get confirmed.'

They looked at each other again, curious, and touched each other's eyes, lips and neck, as if wanting to discover their feel, taste and scent and store them away for when they were apart again. They made love for a second time, with unbridled, almost violent, passion.

Afterwards, when their breathing settled, he asked her, 'Did you storm off because Mama hadn't told us the truth?'

She sat up to look him in the eye, leaning her cheek on one hand.

'How could I be angry? Do you understand what she risked to save you?'

'Then why did you leave?'

'To keep the secret. I knew that if I stayed I wouldn't be able to hide it from you. I left to protect *Zia*'s spell against the Palmisano curse.'

He kissed her full on the lips again and said, 'We should go. That patrol we ran into this morning isn't a good sign. The Germans have been jittery for the last couple of days.'

'What was it you lot were talking about earlier, when I came to the cave? You've got weapons hidden away?'

'The Allies are heading to Matera and we're getting ready to help them out. We've been getting organized to fight and help liberate Italy for a while now.'

'I thought you didn't care about the war, that you only believed in yourself and the family,' she said, with a hint of pride in her expression.

'Just because I don't agree with your friends in the Party or subscribe to any of the groups that fight against Mussolini it doesn't mean I don't hate the fascists and the Germans as much or even more than you all do. They have both brought us misery and robbed us of our dignity.'

'Be careful. I can't lose you, not now,' she said, a dark shadow in her eyes.

'With Il Duce gone, Italy's liberation will be a matter of three or four weeks.'

'Wars are always only supposed to last a short time and in the end they go on and on, getting more and more bloody and merciless. I saw real hell in Catalonia when the Italian planes bombed the Republicans fleeing to the border; I thought I would never see anything worse, but then I saw the horror of the French camps. Then the Germans arrived and I learned of the SS's depravity, their cruelty that's like a habit to them, just another weapon. Who knows what's next . . .'

He took her hand and helped her up. They walked along the gully, retracing the steps they'd taken that morning, with the undergrowth as high as their waists. Vitantonio grabbed a handful of brome grass and threw it at Giovanna's back. Two strands got stuck in her blouse.

'See, you have two suitors,' he said with a laugh.

She played along, but soon grew serious. She grabbed him by the arm and stopped him.

'What are we going to do now? What do I say to Salvatore?' she asked, looking into his eyes.

'I don't know, this is all very new,' he answered. The question had caught him by surprise. 'We were brought up together; can we just, all of a sudden, stop being brother and sister?'

Giovanna looked at the ground and took two steps back. She turned to face him again and answered with the determination she always had in the most difficult moments.

'Let's give it some time. You're preparing to go off to war, and Salvatore is waiting for me to join him in the mountains with a group of communists that have just got out of prison. There is still a long struggle ahead of us – neither the king nor Badoglio are going to do anything to free Italy. In fact, in Bari I got a clear idea of what they consider freedom: they just want to replace one fascist leader with another. When this is all over things will be less confused.'

They approached a rocky pile that emerged from the ravine and led to the path to the Lucignano forest. Giovanna plucked the petals off a bunch of poppies, the last of the season, and left a trail of red along the ground.

'Like a trail of love,' said Vitantonio in jest.

'Like a trail of blood,' replied Giovanna, deadly serious.

Could he be in love with Giovanna? They weren't related, but they had been raised as twins since the day they were born. Wasn't that as good as being blood siblings? Was their attraction natural? It didn't make sense. But the taste of Giovanna lingered happily on his lips.

He walked her to the other side of the Bosco di Lucignano and then he doubled back part of the way to find the Comune forest, following the animal tracks, which led him to a clearing carved out by boars; they had scratched desperately at the earth there in search of some damp dirt to wallow in. Later he went down to the gully so he could return to Matera by following the riverbed, along the same path he'd walked with Giovanna that morning. He passed a woman gathering capers and snails, but he didn't stop – something told him he had to get back to the town quickly.

As he approached the first few Sassi homes, he saw two old men sitting on a rocks smoking herbs. The old men of Matera liked to smoke jimson weed to open their throats: it helped them climb the steep stairs to the city. He knew the two men because they were friends of his *tatònn*, but he also greeted them without stopping. He quickened his step. At the Cappuccino Vecchio church he headed straight for the rocks, planning to enter the town from the back, along the Potenza road. When he got close to the Via dei Cappuccini he found a line of trucks and tanks parked in front of the fascist Milizia headquarters. The Germans had recently begun holding Italian civilians and soldiers there as hostages. He turned back and hid among the bushes of the wasteland that rose in terraces above the official building, knowing it was foolish: he could be seen from there. But he was anxious to get back to the cave and find out what was going on.

Just as he moved out in to the open he heard a huge explosion that threw him to the ground. A column of fire rose up to the heavens: the Palazzo de la Milizia had been blown sky-high. He couldn't see what was going on but, taking advantage of the dust cloud, he set off running and a few minutes later entered the Sassi labyrinth.

Rain of Stars

THE PEASANT FARMERS had erected barricades at the entrances to the Sasso Caveoso using wagons and furniture. Later, Vitantonio learned that they'd also blocked the streets in the Sasso Barissano to keep out the German troops, but the fighting itself was concentrated in Matera's city centre. He found only his grandfather in the cave, gathering items for the barricades; the others had gone out to defend the city's strategic buildings, which the Germans wanted to destroy before retreating. He grabbed what weapons he could find and rushed out. When he reached the cathedral, he saw the first signs of the battle that had broken out unexpectedly just an hour earlier. With a machine gun in his hand, he ran towards the shooting.

By the time he reached the centre, clashes had broken out at two official buildings, the Palazzo del Governo and the Prefettura in the Piazza Vittorio Veneto. It was six in the evening. In square, Vitantonio found Roosevelt and the Professor shooting as part of a group of poorly armed civilians and was shocked to realize that the popular revolt was prevailing.

'We've got things under control here, but the radio

says that it's not going so well in the area around the station. We'll have to go up there and give them a hand.'

News that was spread by word of mouth from house to house, from one end of the city to the other, was called 'he radio'. It was the fastest way to communicate and it never failed them. So they could only assume the information was good and they ran over to the Via Cappelluti. As soon as they arrived there, they saw a fierce battle going on in the station plaza and also fighting in the nearby block of apartments that housed civil servants. On the roof, there were four or five snipers in civilian clothes; they had obviously had army training. This group was led by the unmistakable figure of the Englishman, who was also holding at bay a German detachment that was trying to get close enough to blow up the building. The fresh arrivals, including Vitantonio, started shooting from the other side of the street, together with a group of Italian non-commissioned officers who had armed themselves at the barracks of the Guardia di Finanza. Caught in the crossfire, the Germans retreated.

The Englishman came down to street level: he wanted to capture a German prisoner to be interrogated by the British Eighth Army when it entered the city. Right on his heels, another snipes came down from the roof. He also seemed English or American, and he waved at them with the hand that held his machine gun and vanished in the direction of the Via Roma. Behind him appeared a very young handsome airforce officer.

'Vincenzo Bilardi,' the young man introduced himself.

The group went through the streets, helping the civilians get organized. On the Rione San Biagio, where the fighting had begun, they found Italian soldiers shooting at the Germans. The Professor discovered that the reserve officer who had armed all those men was none other than his close friend, Francesco Paolo Nitti. They hugged; their conversations were what had kept up his link with the world over his years in hiding in Matera. Nitti informed them that in various clashes two men they knew had been killed, and that a group of the electricity company's employees had been shot at its headquarters. The Professor boosted Nitti's morale by telling him that the Germans had suffered many losses in the city centre and that they'd been forced to retreat from the Piazza Vittorio Veneto and the station. It seemed that the insurrection was gaining ground throughout the city.

Narrowly evading an enemy faction on the Via Rosario, they turned back towards the Duomo, to check on the situation in the two Sassi from above. As they neared the cathedral square, a shell exploded right by them and they had to throw themselves to the ground: the Germans had set up a 75-millimetre anti-tank gun in front of the Civilian Hospital and were shooting at the houses around the cathedral, over the roofs of the Sasso Barissano. Up on a roof of the hospital, two blackshirts signalled with their hands to direct the shooting, choosing their targets from among the best-known dissidents in the city. Neighbours watched in silence from their windows, trying to figure out who were these two men in black now in charge of the local fascists. One of them was a huge, hulking giant and the other a young man, but no one could identify them: seemingly they had come up from Puglia, fleeing the advance of the Allied troops.

A second shell exploded even closer to Vitantonio and his comrades. They ran for shelter in a house carved out of the rock. In the deepest part of the cave about twenty people were huddled, but one girl stood at the entrance, watching the German artillery firing. From the depths of the cave, her mother screamed desperately for her to take cover in the safer part of the dwelling.

'What's your name?' Vitantonio asked her.

'Lucia.'

'Your mother is right, Lucia. It's dangerous here by the door.'

Still the girl didn't move. The glow of the tracer bullets fascinated her. She couldn't take her eyes off them.

'It's raining stars,' she said, spellbound. She closed her eyes and made a wish.

'Very dangerous stars,' explained Vitantonio when a third shell blew up just metres from the house.

He offered her his hand and led her to the back of the cave, to join the others. As he did so, there was another explosion right in front of the cave and the force of the impact blew the door to pieces.

Lucia wasn't as young as she seemed, she'd turned

fifteen and was mulling over her wish. The emotions of the day had shaken her: that morning she'd seen a German soldier on a motorbike taking two captured Italian soldiers sitting in the sidecars to the military barracks. They were two young men from Matera she recognized, Pietro Tataranni and Natale Farina. They had abandoned their units on 9 September, the day after the armistice, and they had been caught when they were just about to enter town, after more than ten days of walking. Fate would have it that the motorcycle with the prisoners paused at the door of Pietro Tataranni's girlfriend's house. The girlfriend, who hadn't seen her lover since the start of the war, had walked over to the window when she heard the bike, and when she opened the shutters she couldn't believe her eyes: the young man who had just stood up in the sidecar and was waving his arms at her was her boyfriend.

'Pietro!' she shouted like mad.

'They're taking me to the Milizia, but I'll be back soon. The war's over for us,' he answered excitedly. 'I love you!'

Lucia had watched the scene from the pavement that morning, and had been daydreaming ever since that, one day, a handsome boy would walk across all of Italy for ten days and ten nights to find her and declare his love.

'You should have seen how they looked at each other,' she sighed to all those huddled in the back of the cave. 'I'd like to be there when Pietro Tataranni comes back from the Milizia. They've not seen each other for more than three years because of the war! I want to see the moment they're finally back in each other's arms.'

Outside the cave, the Germans had stopped shooting. Vitantonio signalled to Roosevelt and the Professor that they should take advantage of the lull. They ran out into the streets in time to see that the insurrection was winning. An hour later, when it was already growing dark, the German column was climbing the Potenza road and leaving the city for good.

The uprising of 21 September had come to an end, but the city of Matera had paid a very high price: twenty-six dead.

When the insurgents regrouped, Vitantonio, Roosevelt and the Professor met up with the Englishman, who had managed to capture a wounded German; he had left him under guard at the hospital. The four friends celebrated their victory with a quick embrace, then pulled apart. The Englishman was euphoric; he wanted to leave the city in search of the British Eighth Army, which was approaching from Montescaglioso.

The radio was spreading the news of the at the explosion Milizia headquarters that Vitantonio had seen with his own eyes when he was coming up from the *gravina.*

'The sixteen hostages the Germans were holding there are dead.'

The violence of the explosion had made it impossible to identify five of the victims! but soon word spread of the names of the others: Pietro de Vito, Antonio

Nocera, Mario Greco, Raimondo Semeraro, Tommaso Speciale, Francesco Lecce, Natale Farina, Francesco Farina, Vincenzo Luisi . . .

Young Lucia had just left the safety of the cave and was asking her mother to accompany her to the house of Tataranni's girlfriend; she wanted more than anything to witness the couple's reunion. What she didn't yet know was that her wish would never come true: the last corpse they'd identified from the rubble of the Milizia building was Pietro Tataranni's.

The Liberation of Matera

WHEN THE ENGLISHMAN returned to Matera at dawn he was driving an armoured car belonging to the Eighth Army, which was rapidly approaching along road from the Montescaglioso, and he was wearing the uniform of a British Army lieutenant. Vitantonio barely recognized him: he hadn't seen him in military dress for more than a year, since the day he'd saved him from the *carabinieri* patrol at the entrance to the Sasso Caveoso. In the car with him was the Italian pilot – young Bilardi – and the foreigner they'd seen come down from the roof of the apartment building in the square by the station. Two British motorcycles flanked the armoured car, creating a tiny procession that moved very slowly into the heart of the city.

Hundreds of Matera's residents were gathered in the open to celebrate their liberation from the Germans. When the British armoured car entered the Piazza Vittorio Veneto, the locals started shouting, 'Long live America!' Vitantonio and the Professor exchanged a puzzled look. Only Roosevelt seemed amused by the mistake.

'It looks like in the end we did fight side by side with the Americans,' he said, pleased as punch.

Then he let out one of his booming laughs, lifted his thumb in the Englishman's direction as he was getting out of the car, and shouted, 'Long live President Roosevelt!'

The Trail of Terror

OVERNIGHT, THE ENGLISHMAN had become Lieutenant Donovan. Vitantonio, Roosevelt and the Professor were his troops. The next morning they left Matera, still in the grip of the euphoria brought on by finally entering the fray. They hadn't been permitted to join the ranks of the regular troops, but the British Army had allowed them to act as observers, under the command of their new lieutenant. Donovan spoke perfect Italian and could be very useful to the liberating troops, as both an informant and a liaison officer with the local insurgents.

They were on the heels of the retreating Germans, and charged with reporting back on the state of the transportation routes to the north. They were proud to serve the Allies, but they resented not being able to enlist as regular, real soldiers. Especially Roosevelt, who was baffled not to be considered by the British as at least half American. Vitantonio would have preferred to take the roads closer to the coast, to pass Bellorotondo, because in three years he had returned there only once: to watch his *nonna*'s burial. But their mission forced them to take the inland road towards Grassano, which lay about half way to Potenza.

The first two days of the journey saw them storm ahead to Potenza, where there was no trace of the Germans; but when Lieutenant Donovan's men reached Rionero in Vulture, to the north, they sensed the sinister trail of repression from a distance: the screams and wails of women echoed through the surrounding mountains and rippled through the outskirts of the town. The entire population was in mourning. The Germans just had executed eighteen innocent local men.

The town had been starving for weeks. Only eight days earlier, a group of desperate peasants had broken into a warehouse. The attackers' weak, skeletal appearance so horrified one German soldier that he took pity on them and helped a woman carry off a sack of flour. The next day, his superior officers had him shot.

During those days of hardship, in the towns of Basilicata and Puglia, there were some Italian fascists who managed to earn themselves an even worse reputation than the Germans. Instead of just trying to control the locals, they chose to make survival even more difficult for the poorest, neediest Italians. In Rionero, it was the attempted theft by an Italian commando that set off the punishment executions. A young girl found him in the henhouse and alerted her family. Her father shot the thief in one hand. The Italian soldier and his unit demanded revenge and the Germans decided to compensate him for his wound by killing the father and seventeen other innocent men chosen from among the town's young people. Many of those executed were soldiers who had returned home from the front just hours earlier, having taken advantage of the fact that many of their commanders had abandoned their posts after the signing of the armistice in early September. They had travelled for days to get home.

When, on 25 September, the Englishman, Vitantonio, Roosevelt and the Professor reached Rionero, the eighteen men had been shot less than twenty-four hours earlier; the women were still watching over their bodies. The whole town was deeply resentful of the local Italian soldiers. Many had begged the commandos to intervene before the executions, but they had denied their requests for clemency.

'In the name of Il Duce, there will be no pardon!' they had shouted as their only response.

The townspeople were particularly enraged with two fascist civilians who had urged the Italian and German soldiers on to even greater cruelty. The women who had seen them haranguing the soldiers trembled in fear to remember the scene. The only description they gave was that there were two of them: a tall, hulking man with rotten teeth, and a young man dressed all in black.

As they made their way further north, Vitantonio and his friends came across yet more episodes of gratuitous violence by the Germans, accompanied each time by the enthusiastic collaboration of a few Italian soldiers who remained faithful to their former allies. And soon they discovered that the worst massacres always coincided with the sinister trail of the two strangers who had encouraged the Germans' revenge killings in Matera and Rionero. Their reputation preceded them. Throughout the region, people grew to fear the two fascists as much as the Germans.

When, two days later, the Englishman and his men arrived in Ascoli Satriano, they exchanged the first direct gunfire with the enemy rearguard. Perched up on a hill, a small group of German stragglers were firing a mortar against the helpless townspeople. By the time the Englishman and his band ran them off it was already too late: the shelling had killed ten civilians.

'We've been rationing food for days, because we barely have any left. When we saw they were planning to loot our homes and barns, we stood up to them and the Germans went mad. Two Italians with them egged them on to retaliate with the mortar gun.'

Donovan's group dropped to the ground, exhausted, with their backs resting against the wall of the first house in town. Vitantonio sat alone across the street, facing the others. On the house's façade, a bit above the line of shadow cast by his friends, someone had written: 'Long live Badoglio and long live the king.' He spat on the ground. It sickened him that they were too late again to save the town's civilians; he felt an intense hatred for those responsible for these massacres. And he felt a strong need to come face to face with them and kill them.

In Ascoli, the survivors were better able to identify them. 'They're two bastards from right around here.

From the Mezzogiorno, probably Bari or the Itria valley. One of them is a damn giant, with black teeth rotted away from the venom that runs through his veins. The other is even worse: cruel, heartless. And he acts like it's all a game: he dresses in black from head to toe and calls himself the Black Knight.'

Vitantonio heard the name and felt as if he'd just been punched hard in the stomach. He tried to convince himself that this couldn't be, but he couldn't deny that he'd had his suspicious for a while now. He leaned back against a drystone wall and had a vivid flashback to the palazzo garden on the afternoon of his confirmation.

'Will you teach me how to fight?' Franco had asked him.

'What's got into you? You can't teach fighting. When you're in the right, you fight and that's it,' he'd answered.

Shortly after that they had started playing with the wooden swords Skinny had made for them at the factory. Brandishing his, Vitantonio had donned a white sheet as a cloak and declared, 'I'm Knight Frederic de Castel del Monte, about to set off for the Crusades.'

'I'm the Black Knight. If I win, your people will die by the sword and by fire,' Franco had replied, wearing *Nonna*'s black shawl as his cape.

That night Vitantonio couldn't sleep. He tried to conjure up memories of carefree games and innocent adventures with Franco and Giovanna, but different ones kept rising to the surface, reminding him that he was the only one who had refused to accept a truth that all the others knew and had tried to make him see. He travelled back in his mind's eye to a day in Bari in 1936 when he skipped class and went down to the port to say goodbye to Giocavazzo, who was heading to the war in Abyssinia.

He had found his friend smoking, his right boot resting on a bollard at the foot of the gangway. They hugged and his former school rival joked with him. 'You sure you don't want to come with us? You're really missing out . . . There's nothing to do here, this land is pure misery.'

'There is nothing for me anywhere else. Besides, you think you'll even get there in time? They say the war's almost over.'

'We'll land in late April, just in time for the final assault on Addis Ababa. We'll enter the capital and there'll be a victory parade. You're going to miss it. It's a shame: you'd look good in the photos they'll be publishing in every newspaper in Italy to commemorate our success. I still don't understand how the bravest, strongest guy in the class wants to end up as a lawyer for the poor in Puglia and the biggest coward, your thick cousin, is dying to be a blackshirt.'

Vitantonio looked at him in surprise.

'Didn't he tell you? He's joined the Volunteer Militia. They go through towns burning down dissident meeting places and beating up anti-fascists. In the countryside between Bari and Foggia they've already burnt down one house and two party of Italian Peasants' headquarters.'

‘I thought that stuff was a thing of the past.’

‘The Fascist Party might not encourage it any more, but they still do it under their own steam. When he’s in a group and feeling confident, your cousin is the most aggressive of them all, but when it’s time to fight he’s a little shit. Most of his fellow militia men have volunteered like me and are already in Ethiopia, but he bottled it.’

Giocavazzo lit another cigarette, looked him right in the eye and decided it was time to get a few things off his chest.

‘I don’t know how you can look so surprised. Don’t tell me you didn’t know that he was the one who ratted on Salvatore and got him beaten up . . .’

Vitantonio didn’t wait around for the ship to set sail. He shook his friend’s hand and left the port as quickly as possible. The next day was Saturday and he went up to Bellorotondo. He reached the palazzo around lunchtime and found Giovanna and Franco in the garden, arguing. He was trying to put his arm around her shoulder. When she saw her twin brother come in, the relief showed in her face.

‘Get this idiot off me. I can’t stand him any more,’ she begged as she embraced Vitantonio.

Brushing his sister aside, Vitantonio walked straight up to Franco. He grabbed him by the arm and pushed him into a corner, behind *Nonna*’s azaleas. He pinned him against the wall.

‘I won’t repeat this. As far as I’m concerned, you can act like a big man with your blackshirt friends all you want, as long as you do it far from Bellorotondo. In Naples, Rome or wherever you please but, from now on, stay away from here. Have you heard about the exile your kind is imposing on dissident intellectuals? Well, now it's you who is exiled from Puglia, because if you aren't gone by next month, I'll tell the Vicinos that it was you who informed on Salvatore. And you know that he has a lot of relatives in the mountains who are capable of anything.'

Franco turned white and tried to justify himself. 'You don't understand. Salvatore's no good for Giovanna. He's filling her head with all sorts of ideas. I've already had to defend her several times. She's not escaped the blackshirts' notice and I know people who want to do her harm.'

Vitantonio's anger flared and he slammed Franco against the stone wall again.

'If any of your friends touch her, I'll kill you!'

'I'll protect her, I swear! I just want her to stop seeing Salvatore. She deserves what I have to offer her.'

'You're insane!' he shouted. 'I know you really like Giovanna . . . but for God's sake, she can't stand you and besides, she's your cousin; you'd need a special dispensation from Rome to marry her.'

Vitantonio asked himself if it was confusion or anger that he was feeling, and he decided that, mostly, he despised his cousin and that this time he wasn't willing to forgive him.

'I had hoped you would stick up for yourself, say there'd been a misunderstanding and deny everything.'

He looked at Franco scornfully and spat on the ground. 'You have until the end of the month,' he concluded.

Vitantonio watched Franco leave with his tail between his legs, and wondered if perhaps his cousin had just been trying to act the man in front of Giovanna. All the more reason to make him leave Puglia; hopefully he would forget about her and his new fascist friends. Just as Vitantonio was about to go inside the palazzo he bumped into his sister again, who was waiting for him by the doors to the conservatory. He tried to smile at her, but once again he felt a twisting in his guts: that damn sister of his, everyone was in love with her!

Franco did indeed make himself scarce. A month later, he announced he was going to Rome to study, and a year later he enlisted with the corps of Volunteer Troops to fight alongside the fascist rebels in the Spanish Civil War.

The Hunt

THAT AUTUMN OF 1943 was becoming a waking nightmare. The further north the Englishman's band got, the more bullet-ridden bodies they found on the roads. Vitantonio was losing all hope. He would stare at the murdered civilians and imagine Franco encouraging the Germans to shoot them, and he grew obsessed with catching him and making him pay for his cruelty.

On 1 October, they approached Alberona: before they'd arrived the civilians had stood up to the Germans and in the exchange of fire a girl had been killed. They found her at the entrance to town, laid out on the side of the road, as if she were taking a nap – but the blood on her dress left no room for doubt, nor did the scarlet trail she'd left when trying to drag herself away. Vitantonio's gaze wandered and landed on a swallowtail butterfly zigzagging among the anise-scented flowers of a fennel plant, like the day he and Giovanna had made love by the pool.

'Like a trail of love,' he'd said that morning – that morning that seemed so far in the past now – as Giovanna plucked poppy petals.

'Like a trail of blood,' she'd replied.

For four days and four nights, the German rearguard halted the group's progress, and they were forced to remain at the gates of Celenza Valfortore. At night Vitantonio twisted and turned in his sleep bed as if he had a fever, trying to banish the repulsive image of Franco from his mind, but his childhood and teenage years kept coming back to him like a nightmare. And the memory of a distant day in October 1934 was the one that haunted him more than any other.

They had got up at dawn to hunt the first thrush and quail of the season in the olive groves near Cisternino. At fifteen, Vitantonio was excited. At the beginning of the year Befana the Witch had brought him his first rifle and he'd be using it that morning for the very first time. As soon as they arrived at the olive groves a thrush took flight and he aimed with precision and sent the bird plummeting to the ground. He had learned to shoot with Salvatore's gun and had become a fine shot. Mastega, Salvatore's grandfather's dog, ran to retrieve the bird and soon reappeared with it in its teeth.

By midday Vitantonio's bag was full, with eight thrushes and two hares. Franco, on the other hand, had tried to shoot many times, but his hands were shaky and he was afraid of the gun's recoil. He hadn't hit a single target. He vented his anger by criticizing Salvatore, who was leading their hunting group.

'What a bighead. He acts like he's our leader, but we're not under his command. He's only the son of one of our employees!'

'Cut it out, he *is* the one in charge here. He's older, he knows the land and a lot more about hunting.'

When they moved to another olive grove further up, they got a surprise. Just as they squatted behind some undergrowth they saw a flock of turtledoves take flight, as if sensing their arrival.

'They aren't trying to fly away from us – there must be a hawk chasing them. That's why they keep flying about nervously,' explained Salvatore.

Vitantonio stood up, looking worried. His gaze followed the turtledoves and he hoped they'd get away from the hawk, which had just emerged from behind the trees and was flying in circles, waiting for the moment to swoop on its prey.

Franco stood up as well. 'He's got one!' he shouted excitedly as he watched the hawk sink its claws into the helpless body of a turtledove before carrying it off into the branches of a pine tree. The top of the tree shook as if struck by a sudden burst of wind and a rain of white feathers fell to the boys' feet.

Franco was still shouting eagerly. 'Wow, that was amazing! Did you see how he killed it?'

Vitantonio didn't answer. His eyes were glued to the ground, staring at the feathers of that poor bird. Later, when they went back to the *trulli* with their bag full, they all congratulated Vitantonio on his aim and forgot about the turtledove.

That evening, on the threshing floor, Donata and Concetta skinned the two hares and left them in a marinade of wine, onion, celery, bay leaves, pepper and a pinch of chopped thyme. The next day the two women spent all morning in the kitchen. They sautéed a few pieces of salted pork with half a cup of oil, onion, celery and a couple of carrots. They took the hares out of the marinade, let them drain and then put them to brown in the pan. Then they left them simmering gently. Every once in a while one of them would go over to the pot and toss in a glass of liquid from the overnight marinade or a bit of stock. An hour and a half later, they pulled the hares out and spent more than an hour stripping the meat off the bones and chopping it up into very small pieces.

At midday, when the Vicinos and the Galassos began to arrive with all their children, Concetta hurried to cook up some *orechiette*, while Donata put the pan back on the stove with the sauce and the vegetables and added the chopped meat to it. Once the pasta was ready, they mixed it all together and brought the pan to the table, provoking a storm of compliments, which in turn competed with the praise for Vitantonio's skill with the shotgun. Normally, when the men from the *trulli* had caught good game, they would take it to the town: to the landowners, the doctors and sometimes the priest. Skinny always took the hares he and Salvatore caught to *Nonna*. But that day, the hunter had been Vitantonio and he wasn't obliged to butter up any landowners. He smiled and bowed his head: the praise made him feel both proud and embarrassed.

*

Nine years had passed since that trip to the olive groves of Cisternino, but Vitantonio was now feeling that same impulse to hunt. This time his prey was his cousin and he wouldn't rest until he had made him pay for so many hundreds of innocent deaths. They didn't reach Celenza Valfortore until 5 October, and when they finally entered the town they saw that they were too late again: this time, artillery fire had killed three children and a seventeen-year-old boy. None of Donovan's group had any tears left. That night they again swore that they'd make those responsible pay dearly, but right then the Englishman told them, 'They want us to enter the lion's den: tomorrow we go behind German lines.'

Convinced that the Germans were slowing them down so that they could reinforce their positions in the north, the Allied command pressed Lieutenant Donovan's group to advance behind enemy lines. They needed some accurate intelligence.

They left Celenza with their minds reeling from the terrible image of the three children blown up by German artillery.

'We need to make up for lost time and cross the front line,' urged the Englishman.

It was hard to tell exactly where that line was. It was changing constantly. The marshland between the Trigno and the Sangro rivers was a conflict zone and the many comings and goings made it hard to establish firm positions. Twice they exchanged fire with German soldiers without knowing whether they were retreating stragglers or an advance party in a new counter-attack. Donovan decided to be as cautious as possible: they slept during the day and walked at night.

As they neared the Maiella mountains, Vitantonio was growing more and more anxious to meet up with Giovanna. He thought about her all the time. Maybe he had been too hasty that day at the river when he'd questioned whether they could really be lovers. Now so many miles and months from the day at the pool, he deeply regretted the common sense that had made him say that they were still like brother and sister despite both knowing that they weren't related at all.

At dusk on the third day, when they were about to cross the Trigno river, they happened upon a group of five fugitives who were also heading north to try to penetrate enemy lines and reach the mountains. A huge man, standing at nearly six foot five inches, made way for them.

'They say that in the Maiella there are groups that are getting ready to fight the remaining Germans. We want to join them,' confessed the giant when he saw that they were on the same side and he could speak freely. His name was Primo Carnera and he was leading a small group of Italian former soldiers who were trying to join the partisans.

'Primo Carnera'

After the armistice in early September, Italian soldiers had started returning home. Convinced that things would finally go back to the way they used to be, they found the exact opposite was true: everything had changed. Short of manpower, many families had lost their harvests and their land; those who had avoided conscription had got rich at the expense of the others; women driven mad with loneliness had gone off with opportunists instead of waiting for their husbands to return from the front; young children no longer recognized their fathers and recoiled from them when they suddenly reappeared.

But fate had really sharpened its claws on Primo Carnera. He arrived back to find that his parents had been evicted and hadn't survived the disgrace; his wife had gone off with some passing braggart, and when his children saw him they burst into tears and wouldn't go anywhere near him. It took Primo less than two days to come to a decision. He'd long felt that his fellow soldiers were his family; on the front they had sworn lifelong friendship and he was convinced they wouldn't betray him. He got together with some other soldiers that were as disenchanted as he was and they headed off towards the mountains.

The partisans never knew his real name and he told them that he couldn't even remember it. He liked the nickname he had been given. He was tall, weighed eighteen stone and was strong as an ox. When Primo Carnera won the world heavyweight title in New York, his friends decided that he was just like him and they rechristened him with the boxer's name. From that day on he was always 'Primo Carnera' and proud of it.

Vitantonio and Roosevelt soon adopted him; they quickly saw he was too good a follow to just leave him there alone in that band of hardened men who were regrouping in the mountains. All the partisans were loyal to the cause of freedom, but many were disillusioned and embittered by the war. But Primo was an innocent; he was always willing to give it his all and he trusted everybody. He was like the boxing giant in that way, too.

'You have to prepare yourself for when this all ends. After the war we'll all go home and you'll be left alone,' said Vitantonio, trying to get him to reflect. 'I swore lifelong loyalty to everyone in my class at boarding school and I haven't seen a single one of them since I left Bari. The same thing is going to happen to you.'

Primo laughed and grabbed a fennel blossom, put it in his mouth, and started to chew. Then he pulled it out, pointed the chewed stem at Vitantonio and threatened him.

'You'd better not ditch me! You and Roosevelt are my family.'

'But we met just a month ago.'

'I never had a girlfriend that lasted that long. Not even my wife!'

Then he put the fennel back in his mouth, chewed it a bit more and walked off, laughing.

When they reached the Maiella mountains they found that volunteers were arriving there by the dozens, ready to take the Germans on – even if the odds were stacked against them. They came from all over Italy, willing to see past the ideological differences that had separated them all those years; most of them were former soldiers who refused to accept that the war was over for them. At the first camp they shared with partisans, Vitantonio soon discovered that Giovanna and Salvatore had been in the Maiella mountains for some days.

Overjoyed to know Giovanna was nearby, Vitantonio prepared to search for them. But before he could begin, the Englishman received orders from the Allied command: they were to wait for a partisan column travelling with an American captain, Lewis Clark, a specialist in chemical weapons whom they had to snuggle into the German rearguard. The goal was to find facilities capable of storing and producing mustard gas. The wholly unexpected order may have meant that Vitantonio had to scrap his plans to find Giovanna and Salvatore, but he was about to get an altogether different sort of surprise.

In the Mountains

THE PARTISANS ESCORTING the American wore long coats that reached to their knees, and hats pulled down to their ears, because in that gloomy November the mountain passes were so cold they froze the innards of all who dared to travel through them. Vitantonio saw the American and his escort approaching and watched them from a distance. His heart began to race: Salvatore and Giovanna were leading the column. Their bulky outerwear didn't disguise them obstacle for Vitantonio, he would have recognized Giovanna anywhere. Her laugh was unmistakable.

They hadn't seen each other since that day in Matera nearly two months earlier and he was disheartened to learn that the squad of partisans planned to stay at the camp for only a few hours, just enough time to rest and have something to eat. Giovanna didn't manage to take him aside until the partisans were already preparing to leave. Vitantonio and Giovanna had promised each other that while the war was still going on they would take things as they came, that they wouldn't make plans or talk about their future, but she had some news to give him.

'I'm pregnant.'

He didn't even have time to react. The sun was dropping behind the mountains and the partisan column was already on its way back. Vitantonio accompanied them to the edge of the forest and watched them silently head up into the mountain. Giovanna and Salvatore were again in the lead and when they jumped over a dry riverbed he took her hand and held her by the waist. Vitantonio felt that stab again, aware that while the physical pain would last only an instant, the real pain was deeper and less easily healed. He had found that out long ago, the second summer they'd spent in the countryside, at Concetta's farmhouse.

That summer in the *trulli*, in the afternoons, Vitantonio would sit in the shadow of a walnut tree, and let his mind be carried off in contemplation of that hot, rugged land that robbed them of their energy but somehow still gave them all they needed.

'Harsh but dignified,' said Skinny's father when he talked about life in the valley.

On the other side of the path into the farmstead were two huge oaks, with trunks so wide that not even three men could encircle them. He had always found it amazing that in such dry land there were trees with such enormous trunks and majestic boughs. He didn't know from where those ancient oaks and those tender fruit trees got the strength they proudly displayed in many hues of green: the vibrant greens of the cherry trees, the darker green of the fig, the reddish green of the pomegranate, the muted green of the plum and the light green of the grape vines, which by late August were already turning yellow.

To the right of the oaks was the outline of Bellorotondo's hill, standing proud like a sentry in the middle of the valley. Further to the right, to the east, stood the town of Cisternino, scattered over the slope of the mountain that discreetly folds itself back to let the sea breeze off the Adriatic pass. The sun was going down in the other direction, near Alberobello, and a yellow late-afternoon light spread over the fields, drawing shadow silhouettes on the reddish earth.

When *Zia* and Concetta called them in for supper, in the distance Vitantonio saw Giovanna and Salvatore coming down from the path to the olive grove, walking between drystore walls. He watched them as they slowly approached, sharing laughter and confidences. Grandpa Vicino, who took care of the olive groves when Skinny was at the sawmill, often complained that summer that Salvatore was shirking his duties.

'Luckily you're helping us out,' he would say with a laugh to Vitantonio. 'Lately Salvatore isn't good for much of anything. You know what they say: when your donkey falls in love, you're pulling your own cart!'

Vitantonio couldn't stop staring at the couple as they drew close at dusk, but by the time they'd reached the threshing floor it was only Giovanna he couldn't stop looking at. Sweaty from the walk, her dress clung to her body. He felt that familiar discomfort, but there was also that same strange warmth he'd first felt when she'd teased him in the bedroom doorway the day he was in and she had surprised him by appearing in her dress printed with blue and red flowers, and with cherries dangling from her ears.

That night, at the makeshift camp in the Maiella, Vitantonio slept badly. The cold was awful and he felt sharp needles of pain all over his body. He was tormented by Giovanna's words! 'I'm pregnant,' she had said very calmly. Then she had looked at him with those emerald eyes of hers. She kissed him on the lips and ordered, 'Take care of yourself. Don't be too brave, not now. I need you safe and sound.'

Pregnant? Since when? How long had it been since they'd made love by the pool? Had that meant anything to Giovanna? Was she still sleeping with Salvatore as if nothing had happened? After all, they had only been together that one day and Giovanna hadn't been apart from Salvatore in weeks. They'd been on the move through the mountains since they'd got him out of the Alberobello jail and they'd joined the group of activists that the Communist Party was secretly reorganizing, taking advantage of the collapse of the regime.

Turning and twisting beneath his blanket, Vitantonio couldn't get to sleep in the freezing cold. He stood up, wrapped the blanket around his shoulders like a shawl and spent the night walking from one end of the camp to the other, pacing with his thoughts.

Dr Saroni's Weapons

THEY MET ONLY once more before November ended. This time it was Vitantonio's group that was crossing the mountain range towards the north and stopped in the well-hidden camp of Giovanna's squad. They were there just long enough to rest and restock their provisions, so once again they didn't really have time to talk. They were barely able to give each other a hug and ask how the other was. He didn't have a chance to ask her any of the questions that were tormenting him.

Vitantonio and his comrades still had days of walking ahead of them to take Captain Clark north of Teramo to the forests near Ascoli Piceno, where they were to leave him in the hands of some Allied agents, who would take him on to the Po valley, way past the Gustav Line. In those months, the line between Teramo and Cassino marked the border that divided Italy in two: to the south, the territory liberated by the Allies; to the north, Mussolini's puppet government in the service of the Nazi occupying forces, who in September had freed Il Duce in a bold move under direct orders from Hitler.

'What are we looking for?' Vitantonio had asked Captain Clark the day they set off.

'Chemical weapons.'

Clark spoke Italian with everyone in the group and English only with Lieutenant Donovan. His mother had been an immigrant from Lipari and he had grown up in Italian Harlem, the most Italian part of Manhattan. He spoke his mother's language fluently, making him perfect for the mission. He had been tasked with tracking the chemical weapons that the German troops may or may not have taken out of Foggia in late September, before they withdrew and blew up the most productive chemical plant in Italy: Dr Saroni's factory. If the Germans had managed to smuggle out the chemical weapons, the bombs must have been provisionally hidden somewhere north of the Gustav Line – and Clark had pinpointed, among the possible locations supplied by the Allied spies, where this stockpile was most likely to be. The bombers of the US Fifteenth Air Force stationed in the southern aerodromes were waiting for this last vital piece of information.

'Doctor Saroni's factory in Foggia was one of the world's best. The plant manufactured more than three hundred tons of chemical products each month: phosgene, carbon oxychloride and especially mustard gas. An incredible output!' declared Clark.

Sheltered in a small cave, the group slept little at the end of that first day on the road. Vitantonio had begun to regret accompanying the American on his mission: he had been banging on about chemical weapons ever since he'd arrived. All night he had to listen to him talk about the repugnant subject.

'A single mustard gas bomb can kill hundreds of men and, almost straight afterwards, there's no trace left. We can liquidate an entire German division without firing a single shot or damaging any of their weapons: just hours later we can gather them up intact. Can you imagine?'

Vitantonio hated chemical weapons. Huddled in a corner of the tiny cave, he listened to Captain Clark and started to dislike him as much as he disliked the treacherous war tactics he talked about. His mother had told him of his father's terror in the trenches of the Austrian front; she said that Vito Oronzo mentioned mustard gas in every letter and described with horror the anguish he felt at seeing the contorted faces of the dead soldiers they found gassed in the trenches. With a jolt, Vitantonio realized it was the first time he'd thought about Vito Oronzo Palmisano's experiences of war since learning that he was his real father. And Vitantonio's dislike for that bombastic American who sang the praises of inhumane weapons was rapidly turning into hate.

'*Can you imagine?*' repeated the American, enthused. 'We could take all their tanks and everything. Without risking a single American life!'

Vitantonio could imagine it, and it made him nauseous. He went outside and relieved Primo Carnera from his guard duty.

'That American bastard is sick!' he said in greeting when he reached the gentle giant's post. Primo looked at him, not understanding what he was talking about, and gratefully went to sleep, surprised to be relieved an hour early.

The operation behind enemy lines went better than they'd been expecting. Clark and the spies in the north located the factory, got close to it, saw the trucks entering and exiting the plant, recognized the products they were using and the weapons they were manufacturing and radioed the coordinates to London, so they could send them on to Allied HQ in southern Italy. A week later, the agents left the American near Ascoli Piceno with Vitantonio's group. But when they began their retreat to the south their luck ran out.

On the outskirts of Montorio al Vomano, in a mountainous area not far from Teramo, they were met by a contact who couldn't have been even eighteen years old. All the others partisans had scattered in small groups into the forest, fleeing the German attacks. Approaching the old manor house they had used as a refuge earlier on the way north, Vitantonio and his group decided to surround it first to avoid any nasty surprises. They monitored the house from a distance through binoculars, and Vitantonio spotted a wall doubed with a slogan supporting the king and Badoglio, which was hard to read because it had been painted over with a coat of whitewash. Higher up on the same wall someone had written in a clearer hand: 'Death to Badoglio and the traitor king. Long live Mussolini!' Crouching in the woods, with the binoculars in his hand, Vitantonio had a bad feeling, which was confirmed when he saw an armoured car and two German motorcycles arrive at the house.

The manor had become a vipers', nest of Germans. The group retreated into the deepest part of the forest and when they felt safe they pressed on south. But less than half an hour later they heard voices and had to retreat into the forest again. This time, though, Clark was lagging behind and when he saw the German patrol approaching him, he froze.

Vitantonio watched from a distance as the American was gripped by panic and heard the Germans shout 'Halt!' at him. He saw how they forced him to his knees and rammed a rifle butt into his stomach when he refused to answer the questions they were asking him in a mixture of German and Italian. Then he heard them shout, '*Schnell! Schnell! Svelti! Svelti!*'

He looked up and saw that they were shoving Clark forward, forcing him to march with his hands behind his neck, back towards the manor house. The American was shaking and looked like he was about to faint. Vitantonio followed them continuously until he saw that the Germans had stopped to have a cigarette. Then he took aim at the soldier about to light up and shot him in the back. The other soldier was slow to react. By the time he had grabbed his weapon, Vitantonio had fired again, sending a bullet through his head. Leaping out from cover, Vitantonio went over to Clark, took him by the arm and dragged him up the hillside, until they ran into Primo Carnera and the Professor who were coming down to meet them.

They changed their route. Walking away from the coast, they put same distance between themselves and the German patrols that had infested the area. It took them four days longer than planned to get back to the Maiella mountains. When they reached the camp, they saw that hundreds of Italian deserters had gathered there, along with dozens of Brits, Americans, New Zealanders and Croatians from the prisoner of war camps abandoned after the armistice. And they also found that they had new orders.

'We have to escort the American to Bari before the thirtieth of November,' the Englishman told his men. 'We leave tomorrow.'

But in the morning, a storm made the roads impassable and kept them in camp all day. It was still raining the day after and Vitantonio was beginning to feel desperate. Now that he knew they were going back to Bari, he was hoping to have enough time there to search for Donata: he hadn't seen her since the day she had confessed to being his mother.

On the third day, around noon, the skies began to clear. Vitantonio was at the edge of the camp, leaning against the trunk of a giant oak, with his gaze lost somewhere out on the plain, trying to imagine Foggia, the Gargano and beyond the horizon, the city of Bari. He heard a voice behind him.

'Do you miss it?'

He turned and saw that the commander of the Maiella brigade was watching him.

'I don't know if that's the word. I've been away from

home for more than three years and I suppose I'm used to it by now,' he answered. 'But I have some unfinished business there.'

The man extended his hand. 'Ettore Troilo,' he said.

'Vitantonio Conver— Vitantonio Palmisano,' he stammered.

'You don't even know your own name?'

'It's a long story . . .'

By the time he had finished telling it, the sky had grown overcast again. A flash of lightning lit up the nearest peaks, as if they'd caught fire.

At the back of the mountain range a tiny sliver of blue broke up the cloud cover, making the storm about to hit them again seem even darker in contrast. It was an unsettling sight: he had never seen such a black sky in the middle of the day. Night had fallen suddenly. Another flash of lightning lit up their faces. He saw Ettore Troilo flinch slightly; the booming thunder had caught him by surprise.

'If not for that bit of blue sky and the rays of sun coming from it, this would just be a dark evening like so many others. It's that reminder of the good weather somewhere far off that makes the coming storm seem even worse,' suggested the commander.

Vitantonio looked at the storm clouds again and thought that the partisan leader was right: by the time the storm hits it's no longer something frightening, it surrounds you but you no longer have a clear sense of it. It's only when you see it approaching from a distance, whole and threatening, that the imminent downpour is something to be feared.

He thought that perhaps it was also that light, the hope that they were fighting for a more peaceful, fruitful time, that had him more on edge than he had ever been during the three endless years of exile in Matera. Since he had begun to believe truly that a better time for Italy would soon come, he missed his mother and Giovanna more, and he was increasingly afraid of what might happen to him.

They were interrupted by the Englishman's voice. 'Try to get some sleep,' he said to Vitantonio after shaking hands with the partisan commander. 'Whatever the weather tomorrow, we're setting off at dawn.'

When they left camp the next morning it was still dark; the night was bitterly cold but filled with stars. Some partisans native to those mountains acted as their guides, helping them more stealthily along hidden paths. Twelve hours later, as the sun was setting, they had the Sangro river in their sights.

'We'll wait to cross until it gets dark and the escort comes for us,' announced the leader of the party.

That night, when the escort arrived, they brought good news.

'The British are on the other side of the river.'

PART FIVE

The Bombing of Bari

The Bar Mirror

ON THE SECOND day of December, when he reached Bari, Vitantonio didn't recognize the city: that winter, military vehicles had taken over the main roads and groups of soldiers moved about aimlessly, particularly on the streets that led to the old town and the new port. He left the station and walked along the Corso Italia, following the train tracks for a while. Then he disappeared into the streets of the district of Madonnella. Anxious as he was to start his search for his mother and Dr Ricciardi in the town's civilian and military hospitals, first he needed to wander around, just taking in the city.

He felt the sea breeze on his face and he noticed that he was out on the Lungomare, right in front of the Albergo delle Nazione, the hotel and restaurant where his uncle used to take him. From there, he saw for the first time the cranes in the port, which was a hive of activity. He had trouble recognizing the streets of his last years as a student in Bari. Before continuing, he decided to go into the Albergo for a drink.

Not used to drinking, it felt like the alcohol was burning his insides. He coughed, embarrassed, and quickly straightened up, to save face. When he glanced in the large mirror behind the bar he saw a ship reflected in it, headed to the entrance of the new port, to the eastern dock. If he'd had his military binoculars with him he could have seen that it was the *John Harvey*, an American cargo boat. He remembered the first time he'd seen vessels reflected in the same huge mirror, the day he had argued with Uncle Angelo. That evening, so long ago now, he'd discovered that there was nothing as peaceful as watching the arrival of a ship into port after a voyage filled with uncertainty. It seemed like a thousand years had passed since then.

He paid, decided to take the seafront road to the docks and watch the mooring from up close. Before leaving the bar he glanced in the mirror one last time, wanting to see the boat's exact position and calculate how long it would take it to reach the quay. He looked up: there in the mirror where the *John Harvey* had been was now the familiar figure of his cousin Franco, who was getting out of a car right on the other side of the Lungomare. Vitantonio stood up, his heart racing, trying to penetrate the mirror with his gaze. He saw Franco bid goodbye to the driver, who was wearing an Italian army uniform; then he saw his cousin head away from the hotel towards the Via Dante. Vitantonio bit his lip and clenched his fists, surprised at the impunity with which that murderer was strolling through the city. He had shared his childhood and teenage years with him, without ever questioning the ease with which he so readily ignored such unequivocal signs of evil. Now he hated Franco more than anything.

Earlier, when he had just left the station and was walking through the new part of the city, it had been buzzing with military activity, but it had also felt safe: the Allies had made it their main supply port on the Adriatic and an uprising by the women of the Borgo Antico had kept the Germans from blowing up the docks before evacuating the city. Now, just an hour later, with Franco's appearance, the city no longer felt safe. Bari was at war and his cousin's presence portended every possible horror.

Walking briskly, determined not to lose sight of him, Vitantonio followed his cousin. When Franco turned on to one of the side streets right before the Petruzzelli theatre, he'd almost caught up with him. He could easily recognize his small, sunken shoulders that used to twitch compulsively when they play-fought in the palazzo courtyard. He followed him along the Corso Cavour and, then, the Via Piccinni. When he saw they were approaching the Piazza Garibaldi, Vitantonio knew exactly where Franco was headed. He slowed his pace and, despite knowing where he was going, was still repulsed to see that, indeed, Franco was walking through the doorway of the building where they had shard an apartment in the last year of school, before his cousin had gone off to Rome and then war in Spain. Uncle Angelo had bought it for his son, right after the incident between Franco and Giocavazzo at the boarding school. Two years later Vitantonio too had moved in;

Nonna thought it was absurd to have him boarding at school when they had so much free space in a family apartment.

Vitantonio waited a little while on the other side of the square, watching the entrance. The years spent hiding in Matera and the last few months of guerrilla activity had taught him that things were always more complicated than they first appeared. An hour later he was proved right: the door opened and Franco came out, but not alone; the tall man with the rotten teeth was with him.

Meanwhile, the *John Harvey* had docked at pier 29 on the east jetty; the engineer had only just cut the engines. The pier was crowded with Allied vessels, many of them piled high with ammunition, and the recently arrived ship wouldn't be given any special treatment, so the crew were expecting to have to wait for days before starting to unload.

Vitantonio would have liked to challenge his cousin right there and then, but he let Franco and his accomplice vanish in the direction of the port. After half an hour he finally went up to the apartment, where he decided to wait for them so he could take his revenge. He got in through the window in the hall, which opened right on to the stairwell, just like when they were in school and he'd forgotten his keys.

Sneaking into his former student apartment gave him an odd feeling. It must have been a long time since anyone had cleaned it, because it smelled musty. He opened up the rooms and was revolted to find that the guy with the rotten teeth had taken over his bed; Franco was using the one he always had. The kitchen was covered in crumbs and there was an unbearable stench coming from the bathroom.

When he went into the dining room, he saw through the open balcony door that the sun was setting behind the Bari cemetery. Despite his eyes struggling in the low light, he discovered a radio transmitter and a pile of documents, some in German. He grabbed a handful of files and went over to the balcony to try to decipher them. He read: 'The sun has set on Bari.' And: 'Thirty-one ducks in the pond.' It was signed: 'The Black Knight.'

What did that all mean? Who was Franco communicating with over the transmitter? Was his cousin still working for the fascists of the newly established Italian Republic of Salò, who now shared control of northern Italy with the Nazis? Or was Franco working directly for the Germans? Or maybe he was working for both . . . He supposed that Franco and his sidekick could perfectly well be spying simultaneously for Hitler, Mussolini and any other bastard on the planet.

He went back to reading the files, pacing about the room. What the hell did those messages mean? *Sun? Ducks?* What were they about? Questions ran through his mind until all the sirens in the city went off at once and brought him back to reality. Alarmed, he ran to the balcony and looked out just in time to see people, who just moments before had been happily strolling in the square, running to the shelters.

Unused to the sirens, he decided to stay in the apartment and wait for Franco and the man with the rotten teeth to return home. He sat down on the cold floor, with his back against the open balcony door and facing the Piazza Garibaldi, which was now almost empty. The night was clear. The near deserted square made him uneasy. Time had stopped. Then, suddenly, he heard a deafening explosion only yards from his hiding place. He threw himself to the floor to avoid being hit by flying glass from the windowpanes shattering into a thousand pieces.

The Luftwaffe Raid

THE MEDICAL PERSONNEL in Bari lived in fear of the daily siren drills, because they set the patients on edge. That night, when the patients realized that the sirens hadn't stopped wailing at the usual time, hysteria spread through every ward in the Policlinico.

'If they don't stop that racket soon, I'll go mad,' one doctor complained bitterly as he was leaving Bari's medical school. He was checking on a boy's broken hip and he needed all possible calm to deal with the patient while he manipulated the joint.

The boy had been run over by a British army jeep. The driver hadn't stopped to pick him up. Two women who'd witnessed the accident had carried him and left him at the door of the Policlinico to force the army doctors to admit him. The majority of the Policlinico, Bari's most modern hospital, was under military command and entrusted to the New Zealanders.

'Don't worry, they'll stop soon,' said Dr Ricciardi to ease the tension.

'If that bloody siren doesn't stop in the next five minutes, we'll have to give all the patients—' Donata began, but they didn't hear the end of her complaint.

An enormous explosion shook the city to its foundations, followed by multiple aftershocks, which magnified the noise hugely. Soon, a chain of explosions was ricocheting through the city, closer and closer together.

With the patients screaming in terror, Ricciardi thought they were about to lose control of the ward. Donata shot the doctor a frightened look and saw that he was giving orders in an attempt to overcome his own panic. Just then another, even more horrific, explosion came: the windows shattered and sharks of glass hit those closest to them. The blast ripped out doors and shutters; bottles of medicine broke; the beds moved as if in an earthquake. Doctors on their rounds were sent flying across the room and fell to the ground, only intensifying the general sense of chaos and danger.

Only after a few minutes did they grasp that the chaos was caused by a Luftwaffe attack. More than a hundred planes were flying over the city of Bari and bombing it: it was as if the sky had opened up and rained down at once all the thunder and lightning that had fallen in southern Italy in the last thousand years. At seven forty-five when the bombers would finally leave, the city would be dotted with fires from one end to the other, lighting it up as if it were daytime.

One of the shockwaves had thrown Donata to the floor. When she clambered up look out of the windows, it was to be greeted by the sight of a giant column of fire somewhere, past the old quarter.

'The port is on fire!' she screamed, her eyes fixed on the flames.

More bombs fell again right by the hospital, and the doctor threw himself over Donata to shield her from the window. A hail of debris landed on the other side of the ward and hit an Italian officer who was standing in the doorway. Donata gave Ricciardi a grateful look. Then she glanced at the officer and saw that he appeared as scared as they did. He walked into the centre of the ward with two soldiers who wore Red Cross armbands. He took in the room and shouted, 'We need people to set up a first-aid post in the Borgo Antico straight away. The German bombs are devastating the cathedral and the port; it's a bloodbath.'

Donata and the doctor were the first ones to volunteer.

As soon as they crossed the train tracks they got their first glimpse of the disaster. And by the time they reached the old quarter, they were truly scared: the streets were no more than piles of rubble and survivors were running desperately from one end to the other. Some of them had taken refuge in the Castello, trusting that the thick walls of the fortress would withstand the attacks. Many others were starting to gather at the improvised *posto di pronto soccorso* facing the outer dock; some were bringing in the wounded, and the rest were looking for the comfort of company.

The first injured people that Donata and Dr Ricciardi treated came from the Strada Santa Chiara, but they didn't fully realize the magnitude of the bombing until the survivors of the collapsed buildings on the Via Venezia started coming in. The first ship that the

German bombers had hit had been loaded high with munitions: the explosion had caused a shockwave as strong as a hurricane, which had swept through the Borgo Antico and flattened the ancient buildings of one of Bari's oldest streets.

'The houses fell like dominoes, one after the other, like they were made of cardboard,' explained the eye-witnesses when they reached the medical station.

Among the recent arrivals, Donata recognized a neighbour who was being treated with a seven-year-old boy in her arms. Donata passed her every morning at the door to the cathedral when she left for the hospital. Approaching her to reassure her, Donata picked up the little boy in her arms and saw that he was dead.

The explosions on the ships caused more direct damage to the Borgo Antico than the Luftwaffe's bombs. The buildings crumbled, burying entire families amid piles of rubble that grew as tall as some of the houses had been. Many were also in flames. The air was burning hot and choked with the smoke that streamed off the burning boats. The survivors didn't know which way to go: there were flames in every direction. Suddenly a voice began to shout, 'To the sea! We have to take shelter there!'

A large group of panic-stricken people ran towards the port. Parents carried their children, some seriously injured. Faced with certain death beneath collapsing buildings, they were willing to risk passing by the burning ships in the hope of getting to the sea. By the time they reached the breakwater the entire port was aflame.

Some of the vessels had sunk and others were adrift and burning. The oil pipeline had been hit by one of the first bombs, and was pouring oil into the sea. Hundreds of sailors were desperately trying to stay afloat by clinging to debris or swimming through the burning water: the frantic screams for help sent shivers down the spines of those watching them from the quayside.

When they reached the dock, those survivors whose clothes were on fire jumped into the water too. Donata and Ricciardi tried to convince the injured to turn back and be treated at the *posto di pronto soccorso*. British soldiers also tried to block their way, but the crowd was too large. The bombs and the explosions on the ships terrified them, but there was no way they were going back to those collapsing streets.

Just as the crowd was gathering by the sea, the flames reached the *John Harvey*'s cargo hold. Seconds later, the vessel exploded and the flames rose in a frantic whorl three hundred metres high, lighting up the night. Many of those who had taken refuge by the dock were ripped from the ground, sent flying more than twenty metres and slammed into the walls of the surrounding warehouses. Others were crushed by the cars and trucks that had been sucked into the air by the force of the explosion. Those people thrown into the sea considered themselves lucky and thanked God for saving them.

Windows were blown out five hundred kilometres away. The roofs of the houses in Bari were swept away as if they were leaves on a day when there was a strong north wind. Donata and the doctor, who were still far from the water's edge, were flung along the ground and ended up several metres away, cradled in a buttress of the old city wall.

When Donata grasped that she was one of the very few survivors, she looked at Ricciardi, stretched out beside her, and wondered what would have become of her over the last few months if it hadn't been for him. He returned her gaze, and made as if to say something, but Donata reached forward and placed two fingers on his lips to silence him.

'You are the finest man I've ever known. I love you more than anyone else, after my husband and children. But we have to accept reality – we're too old and too much has happened for us to make a start now.'

They ran to the harbourside and helped pull some of the injured from the sea: even those who had no visible wounds were trembling and in a state of shock. A new explosion sent up a wall of water that dragged more people off the quay. Donata managed to grab hold of an anchor lying abandoned on the dock, but she was soaked by the wave. After rescuing the second round of survivors from the thick, oily sea, they wrapped them in blankets to get them warm. Around eleven at night they heard the siren announcing the all-clear. It seemed like a joke in poor taste: the German airplanes were retreating, but the port was still a raging inferno that showed no signs of abating.

Donata and Ricciardi could no longer see the fires. Nor did they hear the screams of those still struggling to keep afloat in that water covered in burning oil.

They tried not to think about anything at all as they tended to the wounded. Donata was so exhausted that she hadn't noticed that she was drenched in the foul-smelling liquid that floated on the surface of the water. All she could detect was an unbearable stench of garlic.

'These Americans have got a screw loose. Who sends boats filled with garlic to a country like Italy?' muttered someone near her.

At dawn the port was still ablaze, the injured were still filing into the *posto* and Donata and Ricciardi were still treating wounds. They hadn't even had time to go back to their apartment and change.

A Glow at the Window

GIOVANNA HAD OPENED the shutters and was looking out to sea from the hostel on the Lungomare in Barletta whom they had been billeted. The night was clear and filled with stars. Giovanna looked to the south, towards Bari, and thought about how anxious she was to finally get there.

She and Salvatore had walked for two days straight, hoping to leave behind Maiella the mountains and cross the Sangro-river front before dawn on the third day. They had managed to smuggle two American instructors behind enemy lines and had left them in the hands of the partisans of the Brigata Maiella. On their way back to the Allied zone they had escorted a radio operator who needed to get orders from the base in Lucera. They had spent another whole day walking from the front to the outskirts of Foggia before finally finding a truck that would take them to Barletta. The next day they would receive their orders for the following weeks. On Saturday they would take the train to Bari to meet up with Vitantonio's group. And perhaps there they would also see Donata.

'You'll have to find a new partner for your adventures.

I'm going to have to take a little time off,' Giovanna said to Salvatore, still at the window. She was exhausted. She touched her growing belly and smiled.

She missed her *zia*: she was scared about the pregnancy and needed a mother's support. Salvatore drew close and put his arm around her shoulder. For some time now he had stopped thinking of her as a girlfriend and treated her like a sister.

'Tomorrow when we get to Bari airport we'll let your brother's group know and then we'll head into the city to look for your aunt. It'll be good for you to stay with her until the birth.'

When she was once again alone at the window she thought that she was also starting to think of Salvatore as a sibling. She laughed, and from his bed he asked her, 'What's so funny?'

'Nothing, just silly stuff . . .' she answered evasively. She didn't want to get into a conversation about her feelings on how Salvatore and Vitantonio's roles in her life were switching.

Then the sea lit up. From the window Giovanna saw some sort of red glow in the distance, in the direction of Bari. Her laughter stopped cold. Gazing at the intense, deep gleam, she knew that her loved ones were in danger.

A Fear-Struck City

THE SHOCKWAVE FROM the *John Harvey* ripped the whole door off the apartment balcony on the Piazza Garibaldi, and Vitantonio immediately knew that he would have to run to find a shelter; his revenge on Franco would have to wait. He took the steps four at a time but as as flung open the door to the street he saw that the explosions were even more horrifying than he'd throught. He ran like crazy across the square and all the way to the Via Alessandro, towards the train tracks, without stopping. His plan was to get to the other side of the city, far from the port, which seemed to be the prime target of the bombing.

He got stuck around the Via Crisanzio, where buildings had collapsed and buried alive whole families who moments earlier had been sitting around the table eating, convinced that the alarm was just a drill. The rubble stretched on and on, making him think there could more than a hundred dead or one street alone. Firemen, *carabinieri*, local police and soldiers were hurrying around with lanterns. Vitantonio joined those who were scrabbling at the remains of the houses with their hands, trying desperately to find survivors among the mountains of rubble.

An hour later he gave up. They needed heavy machinery to lift the beams and joists, and bombs were still falling very close by. His suspicions that the train station was also a German target were soon confirmed: a goods wagon went flying and sent a heavy rain of olives and almonds over all the surrounding streets. Every once in a while he heard more violent explosions from the port, which must have been caused by the ammunition in the ships' holds that had been waiting to be unloaded for days.

He regretted having gone after Franco before searching for his mother. He looked around him: he knew that she must be nearby but he didn't know where to start. He decided to turn and head towards the Borgo Antico; he seemed to remember Giovanna mentioning an apartment near the cathedral and he resolved to try his luck there.

More collapsed buildings met him at the corner of the Via Piccinni and the via Andrea da Bari and where the Via Abate Gimma met the via Roberto da Bari. It was after midnight by the time he reached the cathedral and found that things were even worse there. For a while, he helped a family search for their son amid the rubble: they finally pulled him out, lifeless. In the Piazza Mercantile he joined a rescue operation to free passengers from a bus where they'd been trapped while trying to get to a shelter: they found all thirty-five of them dead too.

The city had lost all sense of time. It must have been five in the morning when he reached the Via Venezia;

he couldn't have imagined a more devastating scene. It was as if the frontline had been moved right into the heart of the city.

Again, he joined in with those scrabbling through the rubble with their bare hands until they bled, in a desperate attempt to reach a survivor. This time, their persistence was rewarded: just when they had given up hope, they found that the girl was still breathing. They dug with renewed energy, but their hope gave way to bitter disappointment when they realized one of the girl's arms was trapped under a beam that they couldn't move without making the rest of the house collapse. They were desperate. If they didn't get her out of there in a hurry, she faced certain death. A very young surgeon in the rescue crew decided to amputate her arm. Unable to watch, her parents both fainted in terror. Vitantonio was almost crying with rage, but something in the girl reminded him of Giovanna, pregnant, and as soon as she was freed he picked her up in his arms and start running towards the first-aid post he had seen on the outer dock.

At the *posto*, Dr Ricciardi was having a harder time than anyone. The wounded that were coming to him needed experienced surgeons. He was fully aware of his own limitations. He had a good clinical eye, that much was true – with just one look he could come up with a diagnosis, and the young doctors in Bari were constantly consulting him: he was a walking encyclopaedia of the even most specialized medicine. But though he was much more than just a good country doctor, he felt helpless among these sorts of casualties. Donata, on the other hand, seemed born to comfort those poor patients.

Ricciardi watched her proudly. In a strange way, he felt proud of himself as well; it had been his idea to encourage Donata to become a nurse. It had occurred to him shortly after Francesca's death, when he needed help treating a seriously ill patient who couldn't afford a professional nurse. He had watched Donata take doting care of her cousin for over a year and it was clear to him that she was the best option. He had suggested it to her as if it were the most natural thing in the world and she had accepted as if she had been waiting for the opportunity all her life. That job led to others: tending to the sick, making house calls, giving vaccinations and, when there was an emergency at a birth, she also acted as midwife. Soon the doctor's patients and the peasants who received her help started to refer to her as their 'guardian angel'. It was the same nickname that, years later, the Spanish Republicans would give Giovanna when she did all she could to console those poor refugees who had lost everything except their dignity fleeing the Civil War.

Dr Ricciardi looked up again at Donata and thanked a God he couldn't bring himself to believe in, for bringing her to him. Now he only feared losing her. She saw him looking at her and she shifted her gaze, uneasy, just as a group of men and women came in shouting, carrying a wounded survivor. Donata was the first to react and she hurried over to them. When she got close she almost fainted: she had just recognized Vitantonio in the middle of the group, with a girl in his arms.

For a second Donata felt she might burst with joy in the midst of such pain. Every night she fell asleep dreaming of their reunion; now she couldn't believe that he was there in front of her. She shrieked with joy, 'Vitantonio!'

He was focused on the little girl and hadn't seen her yet. But he recognized his mother's voice just as he was looking up to see who would take care of the girl.

'Mama!' he shouted, with the same joy.

Donata drank him in with her eyes. She wanted to hug him. She wanted to touch him. She wanted to ask him a thousand questions. She wanted to know all about those last few weeks on the frontline. She needed to hear him explain how he had stood up to death and won. She needed to convince herself that her son was going to survive. She also wanted to ask about Giovanna. But she allowed herself only a second of gazing at her son. A few hours earlier she would have abandoned everything to be with him and talk. But tonight was different. Just seeing him alive was a gift.

She swallowed hard and asked, 'What happened to her?' Noticing the makeshift bandage around the stump of the girl's arm, she commented, 'It looks like someone did a good job in very tricky circumstances.'

While her mind was filling with more questions, Donata had already extended her arms to take the girl. Mother and son looked at each other for one more second and in that look said everything they had wanted to express since the last time they'd spoken, in Roosevelt's but on the road to Matera. Then she disappeared into the *posto* with the girl and Vitantonio dropped to the ground, exhausted, thanking God. He now felt that everything he'd been through in the Maiella mountains didn't matter any more: not the cold, not the pain, not the fear. Not even the nightmares he'd had could compare to the hell he had seen that night on the bombed streets of Bari.

Occasionally, his mother and Ricciardi would look up and take comfort in Vitantonio's presence at the door to the *posto*. They went out to find him a couple of hours later, when it finally started to get light. At the other end of the harbour, the sun must have risen a while ago, but the smoke from the ships that were still burning obsevred the sky in the old part of the city.

'You want to go up to the apartment to have a sleep and wait for me to finish my work here?' his mother asked him.

'There could still be people buried under the rubble,' answered Vitantonio. 'I have to go back to the area around the cathedral.'

When the day dawned fully, all three of them continued working despite the lack of resources in the *posto*. They had also helped set up improvised clinics in a few churches. Donata, Ricciardi and Vitantonio worked through the afternoon. Around six they took a break; they'd been working for almost twenty-four hours straight. At that point, Bari was still in the grip of panic. The train station was overrun by those fleeing the city: the ones who couldn't get on to the express train travelling directly to Foggia were trying to find space on the *trenino* on the Bari to Barletta coastal line.

Finally, they went up to Donata's apartment, which miraculously stood intact amid the collapsed buildings on the Strada Santa Chiara. For the first time in almost five months, mother and son were alone together, but they didn't talk about the partisans or the missions on the other side of the front. They sat at one corner of the table and Vitantonio explained, through tears, everything he had seen that night on the streets of Bari. Donata watched him as he spoke and silently rejoiced: for her, every day that Vitantonio survived was a priceless victory.

The Secret of Bitonto

AT TEN IN the evening, Donata went back to work at the *posto*. A little while later, close to midnight, Vitantonio reached the barracks that the Englishman had managed to commandeer near the airport some way from town, and everyone piled on him. They wanted to know first-hand what had happened the centre of in Bari over the last twenty-four hours. Vitantonio went straight to his corner and laid down on a blanket that served as his bed. He was dead tired and in no mood for conversation. He summed it up as best he could: 'They pounded us. Bari is a hellhole.'

He turned his back and went to sleep.

When he woke up he saw that Roosevelt was watching him. The shepherd from Murgia was sitting on the floor, his back against the wall of the barracks. From the other room he could hear Captain Clark and Lieutenant Donovan shouting at each other in English. The American seemed nervous, the Englishman angry. Roosevelt put a finger to his lips and Vitantonio crept over to him.

'What are they saying?' he whispered, unable to follow the argument.

'The American just came back from a secret meeting in

Bitonto. All the top brass in the Allied forces in southern Italy were there. It seems the bombing blew up an American ship loaded with two thousand mustard-gas bombs: the *John Harvey*. The water in the port is filled with it and the smoke has spread through the city. In the next few days hundreds more people will die.'

'My mother's there! I have to go back to Bari!' he said, jumping up and starting to head into the other room.

Roosevelt stopped him. 'That's not all. The Americans have decided not to say anything, not to the local authorities and not even to the Allied commanders in the area. They don't want the Germans to find out that they've been stockpiling chemical weapons in Europe.'

Vitantonio stormed next door, walked straight over to Clark and threatened him with his fist. He had never liked him and he'd never understood why Donovan's group was helping a chemical weapons expert. Now he had the proof that it had all been a huge mistake.

'How can you keep this a secret? Are you crazy?'

Clark looked at Vitantonio in surprise and then, with growing horror in his expression, he turned to the Englishman, as if demanding an explanation. From day one he'd assumed that none of the Italians understood English: no one had told him Roosevelt's background. Roosevelt didn't like the American either and had never revealed his past. The day the American had joined them, he'd been excited, especially when he found out clark had been born in Italian Harlem. But as he was going over to give him a hug him he overheard that he had grown up on a block of Pleasant Avenue near 118th Street and he stopped cold. That had been the first street Roosevelt had lived on in New York and they had kicked him out before he'd found work, breaking with their sacred duty to protect new arrivals: nothing good could come from someone raised on Pleasant and 118th.

Clark's panicked eyes travelled between Donovan and Vitantonio, waiting for one of them to speak. He needed to hear them say that they understood the seriousness of the situation and the need for discretion. But neither of them said a word.

'The Germans can't know that we have chemical weapons in Europe. It's a war secret. If you open your mouths, you'll pay with your lives!' he threatened, overcome by panic.

'You bastard!' shouted Vitantonio before punching him in the face and sending him reeling to the floor.

'You don't understand! The future of the war depends on the Germans not knowing our movements,' shouted Clark, lying prone.

'*You* are the one who doesn't understand! Bari is filled with people, just like you and me. I just came from there and I saw *hundreds* of dead and wounded. If we don't warn them soon thousands more will die. My mother is there—'

'I won't let you leave. I haven't shot you yet because you saved my life once; but now we're even. If you move, you're a dead man.'

Clark was looking up at him with hatred in his face.

He had pulled out his revolver and was pointing it at him. He got to his feet and walked over to him. 'You're under arrest.'

'Who's arresting me? *You?* On what authority?'

'In the name of the US army. Move a muscle and I won't hesitate to pull the trigger. Your life doesn't mean shit to me and I couldn't care less about the people in Bari either. This is a war: sometimes you have to sacrifice lives to save many more.'

Primo Carnera had entered the barracks and was watching the conflict, standing disconcerted beside the Englishman. He saw Roosevelt creeping cautiously behind Clark. Vitantonio had also seen him come in and was amazed by how stealthily he moved.

When the American sensed that Roosevelt was behind him, he turned round. Vitantonio took advantage of the distraction, knocking the revolver from the captain's hand just as he pressed the trigger: the bullet lodged in the ceiling. As Clark took aim for a second shot, Roosevelt pounced on him. A shot rang out and the revolver fell to the floor. Primo Carnera kicked it aside. When Roosevelt staggered back from the American, his legs buckled under him. From his left side, just under his shoulder, blood was pouring. Vitantonio caught him as he collapsed and lowered him gently to the floor. Roosevelt was losing a lot of blood and Vitantonio desperately tried to stem the flow by pressing a cloth over the wound.

The American went over to the Englishman and begged, 'I know you're with the partisans, but you're a British officer and you know that it is vital this information doesn't spread to Bari. You have to help me arrest him.'

'Vitantonio is right: you are a bastard!' the Englishman answered. And he punched him in the stomach so hard his knees gave out. 'You're the one who is going to be locked in the barracks,' he added, 'at least until we patch up Roosevelt and Vitantonio has set off for Bari. Then we'll see what we do with you. Anyway, you're the one who's committed treason by revealing secrets from the Bitonto meeting. If you'd like, we can discuss it with your superior officers . . .'

Roosevelt's bleeding from the shoulder still hadn't slowed. Vitantonio wailed, 'Why did you get involved? This was my fight!'

'When he invoked the authority of the US army I had to step in. We had to fight it out between Americans.' Roosevelt turned towards Clark and spat. '*Fuck you!*' he shouted, in his best New York accent.

Half an hour later they had bundled Roosevelt and Vitantonio into a military ambulance headed for the Policlinico in Bari. Just as the ambulance was about to leave, Giovanna and Salvatore arrived from Barletta. When they saw all the blood on the floor, the Englishman reassured them, 'Roosevelt's lost a lot of blood, but he's not in danger: the doctor said that the bullet has shattered his shoulder.'

Without saying a word, Giovanna jumped in the ambulance.

The Stench of Garlic

ONLY TWENTY-FOUR HOURS after the bombing, on the night of 3 December, some of the survivors Donata and Ricciardi had rescued from the water started returning to the first-aid post. They were coming in with burns all over their bodies, with surprisingly low blood pressure and eyes so swollen they thought they were going blind. The queues forming at the door to the *posto* particularly disconcerted the doctors. At midnight the British army doctor who ran the centre called Ricciardi over to ask for his opinion.

'I don't know what to say. Some patients started having problems this morning: itchy, watering eyes, aversion to light . . . It didn't seem serious and at first I thought it was from the oil that had got into their eyes,' Ricciardi tried to update him quickly. 'This afternoon things have got more complicated: they're having trouble breathing, their lungs are burning, their blood pressure has dropped even further but their hearts are racing.'

'That doesn't make sense . . .'

'And that's not all: they're listless and most of them have burns all over their bodies; but none complain of chest pain, or perforated eardrums, or any other symptoms that would be normal if they had blast injuries. I've tried injecting them with stimulants, but they haven't had any effect. Not even morphine! If we had blood I would try giving them transfusions. I don't know what else to do, none of this is described in the medical literature I'm familiar with.'

While Ricciardi confessed his perplexity to the head doctor, Donata lay down on one of the camp beds that had been set up for the medical personnel. Doctor's orders. So wrapped up had she been in tending to all the patients, she hadn't realized that she had burns on her arms and face as well. She'd only noticed that her eyes were stinging, that she kept coughing and she felt a bit tired. Attributing it to the over-exertion of the last two days, she dropped down on to the bed and fell asleep.

In the *posto*, that night, with every passing hour the situation became increasingly alarming: those arriving with burns all over their body swore they hadn't been in contact with the flames. And those with breathing problems hadn't even fallen into the water: they had just breathed in the smoke of the fires from the port, which had lingered for hours over the city, especially in the Borgo Antico. Many of the people queuing for the *posto* hadn't been affected by the bombing at all and yet suddenly they'd started to feel ill. Ricciardi didn't know that at the military hospitals they were just as puzzled, and that they'd already tried blood transfusions. To no avail.

By midmorning on Saturday 4 December, when Vitantonio and Giovanna showed up at the Policlinico to tell the staff that they were dealing with mustard gas, they saw that the doctors had already begun to suspect there was a chemical agent behind their patients' inexplicable symptoms. They told them everything they knew about the *John Harvey*'s secret cargo, but the military doctors didn't like hearing that the source of the mustard gas was not the German Junkers bombers but an American ship, and they refused to listen. Their commanders had assured them that 'the Allied forces in Europe don't have chemical weapons', and the army doctors were unwilling to contradict the High Command's official version.

Giovanna and Vitantonio next tried to convince the local Italian authorities, but they wouldn't listen either: according to the official version the toxic effects were attributable to the fuel that the oil tanker and the bombed ships had leaked into the sea. The pair were worried, but they didn't give up. By midday they were insisting that they wanted to speak with the highest officials of the Secondo Distretto Sanitario, who coordinated all the general hospitals under Allied command; but they refused to see them and threatened to report them for unjustified alarmism.

Meanwhile, in the *posto*, Ricciardi was taking Donata's pulse and saw that her symptoms were developing much like the other patients'. Her eyes were still swollen and there was no explanation for the anomalous behaviour of her pulse and blood pressure: something was eluding him and he was beginning to panic.

Vitantonio and Giovanna went back to the Policlinico. At the entrance, they passed a captain who was on his way out. He was one of the doctors who had listened more attentively to their message. His name was Denfeld.

'It seems clear that we're facing toxic gas poisoning,' he accepted. 'I'm going down to the port. If you are right and this is mustard gas, there must be some kind of evidence there.'

But once they got inside the hospital, they were asked to leave. They went away angry and disheartened: they had information that could save hundreds of lives, but for the military commanders obedience to authority was more important than truth. Roosevelt had almost lost his life for nothing!

By mid-afternoon they gave up and headed to the *posto di pronto soccorso*. When they entered it they looked around for Donata but couldn't spot her. Instead, they went over to Ricciardi who was listening to a patient's chest. When the doctor recognized them, he hugged Giovanna, whom he hadn't seen in weeks, and explained to Vitantonio where his mother was.

'I made Donata lie down. She's been working too hard and she needs some rest. She's over there,' he told them, pointing to a partition at the back of the room.

Then he took Vitantonio by the arm and pulled him aside. 'Since you left earlier, she's been exhibiting very strange vital signs and her body is covered in burns. I'm really concerned: it's the same symptoms that many of the people who were rescued from the water are showing. We can't find any rational explanation.'

'It's the gas!' shouted Vitantonio.

'*Gas?* What gas? What are you talking about?'

'Mustard gas. In the port there was an American ship loaded with eighty tons of mustard gas bombs: the *John Harvey*.'

'No one's told us anything about any gas—'

'And they aren't going to. They want to keep it secret. I've spoken with the Allied doctors and the local authorities, but they swear there are no chemical weapons in Italy and that any strange reactions were just caused by people breathing in the fumes from the oil spilled into the sea by the bombed tanker. We went by the Policlinico and they threw us out, but some of the doctors there have got wind of this and are looking into it, thank God—'

'We're talking about hundreds, perhaps *thousands*, of people! They can't be so immoral! If there really was something toxic in the water, all the blankets and heat that we are applying to the survivors are only furthering their inhalation of the gas. We need to know for sure and alter our treatments—'

'There's no doubt that there was mustard gas in the water at the port and that the smoke has spread through the city. Yesterday, there was a confidential meeting of the Allied High Command at Bitonto, and they agreed to keep it under wraps. General Eisenhower himself has been informed of the situation. I got this straight from the mouth of an American captain who was at the meeting.'

'But this is inhuman . . . You can't hide something like that!'

'For them it's the lesser of two evils: second-class victims are to be sacrificed in order to keep the Germans in the dark. These bastards don't have to answer to anyone, they just make the excuse that the most important thing is the final victory.'

When Vitantonio approached Donata's bed, she had just woken up and flung her arms around Giovanna's neck. They hadn't seen each other since late September. Then she took both of their hands in hers.

'Take me home,' she asked. 'Don't worry about me, I'm fine,' she added to Ricciardi, who made to protest. 'I'll be much better tomorrow. Right now I want to be at home with my children.'

Ricciardi gave in: in any case that night they had to dismantle the *posto di pronto soccorso* and move the patients to the hospitals. More to the point, he still hadn't worked out how to treat Donata's symptoms and he figured he could keep monitoring her just as well in her bed at home as in a less comfortable one at the Policlinico.

They took her up to the apartment. Giovanna gently washed her and changed her clothes, which still smelled of gas.

'You smell like garlic,' said Giovanna with a sad smile.

They laid her down on the bed and the doctor bathed her eyes with a mild salt solution. Then he covered them with gauze to protect them from the light. Now that he knew about the gas, Ricciardi was feeling increasingly worried and he decided to consult at once with his colleagues at the Policlinico. By the time he said goodbye, Donata had gone back to sleep.

'Make sure she doesn't move. I'll be back at dawn.'

At midnight Donata woke up. Despite her burns, she got out of bed all on her own and began gingerly searching through the wardrobe for something. When she limped into the dining room she was carrying two biscuit tins and she put them down on the table.

'These are my keepsakes, and Francesca's. And also the things both your fathers had on them when they died in the Great War; in Vito Oronzo's box there are also some things that belonged to his brothers, little Ignazio and poor Domenico, who was such a good sort. Their captain had Skinny bring it all from the front and we saved it for when you grew up. I've been afraid until now to revisit the past . . . but maybe the time has come.'

She sank into in a chair. She was exhausted and was having trouble speaking. She took the box for, Giovanna and opened it. She had removed the gauze, but her eyes were almost swollen shut and she could no longer see clearly: everything in the tin fell to the floor. Vitantonio and Giovanna looked at each with alarm. Donata made a desperate face, crouched down on the floor to try to pick everything up and started feeling around for the various items. On top of the letters and photos of Antonio Convertini there was a copy of *Little Red Riding Hood*.

'Where did that come from?' asked Giovanna,

surprised to see the book that she had read a million times as a girl. 'I haven't seen it for ages.'

'I found it one day when I was cleaning the house, not long after you left for Spain. I thought you might like to see it again, so I saved it along with your mother's things.'

Giovanna turned to the pages in the middle and opened the pop-up centrefold of the cabin, the forest and all the characters; in the foreground with their backs facing the reader, as if they were the audience, there was a row of rabbits with very long ears looking at the cabin. Then she turned to the first page and started reading: '"*Among the thick trees of a very green forest stood hidden a woodcutter's cabin. He loved his wife, his daughter and his work above all other things. Every day a red angel came out of the cabin, leaping and singing like the birds of the forest who went with her to deliver a basket of food to her sick grandmother, who lived on the other side of the forest: it was Little Red Riding Hood . . .*"'

'When I was little I often dreamt that I was Little Red Riding Hood and that you were both the mother and the father,' she said to her *zia*, looking at her tenderly. '*Nonna* was the sick grandmother . . . and stupid Franco was the ridiculous wolf who always bungled everything.'

'And wasn't I in the story . . . ?' Vitantonio laughed.

'You were the hunter who saved us!'

Suddenly, Donata began to shake violently and they tried to take her back to bed.

She refused. 'I want to spend the night here, with you two.'

More burns and blisters had come out on her legs and neck. She was breathing more and more rapidly, but it was increasingly shallow. Blood began to drip from her nose. Her eyes were now completely shut and hurt more and more. She stretched out on the floor, leaning against the wall, and took Giovanna's hand. Vitantonio placed a pillow at her back. Eventually, she drifted off to sleep.

They looked at each other, deathly afraid.

'She's suffering so much!' said Giovanna through her tears.

All night long, they kept watch over Donata, attentive to any slight movement that might help them assess her condition. In the end, Giovanna fell asleep too. She dreamt that she was Little Red Riding Hood, but now the forest was filled with big, bad wolves and they weren't as clumsy as little Franco: now, the wolves wore brown- and blackshirts and carried red flags with swastikas on them. Vitantonio watched her, his heart bursting.

As his mother woke up, he placed a hand on her shoulder. She was racked with pain. Shaking and sweating, she was overcome with a terrible thirst. Vitantonio got her some water but after she drank it she looked even paler. He took her pulse: irregular. Her breathing was now so urgent, as if she was desperate to take in even the smallest breath.

Vitantonio studied carefully the sleeping Giovanna's

belly, which was beginning to look clearly pregnant. Then his gaze travelled to the increasingly livid burns covering his mother's body. He had a bad feeling: one life was about to start, but, unexpectedly, another life was slipping away from them.

The Heart of a Palmisano

'LET ME TOUCH you,' his mother said hoarsely. And she ran the fingers of her right hand over Vitantonio's profile.

Her hand was trembling. She knew that her strength was leaving her, but she was still able to make out his eyes and his lips. She stroked them. Then she ran her fingertips over his cheeks and down to his left shoulder blade: she was looking for his birthmark. When she felt the Palmisano heart beneath her fingers she traced it with a smile on her lips.

It was the last smile her son would ever see from her.

'The day he declared his love for me, he took my hand and ran it gently over the outline of the red mark and said, very seriously, "Now my heart is yours." And I knew that Vito Oronzo Palmisano was my man.'

Donata made a last effort to bring her lips to the birthmark and kiss it. Then she still found a thin whisp of voice, almost inaudible amid her desperate, rasping attempts at breathing. Vitantonio brought his ear to her lips.

'Take care of Ggiuànnin: as a woman or as a sister! But don't let anything happen to her! I promised her mother.'

Her eyes gleamed as she remembered Francesca. 'If we have a boy and a girl, we can marry them,' she'd said when she found out they were both pregnant.

Donata slowly moved her head back to look at Vitantonio one last time. Her eyes were so swollen that she couldn't open them at all now. She placed her hands on his face again.

'We haven't had an easy time of it, my son,' she said in a choked voice. 'But we are beating fate. Even if I could go back, I wouldn't change a thing.'

Those were her final words. Her head fell on to the heart-shaped birthmark and Vitantonio knew that he had lost her.

The Biscuit Tin

GIOVANNA AND VITANTONIO had always known they were different from other children: their father had died in the war before they were born and they were only five years old when they'd had to bury Francesca, the first of the two women they shared as mothers. Maybe that was why, since they were little, they'd always had a natural instinct that made them stronger than others: they didn't know where that strength came from, but it had allowed them to overcome their misfortunes with grace. But the death of their *zia* was different. They weren't prepared for it: they had thought they were the ones taking risks in this war, especially when they were smuggled behind enemy lines on sabotage missions; Donata was working in a hospital as a nurse, she should have been out of danger. For the second time, they lived through a mother's death. It was more than they could bear.

When he felt his mother lying motionless on his chest, Vitantonio let out an angry cry, just like the one she'd given at Roosevelt's but on the day he'd announced he was going to war. The cry woke Giovanna up with a start, and she woke to learn that Donata was gone. She and Vitantonio embraced each other and *Zia*, in their own personal wake.

They hadn't said a word for some time. Giovanna just sobbed and, every once in a while, moaned, '*Zia!*'

Vitantonio was curled up like a helpless child.

Earlier that night they might have wished her a speedy death to spare her such suffering; now they would have given anything to revive her for a moment and give her one last kiss. For the next two hours time stopped. Or maybe it was longer, because, so overwhelmed with tolling for the dead, the Bari church bells had stopped ringing the hours, making it hard to measure the passage of time. The candle that lit up the room had burned down and they were left in the dark. They remained motionless, keeping watch over Donata's lifeless body. When the morning came, Vitantonio rested his mother's head on Giovanna's lap and lit another candle.

Suddenly, the freezing north wind blew in through the windows shattered in the air raid, and light filtered through the room, making Donata's biscuits tins glimmer. The gleam caught Vitantonio's eye. He had sat down at the table without even realizing it. He pulled the lid off the tin: there were letters, medals, photos, newspaper clippings, ID cards and other kinds of documents. There was also the wallet that his father had on him, on the last day of the war when he was killed by an Austrian sniper.

He took everything out and picked up the wallet; it was exactly as Skinny had handed it over on that day when he brought Vito Oronzo Palmisano and Antonio Convertini's personal effects over to the Widows' House. That wallet was the closest Vitantonio had ever come to touching something of his father's and he opened it carefully. The first thing he saw was a photo of his mother, very young, wearing the calm gaze that had always made him feel at peace. As a boy he had taken refuge in those brown eyes and he imagined his father must have, as well. He imagined Vito Oronzo in a trench at the front, kissing that photo every night and letting her gaze lull him peacefully to sleep.

The wallet also contained some of his father's personal documents, including the permission for leave from 14 to 26 October 1918, and the last letter that Donata had written him, the very day after saying goodbye at the Bellorotondo station. In fact, she had put it in the post while his father was still on his way back from leave, headed towards Vittorio Veneto, where he would meet up with his company, already engaged in the war's last offensive.

Vito Oronzo Palmisano
94° Reggimento Fanteria
Bellorotondo,

Friday 25 October 1918

My love,

I am dictating this letter to Francesca, because this way I won't be so embarrassed as when I dictate them to the local scribe and I'll be able to tell you more things, our things.

Yesterday – Thursday – when I came home I could still smell you and I missed you more than I ever have before. Since you've been gone, every time I look at the kitchen table I tingle all over and I yearn for you. Oh, how I wish I could cover you in kisses and caress the red heart you have engraved on your collarbone. Is that heart really all just for me? I wear mine on the inside, but it too beats like mad for you.

How are things at the front? Do you still believe this damn war is coming to an end? Do you promise you'll be home for Christmas? I like imagining that we'll go to the Immacolata together for the next Midnight Mass, walking into the church arm in arm and sitting in the front pew, like the landowners. After almost four years of war you've earned the right to have everyone see you seated up front, with your head held high. Father Constanzo, the new priest, might even say a few words of welcome especially for you.

Next week we'll harvest all the olives. Today we gathered up the last two rows of rosse olives and next week I plan on finishing all the ñastre behind the house. Francesca, my sister-in-law Concetta, and my cousin Bruna, plus Vicino's wife, all help me. Maybe you'll be back in time to help me spread the olives out on the table to choose the best ones, and maybe afterwards I'll let you lay me out on it and undo the buttons on my blouse, one by one.

Take care, I need you home safe and sound. Honestly, I don't know what I'd do without you. I'd die.

Write and tell me about everything you're doing and everything you're thinking. I send you a thousand kisses and a very big hug. I love you like mad.

Your Donata

P. S.: Francesca is teaching me how to read and write. She says that soon I'll be able to do it all on my own.

Another big kiss.
Donata

Vitantonio felt a knot in his stomach and he started to cry quietly. He picked up two bunches of letters, which were tied delicately with a white ribbon, and held them in his hands for a while: they were the other letters that his parents had written while Vito Oronzo Palmisano was at the front. There were about thirty in each bundle: they had written to each other regularly for three years, at least once a month. He put the letters to one side, for later, and started to sort through his mother's other small treasures, one by one.

He pulled a gold locket, in the shape of a heart, out by its chain. He opened it and found the faces of his mother and father and remembered that she had worn it at every special family occasion when he was a boy. It saddened him to recall that it had now been three and a half years since he'd left Bellorotondo and they hadn't had a chance in all that time to celebrate anything. He pulled out two gold earrings with a pearl that *Nonna* had given his mother when she turned forty and he laughed because Donata had thought they were too nice and was embarrassed to wear them.

Then he started to leaf through more keepsakes of his father's: first of all, his membership card to the Confederazione Generale del Lavoro, which didn't surprise him because skinny had already told him about that at the factory that day when he had asked about his father, when he still believed he was Antonio Convertini's son. He found another card and discovered – and this one was a surprise – that his father had been a member of the Partito Socialista; that explained some things that years earlier had baffled him.

In the pile there was an official document that was folded more carefully than the others and when he opened it up he found that it was the death notice for his father; the document was just as the lieutenant colonel sent from the 94° Reggimento Fanteria had given it to the mayor of Bellorotondo, so he could officially inform the family of the last Palmisano's death. Only twenty-five years had passed and Europe was again experiencing the savagery of war: Vitantonio thought that if his father hadn't died on that last day of the Great War they might have called him up again and forced him to return to the front.

He was still thinking about that when he realized he had a newspaper clipping in his hands, underlined in pencil. It was covered in enthusiastic annotations, which must have been by his mother because they were in the earnest handwriting of someone who had learned to write as an adult. He saw that it was a clipping from *Il Seme*, the socialist newspaper of Bellorotondo, from September 1914, and he started to read the article, by a certain Giovanni Gianfrate.

'O mothers of Italy!

O mothers of Italy, these words go out to you!

They're inebriating your sons with tobacco, champagne and rhetoric and they're leading them to war. Rush to help them, O mothers!

They snatch them from your breasts and send them far away, to fields ravaged by shrapnel and fire. Mothers of Italy, hold them close!

Hundreds, thousands, have been sent to the slaughter. They've robbed us of our sons, they've robbed us of our husbands. You nursed them to live, not to die . . . Mothers of Italy, stand up against this!

Your sons are good and they vilify them; they are healthy and handsome and they deform them; they are docile and they teach them to kill . . .'

Donata had traced a thick line under a particularly fierce section of the journalist's polemic but it looked like it had already been underlined earlier, perhaps by Vito Oronzo himself. On one side of the page his mother had written '*Bravissimo!!!*' with three energetic exclamation marks and beneath that a small note with a very large question mark: 'Read to Vitantonio?' He felt his stomach contract again and he couldn't continue reading.

My God, how his mother must have suffered, to have held on to those inflammatory words against the war as if they were a treasure! If she had given them to him to read, would they have changed his decision? He supposed not, but they would have certainly made his decision to take up arms and fight more painful. The words from *Il Seme* were as filled with passion as they were with common sense: that had been proven right by those last few months of war. But that was precisely why they now had to fight and defeat the Nazis and the fascists. He put those thoughts aside, wiped his eyes and continued reading.

In the tin there were two more front pages from *Il Seme*, which were folded very neatly. One was a copy of the Italian Socialist Party manifesto defending Italy's neutrality in the European conflict. The other opened with another anti-war editorial: '*Abbasso la guerra!*' He was surprised that his mother had never told him about his father's political involvement. Not even in these last few years. Her attempts to protect him from war had led her to try to hide all traces of it. And she had been particularly careful to distance him from any sort of political commitment.

He put the clippings back in the biscuit tin and grabbed a pile of photos. In the first one he saw his father in profile, dressed in army garb, with his mother at his side, and bringing his lips to her cheek, about to kiss her. She was facing the camera and looking at him mischievously out of the corner of her eye. They were both laughing and looked happy, convinced that life promised them wonderful things and that nothing bad could happen. It must have been taken during that leave in the autumn of 1918. When he brought it close to the candle's flame, he was shocked at how much he resembled his father; they had the same face, the same long neck and especially the same broad shoulders. He looked in the mirror over the sideboard and smiled. He pulled out a second photo. In front of an exotic backdrop of Dutch windmills painted by some keen artist, his parents appeared arm in arm, next to Antonio and Francesca, Convertini and he was even more shocked: it was hard to believe that the young woman in the photo wasn't Giovanna. My God, that long black hair, that brown skin and those green eyes on Francesca were the same ones that hypnotized him when he looked at Giovanna. Both mother and daughter had such a fierce, wild beauty that sometimes it hurt to look at them. But their laughter, like Francesca's in the photo, was so good-natured that it softened them.

He put the photos to one side and picked up the letters again. Untying a ribbon, he read them all one by one, hoping to find something in them that helped him imagine what his parents were like and what they talked about in the little time they were able to spend together. But the letters were nearly all the same, filled with repetitive declarations of love in the same conventional formulas, and he remembered that they'd both had to use a scribe, who always wrote the same banalities.

When he was just about to put the letters back into the tin, he saw that there was one by itself, in a different hand. It had been written that very year, just a month earlier.

Bari, 2 November 1943

Dear Donata,

The day when we will have to say goodbye for ever is rapidly approaching and I wanted to write to you a few words of acknowledgement and respect. These last few weeks at the hospital have confirmed what I already knew, that you have a special gift for comforting people. Have you suffered so much that you can recognize pain at first glance? Have you been so afraid that you are able to identify it in others, before they even ask for help? Have you sacrificed so much that you don't mind sharing the little you have left? The more I see you devote yourself to comforting others, the closer I feel to you and the more I curse this country that has failed either to make the most of its finest sons and daughters, or to grant them any opportunities.

We are living through terrible times, in which only your company at work has kept me going and helped me to keep looking towards the future. It's so painful to see men come from the front with wounds that will never heal completely. The terror etched into their faces! How they suffer, even in their dreams! And yet you are able to calm them with loving words from your heart, you care for them just as you would for Vitantonio and Giovanna, if they were the ones who had been wounded.

I have always admired your courage, but now I know that over time my admiration has turned to love. I would have done anything to make up for everything that has happened to you, to give you back a little bit of what you've given others. Perhaps far from this thankless land we could have built a paradise for our old age. But now that you have recovered your son, you'll never be able to leave him again. I am sorry to lose you, but I'm happy to see you near Vitantonio and Giovanna, finally without secrets or lies. I have always considered them a little bit mine too, since that night you and Francesca involved me in your secret. Watching them grow up, I've always felt proud of them and had the opportunity to see how valuable your sacrifice was.

When this horrible nightmare ends I will go far, far away. They say that miracles happen in the

Promised Land. You know that I don't
believe in gods and miracles, but I can't
help but acknowledge the miracle of a town
that history has treated with such cruelty but
that remains standing despite it all. You decided
long ago that the Palmisanos were your only
homeland. Now I know that the Jewish people
are my family.

I will always carry you in my heart. With
deepest affection,

Gabriele Ricciardi

Vitantonio heard Giovanna stirring awake again. He tied up all the papers and things he hadn't looked at yet and put the tin in the sideboard. Lying down by her side, he put his arm around her and leaned back against the wall. He looked out towards the balcony: the dawn was just breaking and he was surprised by the calm of the freezing December night. The only reminder of the tragedy was the stench of burning still emanating from the port. Vitantonio looked at Donata's lifeless body and it all seemed unreal. He placed a pillow at Giovanna's back and put his other hand on her belly. Suddenly he noticed that he was still holding Dr Ricciardi's letter and he said, 'You have to read this. It's from Ricciardi to my mother.'

His revelation didn't achieve the desired effect. Her expression was amused and all she said was, 'There is nothing in that letter that I haven't read a thousand times in Ricciardi's eyes. I've seen the love in his gaze, all these years, whenever he looked at her.'

She leaned forward and kissed her *zia*'s forehead and cried.

The Ducks in the Pond

THEY WERE STARTLED by a knock at the door. They looked at each other, wondering who it could be that early and Vitantonio shouted, 'Ricciardi!'

They'd forgotten about him. The doctor had spent the night at the Policlinico, on duty with patients who were getting sicker by the hour, with no apparent cause. Opening the door, Vitantonio was hit by another wave of grief: the white-haired man waiting in the doorway looked defeated. Dr Gabriele Ricciardi had aged all of a sudden; he was thinner than ever, he hadn't shaved in days, he had dark circles under his eyes and his clothing still smelled of mustard gas. It was the first time Vitantonio had noticed the passing of time in his doctor's exhausted face. Ever since he was a boy, Vitantonio had thought that Ricciardi, with his neatly trimmed crop of white hair moustache, had an elegant, mature air. And over the years the doctor maintained his tidy, ageless appearance. He was quick to laugh, passionate, upstanding, educated, polite; 'charming' was the word his mother always used. Now he seemed shrunken and ill.

'How is she?' Ricciardi asked as soon as he walked in, hoping to find Donata feeling better.

Vitantonio pushed open the door to the dining room and moved aside. The doctor saw Giovanna stretched out on the floor, crying and hugging Donata, and he understood that he was too late. A grimace of pain contorted his face and his legs wobbled. Stepping forward, Vitantonio held the doctor to stop him collapsing. Ricciardi leaned one arm against the door and tried to stand up straight, but he seemed disoriented, as if he were hesitating between entering the room or leaving it. Vitantonio turned his back to him: he had just read his love letter and felt he had violated his privacy quite enough for one day.

Giovanna got up and hugged the doctor. He had often been like a father to her and she'd always noticed how happy her *zia* was when he was around the house. She and Vitantonio exchanged a look, discreetly communicating they should leave the doctor alone with Donata's body. When they left, the doctor dropped to Donata's side and broke down in sobs. He still had so many things to tell her, and he began speaking to her lifeless corpse.

After leaving him there alone for more than an hour, they finally went back in to the dining room. Ricciardi's eyes were red and he was wiping his face on his sleeve. He looked up from the floor and addressed Vitantonio. 'She wanted to trick fate the day she handed you over to Francesca, but the gods made her pay dearly for it. Every time she thought happiness was with in reach, life played another trick on her. But she never gave up. I don't know where she got the strength to start again and I don't know how I will do it now. I don't know if it's worth fighting on without her.'

'The war will go on for much longer than we thought and in the end we'll all pay a much higher price,' agreed Vitantonio. 'I turned my back on my family to defend freedom beside the Allies and fate has repaid me with the worst betrayal: American bombs have robbed me of my mother, just when I had just found her again. But we can't stop fighting. You said it yourself, she never would have given up.'

'I don't know what more could happen to us,' said Giovanna. She was staring down at the floor, aware that she wasn't really asking a question she expected Ricciardi to answer.

'If God were just, nothing more could possibly happen to us,' declared the doctor. 'Or to this city. No one can pay such a high price or be so unfairly punished. The authorities refuse to reveal the number of dead to cover up the gas disaster, but today they made an official tally of the damage to materiel and admitted that the bombing was the worse catastrophe suffered by the Allied troops since Pearl Harbor: the German planes sunk seventeen of the thirty-one ships that were in the Bari port that night. Thirty-one easy targets in an enclosed area, caged like helpless animals, because now we know that the radars that should have alerted the anti-aircraft defences were out of order. When they make public the final death toll we'll see the full extent of this brutal attack—'

'One second, say that again,' said Vitantonio, cutting him off. His face was tense and his eyes were wide.

'Say what again?'

'That part about the boats in the port being like helpless animals. How many did you say there were?'

'Thirty-one . . .' repeated the doctor, not understanding why that particular figure was of interest.

'*Thirty-one ducks in the pond*: they're the thirty-one ships in the port! The bastard! And *the sun has set on Bari* must have referred to the sabotaged radars . . .'

'What's going on?' Giovanna and the doctor asked at the same time. 'What are you talking about?'

He didn't answer. He was staring at a bundle of photos he must have forgotten to put back in to his mother's tin. The first rays of sun streaming through the broken window fell on the image of a nude girl and he went over to look at it. She had the eyes of an angel and a curvaceous body that would have driven the devil himself mad. He looked at her curiously, unaware that he had just met Domenico Palmisano's girlfriend. When he picked up the card, his smile froze: beneath it was a photo of him and Franco in the palazzo garden, on the day of his confirmation. His cousin was sitting on the bench with his legs dangling, wearing socks up to his knees and dark, very shiny patent-leather shoes; Vitantonio saw himself, standing beside the bench in his solemn confirmation outfit. Franco was looking at him and saying something.

Vitantonio felt rage burn his throat and redden his cheeks. He tore up the photo and went over to

Giovanna. He looked her in the eyes and implored her, 'You have to take my mother's body to Bellorotondo to be buried beside my father, in the Palmisano grave. The doctor will help you.'

Ricciardi's eyes were still wet, but he knew that he had to pull himself together. He nodded. 'And you?' he asked.

'I have to settle a debt with a bastard who is never going to hurt anyone ever again . . . I'll catch up with you two later.'

The rage of the past few months churned inside him, as he walked set on to the street. He knew perfectly well what he had to do; his mind was made up. But once outside, instead of heading towards the cathedral and finding the quickest way out of the old quarter, he went to the Via del Carmine and continued in the opposite direction, towards San Nicola and the sea. At the port he saw the seventeen sunken ships and remembered the bodies floating among the flames on the night of the air raid. It had only been three days ago, yet it seemed like an eternity. He relived the desperate howls of the sailors shouting for help from the water. He saw the corpses mangled by debris. He left the port and headed up the Via Venezia, passing the houses that had fallen one after the other, like dominoes. There were kitchen utensils and bits of clothing amid the rubble and he again felt the impotence of the rescue teams who were unable to dig out that girl until the surgeon sedated her and amputated her arm. Further on, he passed the shelter that had filled with water, where some twenty-odd people had drowned, and soon after he walked by a house in ruins where a woman and her seven children had been buried alive.

'God has turned his back on us,' someone had lamented the night of the bombing as they pulled the dead body of the youngest child out of the rubble.

But this, this was not a matter for the gods. The guilty parties were of flesh and blood, and after reliving the terror of the worst hours of his life, Vitantonio knew that he was finally preparing to do what he'd sworn as he left Matera, as they travelled north in the wake of cruel German repression. Only then did he hasten his step, leave the Borgo Antico near the Corso Vittorio Emmanuele and head decisively towards the Piazza Garibaldi.

Shootout in the Piazza Garibaldi

WHEN HE ENTERED the lobby of the apartment house in the Piazza Garibaldi, he thought for a moment he saw someone slipping out through the back entrance, but it was dark and he didn't make too much of it. He was in a rush to get this over with and get to Bellorotondo. He took the stairs two at a time and when he reached the third-floor landing he heard some noise and knew that Franco was at home. Continuing up the stairs, he hid in a corner of the stairwell to catch his breath and load his gun. When he felt ready he went back down, kicked in the door and caught the Black Knight by surprise.

Franco screamed. Then, when he recognized Vitantonio, his panic changed to puzzlement.

'I thought you were still in the mountains.' He saw Vitantonio's weapon and asked, 'What are you doing with a gun? You aren't planning on shooting your cousin, are you?'

Vitantonio didn't answer. He went over to the table and swept off all the papers with his arm. Then he picked up the radio transmitter and threw that to the floor as well.

'Are you still working for the fascists or are you now working directly for the agents of the Germans?' he asked him, beside himself.

'I am a patriot and I do my duty,' Franco said in his defence when he saw that the game was up. 'The Germans are our allies.'

'You bastard!' Vitantonio spat out, looking straight into his eyes. 'Do you know what you've done?'

'The king and Badoglio are just puppets . . .'

Vitantonio lost his temper completely. He couldn't stand his cousin's false naivety; he couldn't believe that Franco was really incapable of telling the difference between good and evil. He went over and hit him, hard.

'They have nothing to do with this. I'm talking about the good people that are dead because of you. All your life you've spread pain around you. You and your friend are sick, and you're going to rot in hell.'

As soon as the words had left his mouth, he realized that Franco's accomplice wasn't in the room. In his anger, he had forgotten about him. He turned toward his old bedroom, but it was too late: the door was just opening and the man with the blackened teeth was already firing.

After the first shot, everything happened very fast. Vitantonio felt a burning sensation on one side of his forehead: the bullet had grazed his temple. But he kept his cool and fired back twice; both bullets lodged in the chest of the man with the rotten teeth, and he suddenly crumpled, like a puppet whose strings have been cut. Vitantonio ran his hand over his temple and felt an unpleasant, viscous mass of blood and hair that had been ripped away by the bullet. Warm blood streamed down his cheek, but he didn't let himself panic.

However, before he had time to react, he saw the main door open and a new character enter the stage. At first he didn't recognize him, but he soon registered the uniform of an American army officer. Captain Lewis Clark held a revolver in his hand. He fired, and this time Vitantonio felt a burning in his stomach and he had to lean against the table to keep himself from falling.

'I gave you a chance to keep quiet and save your life but you refused. Now I'm going to have to kill you. I can't let you spread any more rumours about chemical weapons and endanger many months' worth of work.'

But just as the American was about to shoot him a second time, another figure emerged from behind the door and hurled himself between them. Two more shots rang out and Vitantonio saw Clark limping out of the apartment with a bullet in one leg. Then, from the back, he recognized the new gunmen, now on the point of collapse: it was Salvatore. He ran to hold him up, but didn't reach him in time. Salvatore collapsed, bleeding profusely from an ugly chest wound. When Vitantonio sat down next to him, their blood pooled together on the floor. He tried to get him talking, to calm him down.

'You were the one hiding by the back door earlier on . . .'

'I was waiting for the man with the black teeth, to

settle a score that's been eating away at me for years. When I saw the American following you up the stairs I knew I had to intervene to make sure you didn't get caught between two gunmen. Before Roosevelt and the others left for the airport they told me about the fight you'd had . . .'

Suddenly Salvatore was quiet but a flicker in his eyes showed he was on the alert. Vitantonio turned and saw that Franco was preparing to fire the revolver that his accomplice had dropped. His hand was shaking and he missed. Killing was what Franco liked best, but he was so useless at it that he always needed someone else to do the dirty work for him. Vitantonio stood up. He was just the opposite: he didn't enjoy shooting, but it came easily to him. He saw that Franco was still shaking as he tried to pull the trigger again, but his finger froze. Vitantonio watched him with a disgusted expression and took aim.

But something made him hesitate. He remembered him pestering Giovanna in the garden of the palazzo, the day that *Nonna* punished him by cancelling his confirmation; he saw him a year later playing with the wooden sword, dressed as the Black Knight; he relived Salvatore's beating at the hands of the fascists; he thought about little Michele, at the bottom of the *gravina*, and about how Skinny had been was sacked and Dr Ricciardi exiled. In his mind's eye Vitantonio saw the Matera Milizia barracks blown sky-high; he saw the eighteen men executed in the town square of Rionero, and all the others he had found as he climbed the road to the Maiella. Then he relived all the horror of the bombing of Bari and he knew there was no turning back.

He cocked the revolver. His last thought was of his mother, that very morning, when she was desperately trying to take in a breath. Then he angrily fired two shots into Franco's forehead. His head jerked back violently, as if yanked by a cord, and his legs folded under him as if they were made of soft butter. Without time even to reflect his incredulity in his face, the Black Knight fell down dead. Vitantonio stood stock-still, his gaze fixed on the blood that splattered the wall. Through that gory mess he saw two holes near the balcony: the bullets had exited the back of Franco's head and lodged in the wall, making the plaster fly. He lowered his eyes and took a look at his cousin's lifeless body. He stared at it for a good long while. And he felt nothing.

He then ran to Salvatore's side, and found he was choking on his own blood. Vitantonio took off his shirt and used it to try to staunch the flow. The blood streaming out of the bullet's entrance wound was making little bubbles on Salvatore's chest, as if air was escaping from a bicycle tyre. The bullet must have punctured his right lung. Salvatore coughed and more blood came from his mouth. He opened it as wide as he could, gasping for air, but must not have been taking any in because his face was turning purple. Then, still struggling to sit up, he surprised Vitantonio by speaking in a very clear voice.

'Your work here is done: now leave quickly and go to Giovanna.'

'We need to get you to a hospital ...' protested Vitantonio.

'We can't,' answered Salvatore. This time his voice was much fainter and Vitantonio had to lean in to hear him. 'We shot an American officer and no one will believe us when we tell them what he did.'

Until that moment, Vitantonio hadn't grasped the danger he was in. He could be considered a traitor: in just the last few hours he had challenged a captain of the American army twice and had killed two fascists who were most likely passing themselves off as loyal to Marshal Badoglio's government. He rapidly started assessing the situation and tried to guess what might come next. The fact that his attacker had fled might mean that he was keen not to attract the attention of the military police. A shootout wasn't something an army expert on chemical weapons wanted to get mixed up in, especially when he was part of a special unit that didn't officially exist and secrecy was his top priority.

Vitantonio coughed and his stomach wound started to gush more blood.

'You have to see a doctor and leave Bari, before they start searching for you in all the city's hospitals,' Salvatore said. 'I don't like the look of that wound.'

'I'm not leaving without you.'

'My time has come.'

Vitantonio saw the increasingly bluish tint of his friend's face and sensed that he was right: Salvatore's life was slipping away from him. But he was still unwilling to abandon him.

'I won't leave you. We'll go to a hospital together.'

'Don't try to be a hero! You have obligations now. It's all over for me.' He turned his head and looked at the corpse of the man with the rotted teeth. He grabbed Vitantonio's arm tightly, looked into his eyes and said, 'Thank you.' He gave him an enigmatic smile, put his arms around his neck and kissed him on the cheek. 'Give Giovanna a kiss from me,' he said, kissing him again, this time on the forehead, and added, 'and the baby too when he's born; they say he'll be a boy because her belly is high.'

He laughed, which made him cough and robbed him of the little energy he had left. He kept looking at Vitantonio with a smile on his lips and revealed, 'The baby is yours, from that morning when Giovanna went up to Matera . . .'

Vitantonio felt his heart racing. He was about to say something, but Salvatore, still gripping him tightly, lost consciousness. When Vitantonio tried to bring him to, he felt his arms hanging limply and he realized that he had stopped breathing. He hugged Salvatore's lifeless body, crying, like he had done that morning with his mother's, wondering aloud, 'God! What more do you want from us?'

He embraced him tightly once more, breathing in the scent of the black leather jacket that Salvatore had worn since those distant September days when he gave him a lift on his motorcycle to school in Martina

Franca. In a matter of seconds he relived the entire summer at the farmstead, when he had decided to adopt Skinny's son as an older brother. And gripped by the memory of a summer haze, Vitantonio too passed out.

In the Crypt

HE WAS WOKEN by the voices of children running in the square outside, oblivious to the city's tragedies. Vitantonio wanted to get up, but his side was hurting badly. He was dizzy. He stayed still for a little while, waiting for everything to stop spinning. Closing his eyes, he focused on his breathing. When it seemed the world was no longer spinning, he opened them and saw two red and white candles. He took a deep breath, looked around him and found that he was in the crypt of the church of San Nicola. He had no idea how he had got there.

When he heard the distant voices from in the square he recognized the strange feeling he knew from his childhood – when he lay in bed ill, and heard children playing in the Piazza Santa Anna, while he read or looked through the window at the shadows the afternoon sun drew on the grain lofts that topped the homes in Bellorotondo. It had always made him feel that there were two worlds: the real world was the one those children in the square inhabited, but his imaginary universe began and ended in his room. They were worlds that almost touched but were actually so distant that they never overlapped. This often made him feel that he was on the other side, far from the others: that sensation was sometimes comforting and made him feel special, but other times it was unnerving. Like now.

He wanted to stand up but again he felt light-headed and he decided to take it in stages: first he sat on the nearest pew, then he leaned against the wall and finally he walked from pew to pew until he reached the wall of the crypt that gave on to the square. He got up on a pew and watched the children playing from one of the windows at ground level. He was surprised at the amount of rubble on the Largo Urbano II, as if the Germans and the Allies had moved the trenches right into town.

It had been three and a half years since he'd seen children running and playing beside San Nicola in Bari. After an afternoon of exams he had left the law college happy because he was feeling sure he was well on his way to becoming a lawyer. He recalled that on that June day, almost evening, it was incredibly hot and everyone in Bari had brought chairs out on to the street to wait for the wind to come in off the sea. He could have written an essay on the art of catching a breeze in the Borgo Antico. He never tired of watching them: some people took their chairs right out into the middle of the street; others stayed in their doorways, and there were even those who preferred to remain discreetly in their halls, with the door wide open. But if you looked closely you'd find that they had all positioned themselves precisely in the airiest spot, and they all maintained eye contact with their neighbours to keep up a lively conversation. They were like actors on a stage, but actually those cooling off were the audience, enjoying the spectacle of the passersby walking through the city.

When Vitantonio gingerly got down from the pew and moved away from the window, he lost his balance, just as a man entered the crypt. He recognized Father Cataldo, Father Felice's favourite student. His appearance was quite a surprise because Vitantonio didn't know that he'd been named prior of San Nicola. The priest rushed over to catch him just as he was falling to the ground.

'You shouldn't move. You've lost a lot of blood.'

'What am I doing here, Father? How did I get here?'

'You were brought here by a giant with a kind face. When I saw that you were wounded, I wanted to take you to a hospital, but he asked me to hide you in the crypt. Then he went to find a doctor and some transport. I couldn't refuse to help you when you needed it, so I didn't ask any questions.'

Vitantonio wondered how in the world Primo Carnera had known that he was in Franco's apartment in the Piazza Garibaldi, wounded, and needed help urgently. And he also wondered how he must have looked, a gentle giant lugging a dying man on his back through the streets of Bari to San Nicola. The image made him laugh and he thought that the city must be hard to shock these days. They had seen much worse things.

He dropped down, exhausted, on the pew, unable to stop himself sinking back into sleep. He dreamt that he was being chased by the Black Knight and the man with the rotten teeth, and when he stood up to them and defeated them, they reappeared somewhere else and attacked him all over again. He woke up and heard voices he couldn't identify; they spoke very slowly and seemed very far away. When he woke up for the second time it was pitch black and someone had bandaged his wound. Primo Carnera was once again lugging him over his shoulder like a big sack. It didn't seem to be an effort for him.

'Where are we going?' asked Vitantonio.

'I have to take you to Bellorotondo. Giovanna will know what to do. You've lost a lot of blood.'

'How did you know I was in Franco's apartment?'

'I followed you. Giovanna asked me to keep an eye on you.'

Outside, the north wind began to blow again and Vitantonio was grateful for the freezing December air on his face. Primo Carnera left the Piazza San Nicola and took the narrower streets, all the while carrying Vitantonio. Father Cataldo walked a few paces ahead to warn him of any checkpoints. Nearly all of the commotion was still at the port and on the Lungomare, and they were able to reach the door of the seminary without incident. Primo laid him down in the backseat of a British army jeep and started the engine, gesturing his thanks to the priest, who was already slipping discreetly back into the courtyard of the seminary. The car left the Borgo Antigo along the Via Corridoni, found the Corso Vittorio Emmanuele and got lost among the city's traffic.

Lying in the back, Vitantonio saw the tops of the buildings stream past him in the near dark. He remembered that the day of the air raid, when the Germans had already dropped half of their bombs, the city looked like a lantern lit expressly to attract the firemen's attention. The pain in his stomach was getting sharper and sharper. He almost screamed when he saw giant flames devouring an apartment building somewhere he couldn't quite identify.

Primo had also seen it. 'Hide under the blanket!' he ordered. He saw a boy come running from the direction of the fire and he called out to him, 'What's going on?'

'Number 17 in the Piazza Garibaldi just went up like a tinderbox!'

Primo Carnera recognized the address. It was Franco's apartment that was on fire.

'It must have been set on fire by some of your cousin's accomplices, who wanted to destroy any evidence, keep the police off the scent,' shouted Primo Carnera towards the back of the jeep. 'Or maybe the American went back and decided he didn't want to be linked to that hest of vipers! It's a stroke of luck for us, they won't turn you in to the police,' he added, trying to reassure him as he sped up and drove towards the station.

Vitantonio didn't hear him. He had lost consciousness again.

The Englishman was waiting for them at the station. The Jeep Primo was driving was his, and his British lieutenant's stripes helped get them past all the controls. They put Vitantonio in the last carriage; he was still unconscious.

'I wish I'd had a chance to say goodbye to him,' said Lieutenant Donovan. 'I'll see you in three days, in Foggia,' he shouted to Primo Carnera when the train started off.

There were people hanging off a freight car and they had even taken over the engine footplate, which was making the driver's manoeuvres difficult. Three days after the bombing, rumours of chemical weapons at the port had spread throughout Bari and people were still fleeing the city.

When they had passed Putignano, Vitantonio woke up shouting, 'Salvatore's body was in the burning apartment in the Piazza Garibaldi!'

'While you were in the crypt I took him out on to the street and left him among the ruins of a house on the Via Abate Gimma. When they find him they'll think he died the day of the raid,' Primo reassured him.

Vitantonio relaxed and again lost consciousness.

When they got off at the Bellorotondo station the cold had lessened, as if it were about to snow but, to Vitantonio, it still seemed to be the bitterest night of the year.

'Take me home, to the Piazza Santa Anna. I'm freezing.'

'You can't go home. That's the first place they'll look for you.'

Primo Carnera saw his face and was alarmed. He couldn't take him anywhere in that state. He took a risk and knocked on the first door he found. It was the Raguseos' house: the woman recognized Lady Angela's grandson and ushered them in. They lay Vitantonio in Pasquale's bed; their son had just been shot by the Germans in Cephalonia. While Primo Carnera went out to look for Giovanna, the women of the house took care of Vitantonio as if he were their own Pasquale.

The Cherry Tree

THEY REACHED THE palazzo after midnight and entered under cover of night, but as soon as they opened up the office they could see that the house had been ransacked. *Nonna*'s files were scattered everywhere, and the desk drawers lay on the floor. The paintings of red and white flowers had disappeared from the living room and the little inlaid boxes and terracotta pieces were gone from the library.

When they went into the playroom they found that the window was broken, because a gust of wind put out the candle they were using to see the way. They assumed that was how the intruders had got into the house. Giovanna lit the candle again, this time protecting the flame with one hand. The light projected shadows on the walls and around the room, revealing books and toys strewn all over the floor. The electric train itself had disappeared, but there were pieces of the track and the mountains everywhere. Vitantonio pushed a few aside with his foot; they were the little houses with snow-dusted roofs.

In the living room the looters had opened up the china cabinet and emptied all the shelves.

'Will you manage to get upstairs?' Giovanna asked him.

'I'll be fine here.'

Vitantonio gripped an armchair and slowly lowered himself on to the carpet. Giovanna looked for a cushion and placed it under his head.

'Wait, I'll bring down a mattress for you.'

'No!' He held her back. 'I wouldn't know how to sleep on one any more. I'm better on the floor.'

He was burning up with fever. Sweat drenched his face and dripped down his neck. Giovanna went to the kitchen and came back with a damp cloth to clean his face. She was exhausted and when he fell asleep in her arms she closed her eyes too.

She was woken up by thin streams of light entering through the sliding doors to the conservatory. He was gazing at her and gave her a smile.

'Open the curtains. I'd like to see the garden.'

Giovanna stood up and pulled back the velvet drapes. Then she undid the shutters and noticed that the servants' entrance had been left open and they could see through to the town square, which was deserted at that time of day. She went over to the sliding doors, which had come out of their track. She pushed them with all her weight, until they moved.

'Help me over to the conservatory,' Vitantonio requested.

Sunlight flooded the room and she was alarmed to see that his wound was bleeding again and his face was paler than ever. She helped him get up and led him over to the conservatory. Vitantonio leaned against the leaded glass, his gaze fixed on some indeterminate point in the garden. It had been some time since anyone had worked on it. There was an abandoned bucket and basin on the tiles of *Nonna*'s arcaded terrace. Half-rotten leaves carpeted the flowerbeds and paths. The leafless trees looked like corpses left on a battlefield, like the partisans fallen in the mountains of the Maiella. Like the sailors gassed in the Bari port. But the trees would have green shoots again, come spring.

His wound had reopened from the walking. Giovanna didn't have anything to stop the haemorrhaging and she was starting to panic. If Skinny or Concetta didn't send help soon, this was the end. She looked at his face, which grew whiter by the moment. He was having trouble breathing.

Vitantonio closed his eyes and in a thin, barely audible voice said, 'It's not fair.' Then he was silent.

She thought she had lost him and she burst into tears. Then he surprised her by speaking again, this time in a stronger voice. 'Soon the whole garden will start budding, but I won't be here to see the cherry tree bloom. Isn't it strange?'

'Did you see?' she said, encouraging him to keep fighting for his life. She pointed to a flowering geranium she'd just spotted amid all the plants withered by the cold. *Nonna*'s azaleas looked half-dead, but their giant pots must have protected that geranium from the wind, as if it were in a greenhouse. Its flowers were of a vivid blood red and hung like a cardinal's cape.

He made a last effort and managed to open his eyes.

He saw the crimson geranium that Giovanna was pointing to. Then he looked at her belly and asked, 'What will you name him?'

'Vitantonio . . . Vitantonio Palmisano. He will bear your name openly, so everyone in town can see.'

He replied with a sad smile and said, 'Destiny is not set in stone. The curse is killing me, but the little boy you are carrying is proof that we have once again won the battle . . . All my life I've made my own choices. There is only one thing I was unable to choose freely: who I was born. I was born a Palmisano. I couldn't pick a different side. That's why I've loved the Convertinis like mad and I'm proud to be a part of the family, but I've always stayed true to my own: I will die like a Palmisano. Just like in the war, where I tried to switch sides and I devoted myself to the Allied cause, but they never really considered me one of them. In the end, it's an American bullet that's killing me . . .'

'Don't speak. Rest.' Giovanna wiped the sweat from his face and put a clean cloth on his wound. Without realizing it, he had begun singing something in French.

'What are you singing?' she asked him.

> "The Time of the Cherries'. The French Resistance fighters sing it:
> 'Mais il est bien court, le temps des cerises
> Où l'on s'en va deux, cueillir en rêvant
> Des pendants d'oreilles.
> Cerises d'amour aux roses pareilles,
> Tombant sous la feuille en gouttes de sang . . ."

Seeing that he was barely breathing now, she began to despair again. She was about to lose him. How many men will have died altogether when, in just a few months' time, those trees begin to bloom? Vitantonio was right: the cherry tree will flower and bear sweet, juicy fruit. The time of the cherries would return, oblivious to the drama the blighted people of Puglia were living through. They tried to remain loyal to the cause of freedom, but they had to fight against both the loathsome betrayal of their own leaders and the contemptible distrust of the Allies. They deserved better.

Vitantonio must have read her thoughts because he smiled one last time. He imagined the garden in bloom and the cherry tree loaded down with red, ripe fruit. In his mind's eye, Giovanna led a boy by the hand and they both laughed and smiled. Then, from some very distant place, he found the strength to make one last plea.

'When our boy starts to walk, make him some cherry earrings, for me.'

Just then, a Jeep with a big red cross painted on the canvas roof parked in front of the side door that opened on to the square. Standing in the window, Giovanna saw Dr Ricciardi step from it.

Epilogue

24 August 2012. Late evening.

The sun had already disappeared behind the hills of Alberobello. In Bellorotondo's town square the day was slowly fading. It was one of those summer evenings that linger languidly: the light was waning but resisted giving way to night. A swirl of breeze came off of the sea, from the direction of Ostuni. The temperature was rapidly dropping, and after an unbearably hot day, it was starting to feel pleasant again.

The first lights came on in windows and the streets filled with groups of young people strolling and laughing. Many people had brought chairs out on to the street to savour the breeze. From the modern avenues in the commercial district came the sounds of cars and motorcycles, poople out and about just to see and be seen. Suddenly, Bellorotondo looked like a different town.

The cicadas in the carob trees sang louder, to overcome the competition they were facing from all sides. There were couples relaxing on balconies and in the centre of the square mothers chatted while keeping one eye on the children playing hide-and-seek behind the monuments to the victims of the two world wars.

A woman shouted from a nearby window, '*Nonno!*'

The old man slowly got up from the bench with the peeling paint and began to walk back to the southern side of the square, but he stopped at the monument to the victims of the Second World War. He drew close to the memorial, hunched over the list of the dead and traced it with his hand, letting his fingertips glide very gently over the names etched into stone. He straightened up just as a young woman arrived to urge him to return home.

'Papa says that if you don't come right now you can eat in town, because at home the kitchen closes at nine . . .' said the woman, laughing.

'You see? When you're ninety-three years old they start scolding you like a child again,' he replied.

The young woman was still catching her breath. She must have been in her early thirties and was very beautiful. She wore jeans and a spaghetti-strap top. She was dark, with green eyes and very long black hair that was pulled back in an elegant ponytail that had come somewhat loose from her running to tumble over her left shoulder.

Taking his granddaughter's arm, the old man turned to leave. As they set off, she swung her hair back with a toss of her head and exposed her collarbone briefly. The motion revealed a fleeting shadow, like a birthmark: just for a second the outline of a red heart seemed to appear there before she turned away again. They walked haltingly towards the other end of the square, where they reached the palazzo's garden wall that marked the southern side of the large terrace. The old man paused, lifted a hand as if in a last goodbye and disappeared through the side entrance.

Author's Note

This is a work of fiction, so all the events and characters described here come from the author's imagination. However, the historical setting and events of the wars are strictly true: that is the case with the pacifist mobilization in Locorotondo and the chaos on the Italian fronts during the Great War; and also the Matera uprising, the bombing of Bari and the explosion of the *John Harvey* in the Second World War. In that sense, the novel is a homage to all those southern Italians, so often forgotten by history, who rose up against the Nazi–fascist alliance without adequate resources or clear leadership.

The scenes set during the bombing of the Bari port on 2 December 1943, and the explosion of the mustard gas cargo on the American ship, owe a debt to the Italian edition of the book *Disaster at Bari*, written in 1971 by Glenn B. Infield, a British former major in the American air force, who was an eyewitness. I used the most recent edition published by Mario Adda Editore, with a preface by Professor Vito Antonio Leuzi, also the author of *Inferno su Bari*. As for the events of 21 September 1943 in Matera – the other big episode of the Second World war in southern Italy that has not been sufficiently considered by history–there are still some contemporary reports by Allied officers on the ground that have yet to be declassified, but recently *Matera Atrocities are Murders*, by Vittorio Sebastiani (Edizioni Giannatelli), was published, the most complete contribution to date on the British investigation into it. *Voce di sassi*, by Antonio d'Ercole, is an account of daily life in Matera and its language, and also contains direct testimony of that day.

Bellorotondo is a product of the author's imagination, but you will find many traces of it in Cisternino, Martina Franca, Altamura and especially Locorotondo, a wonderful town in the Itria valley, which I enthusiastically recommend. In fact, if you are still unacquainted with that part of southern Italy, don't miss the land of the *trulli*, as well as the rest of Puglia and Basilicata, home to an unparalleled treasure: the Sassi caves in Matera.

Acknowledgements

This book would not exist without all the people of Puglia and Basilicata who I've met over these last few years: farmers, booksellers, teachers, doctors, professors, gardeners, chefs and timber importers, who always treated me with kindness and a trust that went far beyond my expectations. I don't know if I was able adequately to convey my thanks in person and so I would like to now acknowledge here my most sincere gratitude.

I want particularly to thank Professor Fernando Mirizzi, of the University of Basilicata, for his patience over our stimulating correspondence that began after our first meeting in Matera and a wonderful second conversation one June afternoon, in the square of the Altamura cathedral. And the historian Angelantonio Spagnoletti, who opened up his home to me and revealed Molfetta's secrets. And the historian Vito Antonio Leuzzi, for receiving me in his office at the Istituto Pugliese per la Storia dell'Antifascismo e dell'Italia Contemporanea 'Tommaso Fiore'. And Alberto Pelegrini and Paola Locascio as well, both professors of history in Barcelona, who taught me about the speeifies of Italian historiography.

I would also like to thank Anna Maria Aprile for welcoming me warmly into her farmstead in Locorotondo and for trusting me with her albums of keepsakes on the region's twentieth century history. And Franco Basile and Graziella D'Onofrio, who generously gave of their time and shared their memories of school in Puglia in the first half of the twentieth century.

Nicola Furio and his mother, Maria Campanella, revealed the secrets of fishing and the traditions on the Savelletri coast. Signora. Maria was kind enough to receive me in her home, presided over by a large portrait of Padre Pio, the most popular saint in Italy. 'In the winter, when my son goes north to work, I live alone. Alone with Padre Pio,' she told me on that day in July.

Maria Lucia Colucci, with her exceptionally lucid memory, explained 'the rain of stars' that she imagined, when she was sixteen, watching the German artillery's tracer bullets from the shelter of a cave near the Matera cathedral, the night the city was liberated. Nicola Frangione was invaluable in my research on the scenes of the popular uprising and for putting me in touch with some eyewitnesses.

I received much help on the food and produce of Puglia from Margheritta at the U Curdunn restaurant and Giovanni Loparco at the Trattoria Centro Storico, both from Locorotondo, but the recipe for *orechiette a la lepre* comes from brothers Franco and Giuliano Lombardo, chefs at *le cinque terre,* who prepare it with *papardelle* at their restaurant, Tramonti, in Barcelona.

Dr Josep Arimany, a specialist in medical jurisprudence, introduced me to the secrets of forensic medicine and Ds Antoni Mirada and or August Andrés answered my questions about medical specialisms in the period between the wars. The notary Juanjo López Burniol helped me understand the Italian figure of the custody judge.

I had long conversations with Quim Español, Josep Maria Fonalleras, Pep Nadal and Arturo San Agustín on various aspects of the book while the manuscript was taking shape and I must thank them for their patience and comments. Andreu Pulido always gives me tons of good advice about language.

Ester Pujol is my editor and to her I owe the magnificent editing of this book. She and Berta Bruna were the first to see my travel notebooks with the original notes for the novel and the first to read the manuscript; they both threw themselves into it wholeheartedly. As did the entire team at Columna and Destino, headed by Emili Rosales, who accompanied me throughout with enthusiasm and professionalism. As did everyone at the Pontas Literary Agency, Marina Penalva, Ricard Domingo and Anna Soler-Pont, who not only represent me but also make my life as easy as they possibly can. I am truly grateful to them all.